CHEMISTRY OF MAGIC

UNEXPECTED MAGIC #5

Patricia Rice

Chemistry of Magic

Patricia Rice

Book View Café Publishing Cooperative
P.O. Box 1624, Cedar Crest, NM 87008-1624
http://bookviewcafe.com
ISBN 978-1-61138-665-3

CHEMISTRY OF MAGIC

Patricia Rice

Author's Note

VIRTUAL HUGS AND KISSES to my faithful readers, without whom I wouldn't be having so much fun writing this series!

To my new readers: Don't worry. You needn't have read any of the other volumes to enjoy this one. The characters may be recurring, but each story and couple stands alone. The only problem you might encounter is if you're a stickler for title usage and don't realize Lady Aster is the daughter of an earl and thus entitled to be called Lady Aster instead of Lady Theophilus—not that the Malcolms care overmuch about titles anyway.

I usually attempt to give my Malcolms "gifts" that have been discussed for centuries as possible but never scientifically proved. Although many people swear by Reiki healing, what Emilia does goes a step further. We can all dream of a little magic, can't we?

Acknowledgments

FIRST AND FOREMOST, to Mindy Klasky and Jennifer Stevenson who keep my nose to the grindstone and force me to add those little details that make a book come alive. And as always, to the hard working Book View Café crew who handle all those pesky technical details I don't understand and who offer me a wonderful company of talented professionals with whom I can talk writerese.

I can't thank Kim Killion enough—for her fabulous covers and also for translating my "He's dark and she's fair and they're magic" into reality!

And hugs to my wonderful husband who handles my authorial technology and doesn't complain when I ask him for just one more link. Or three.

One

"DOES LORD DARE NORMALLY generate the smell of sulfur?" Miss Emilia Malcolm McDowell inquired anxiously, holding a handkerchief to her nose as she traversed the back hall of that gentleman's London home.

She'd occasionally heard family members refer to the viscount as Devil Dare, but she'd rather thought it referred to his bold and reckless approach to life, not the actual stench of Hell. Still, if he was as ill as her mother had said, one could make exceptions for odd odors. She, of all people, knew better than to be superstitious about peculiarities.

Lady Dare, the viscount's widowed mother, bobbed her cap-covered graying curls. "He produces the most vile odors one can imagine. Perhaps I should not have insisted that he leave the window open even in winter," she said worriedly. "London air can carry terrible diseases. Perhaps his illness is all my fault."

"Then we would all be ill," Emilia said, trying to reassure the lady while mentally re-evaluating her mission here. The viscount regularly generated the stench of sulfur and *other* vile odors? What kind of illness was that?

Before she could lose courage and flee, however, the lady shoved open a door without knocking. "Dare, you have a visitor."

"Not now," a deep male voice called impatiently from the interior. "And where is Jackson if you're performing his duties?"

"I did not think it appropriate for a lady to visit without my presence," the viscountess responded tartly, expressing the same impatience as her son. "Miss McDowell, I apologize for my son's rudeness. He does know the niceties when he chooses to acknowledge them."

"I've told you I don't need any more ladies bringing me soup and patting me on the head," he roared.

And then the room exploded. Glass shattered.

Emilia stepped in front of the much shorter, stouter Lady Dare, blocking her from the black, malodorous cloud billowing through the open door. She held her breath and ducked her head so that her wide-brimmed hat blocked the smoke from her face.

Voluble cursing from inside the chamber, combined with a hacking cough, led her to conclude the devil had only blown up the room, not himself. "My lord, are you injured?" she called, unwilling to enter hell unless he could not escape on his own.

A large, blackened gentleman emerged from the baleful haze, brushing ash from his unbuttoned waistcoat and shirtsleeves.

She had been led to expect an *invalid*. She swallowed hard and again re-thought her purpose here. Lord Dare was so far from being an invalid as to resemble a veritable dragon—taller than she and twice as broad, larger than she remembered from her one brief introduction. Instead of dragon scales, however, he sported loose linen plastered with sweat and soot. Undisguised by gentlemanly attire, his powerful shoulders and solid chest created an illusion of virile health.

Only his hacking cough revealed the deteriorating state of his lungs—a dragon whose fire had died.

She recalled his hair as golden-brown, but she could not tell through the smoke. The apparition removed his spectacles to rub his eyes, leaving a ring of white around his singed dark lashes. Perhaps he did appear a trifle pale beneath the filth, she told herself. She was that desperate. And the sweat no doubt indicated fever since no actual fire emanated from his cave.

"Irritated, not injured," he said, rudely looking her up and down. "No soup? No posies?"

"Dare, I swear. . ." The lady bit off her irritation. "Miss McDowell has a business proposition for you." Her eagerness was obvious.

A few minutes ago, Emilia had been eager and anxious too. She'd waited years to tackle this task, studying the problem from every angle. She thought she'd finally found a perfect solution—

Faced with the devil, she was now back to *wary* and anxious. The frail invalid of her imagination was not quite the same as the querulous reality. Remembering all the sick people who counted on her, the future of pharmaceuticals, and the health of a kingdom—she drew a deep breath and met his cynical gaze without flinching. She had no other choices left.

"Lord Dare, perhaps this is a discussion we should have in private," she suggested with as much hauteur as breathlessness could achieve. She wasn't good at small talk, but she knew how to be direct.

"Do I know you?" Now that he'd stopped coughing, he cleaned his spectacles on the shirt tail he pulled from his trouser band.

Sympathizing with his mother's irritation, Emilia refrained from rolling her eyes at this familiar refrain. It wasn't as if her height rendered her invisible, but for whatever reason, men didn't notice her, no matter how outrageously she dressed. "We met last year in Iveston, my lord, when you came to discuss glass for microscopes with Lord Theo."

He frowned, dropped his spectacles in his waistcoat pocket, and without permission, grabbed her lovely wide-brimmed hat adorned with lavender roses and removed it. She glared and snatched it back, just barely avoiding swatting him with it.

"The woman with the violet eyes," he exclaimed in pleasure, as if he actually remembered her. "Why the devil do you hide beneath that appalling flower garden? Come in, if you can bear the stench. I need to clean up before the soot settles. Mother, have Jackson bring the lady some tea." He held the door open wide to reveal the blackened ruins of a... study?

"Don't be improper, Dare," his mother scolded. "You must at least come into the sitting room where you can be chaperoned."

Wiping his face with his shirt tail, Lord Dare gazed upon his mother with a droll expression. "I think a dying man can be trusted to behave with all due respect for fear of what waits on the other side, don't you agree, Miss McDowell?"

She did not, but she'd been the one to suggest a private discussion. Lady Dare had some notion of her mission since she and Emilia's mother had discussed the problem of their recalcitrant offspring in advance. But Emilia preferred the terms of her proposal to be private.

"I think I can trust you to be a gentleman in your own home, under the same roof as your mother and sisters," she replied primly, avoiding the subject of what awaited on the other side of death. "Although I'm not at all certain that I can trust the room won't explode again."

"I've turned off the burners. You'll be safe." Lord Dare caught her elbow—he caught her elbow!—and dragged her inside the dimly lit chamber, closing the door on his mother.

He was fortunate she did not expire on the spot. The discomfort of his disease shot straight up her arm in pinpricks of warning.

"WE WON'T BE SAFE, not in this cesspool," the tall, be-flowered lady argued, rather dramatically wrenching her arm from Dare's hold and putting distance between them. "You cannot breathe properly in this soot. Where is the sitting room?" She looked about as if she might find a magic door.

"I'm covered in grime. I can't pollute the sitting room. Tell me your business and you needn't admire my décor for long." Dare grabbed cleaning rags from his desk drawer and began wiping down his glass beakers. At least, this time, he'd not set the draperies on fire, since there were none. He'd had the window boarded.

His damnable coughing started up again. He had no clean handkerchiefs left, so he used his shirt tail. Bad choice. When he came up for air, the lady was looking at him with a glimmer of sympathy. *That* was the look he despised most. He wanted to prove to her that he wasn't exactly dead yet, except he'd more or less promised his mother to behave while they shared the same roof.

That he had sacrificed his private quarters and laboratory grated, but his remaining time in this world shouldn't be selfishly spent sending good money after bad.

"You must lie down," his guest said, blessedly not offering the usual weeping platitudes. "Your lungs and heart work harder when you stand. Lie down on that filthy piece of furniture over there and give your organs a rest." She pointed at the settee that had once been a silly bit of green silk when his mother had installed it a year ago, after the last fire.

Organs? The lady dared say *organs*? Impressed, Dare still ignored her admonitions and returned to polishing.

She returned the horrid hat to her lustrous black hair. "We will discuss nothing unless you exhibit a modicum of good sense. I cannot deal with a suicidal madman. I apologize if I've wasted your time and raised your mother's hopes."

"I need the glassware to be clean, and it won't be if I lie about admiring ceilings. You may speak or leave, it's no matter to me."

Dare knew he was being abominably rude, but faced with the kind of woman he could no longer have, he'd rather she walked out than taunt him with his fate.

To his surprise, she took the beaker from his hand. "Do you keep vinegar or alcohol in here?"

His nose had almost lost its ability to smell, but she carried an air of. . . freshness. . . with her, as if the stench of his work didn't touch her. Out of curiosity, he located the bottle of clear alcohol and handed it to her.

"Go lie down. I will clean and we will talk."

Dare watched in fascination as the lady stripped off her gloves, expertly dipped a rag in a bowl of alcohol, and began vigorously polishing the glass as if she'd been doing it all her life. Those soft hands had most definitely not spent hours cleaning glass. They did, however, raise lewd notions of better uses for those slender fingers. In shock, he thought he needed a good lie-down. To his knowledge, ladies did not clean glass or even recognize the need for glass to be cleaned.

His reaction to her unusual beauty was far less surprising. The combination of gleaming black hair, brilliant purple eyes, and fair skin reminded him of a common flower he'd seen in the market—not glamorous but striking.

Coughing again, he did as told and crumpled onto the settee. In truth, he needed to find breath for a discussion, and it was damned hard while breathing heavily down her delightfully long throat. Not that he was capable of breathing heavily any longer.

"That's better," she said in satisfaction, setting aside the sparkling beaker and picking up the difficult-to-clean, extremely expensive glass tubing.

Dare didn't know if she referred to the glass or his position. He leaned against the pillows on the high end of the cushioned settee so he could watch her. She was tall for a woman, but the rest of her was disguised in sleeves wider than she seemed to be and skirts that belled out from her too-slender waist. "You can lose the hat. I can't discuss business with someone whose face is concealed by all that flummery."

She pinched the hat brim delicately between two fingers so as not to add filth to the lavender, removed it, then looked around for a safe place to set it down. There wasn't any.

"Open a drawer. There's nothing in them but supplies, but the interior stays clean." Dare propped an arm behind his head and admired her graceful sway as she opened the begrimed desk and found a suitable resting place for her prized confection. Somehow, she did not strike him as a woman who cared about her attire, but she was garbed in what he recognized as the highest fashion. Living in a household of females, he was forced to notice such things.

She found his cleaning wires and cotton and began cleaning the tubing she'd left soaking in the alcohol. By damn, she knew what she was about. "Your proposition?" he asked, consumed with curiosity now.

It took a great deal to distract him from his goals these days, but this tantalizing female had managed it. Studying her, he decided her bosom probably wasn't large, but it was high and firm above a waist so slender he could probably snap her in two. And those impossibly violet eyes... Where had she been when he'd been stupidly swaggering through the ballrooms of society?

Her fair brow drew down in a thoughtful line as she posed a response to his question. "My maternal great-grandfather left me a substantial estate. We had much in common, and he wished me to continue his work."

"Which is?" Dare asked, because he was suddenly consumed with a desire to know everything about this woman of lavender mystery.

She hesitated, then said reluctantly, "Developing a truly accurate pharmacopeia."

His interest immediately waned. "Female potions and witchery belong to the last century," he said in dismissal. "Grass does not cure anything. Modern medicine requires experimentation and will surely encompass elements of which we know nothing yet."

She looked down her nose at him. Perhaps her nose was a little long. And a bit sharp. Her lush lips thinned considerably with her disapprobation. And those bold black eyebrows formed jagged points of censure, which perversely thrilled him—perhaps because those huge purple eyes focused on him and him alone.

"Botany is a well-respected *science*. The women of my family were botanists long before the term was coined. Just because men have the freedom to explore other countries for new specimens does not make them better botanists than women," she said coldly. "We have been using curative herbs and salves for centuries."

Ignoring his snort of dismissal, she continued her lecture. "I am always interested in other cures, of course, and I most certainly experiment to determine the effectiveness of my formulas. . . unlike most apothecaries, I trust you realize. We are what we ingest, and if we ingest foreign chemicals, we cannot expect our bodies to do anything but reject them, often in a disastrous manner. That is not the point and is neither here nor there, however."

"You are wrong about the effectiveness of chemicals," Dare argued. "My physician prescribes Fowler's Solution, a chemical mixture that has *cured* disease, including malaria and asthma." And syphilis, but Dare refrained from shocking the lady with his sordid research. "It's still in the experimental stage for consumption, but otherwise, I believe its effectiveness has been proven."

She heaved a sigh of exasperation and picked up the next piece of glass to be cleaned. "I did not come here to argue over medicine. This is a *business* proposition. I have been reliably informed that your family will be thrown from their home upon your demise, a situation which you seem unwilling to rectify."

Dare closed his aching eyes and rubbed his pounding temple. *This* was the reason he'd given up his private quarters—to save money. "My funds are all invested. They will pay off eventually, but they are not liquid enough yet to buy houses. I regret that, but short of finding a cure for consumption, I don't see how you can help. Perhaps you could shoot my heir?" he asked hopefully, with an element of sarcasm, to be sure.

"An interesting solution," she retorted in the same tone. "I suppose the lawyers could then consume your estate searching for a new heir. My solution might be a trifle archaic, but more apt to succeed for both of us. You see, my great-grandfather was an old-fashioned sort of gentleman. He believed women should be married. So I cannot take charge of my inheritance until I am wedded."

Dare pried open one eye. She seemed serious. She frowned as she polished a graduated cylinder. She wasn't even looking at him. He ought to be insulted. Most women flattered, flirted, and fawned all over him. Instead, he was fascinated by her lack of feminine wile, reflecting the perversity of his mind, he fully acknowledged.

A maid rapped at the door, and the lady called for her to enter. Once the tea tray was settled, the maid scampered out. Dare watched as Miss McDowell poured tea in the genteel manner instilled in all ladies of quality. She was everything society expected her to be. . . but unless the disease had eaten his brains, he was quite certain she was not at all what she seemed.

She offered the cup to him, and Dare shook his head. He'd have to sit up to drink, and he thought his head might roll off his shoulders if he tried. Despite what the poets said, there wasn't a damned thing romantic about this damnable disease. The body he'd taken for granted for thirty-one years was deteriorating faster with each passing day.

"How sizable is your great-grandfather's estate?" he asked after she'd sipped her tea, because his brain wasn't completely gone yet, and he thought he knew where this *discussion* was headed.

She almost stopped his heart when her wide lips curled upward and her lustrous-lashed eyes sparkled in approval.

"Grandfather's estate is large enough to purchase the townhouse your family will need when your heir evicts them. Large enough to establish the laboratory I need for my experiments. And the house and land pay for themselves," she said in satisfaction.

"Laboratory?" A bout of coughing prevented finishing the question.

He didn't realize she'd approached until he felt her hands on his chest, pushing him back down into the confounded hard settee. Coughing too hard to object, Dare tried to concentrate on a woman's hands on him for the first time in forever. They felt good. They felt more than good. It was as if she were pushing warmth into his lungs, forcing them to open up. He almost choked taking a deeper breath than he'd been able to take in months.

She hastily backed away and stared at her now-filthy hands as if they were as diseased as he was. Her voice was a little shaky but did not reflect distaste. "Does your physician use one of those new stethoscopes?" she asked, returning to his table to clean off the soot. "The damage seems worse on one side than the other."

What the devil did that mean? And since when did ladies lay hands on gentlemen to whom they were not related?

He used a dirty rag to wipe his mouth, wadding up the bloody stain and flinging the rag under the chair. Now that he was breathing again, his coughing settled. "Yes, he uses a stethoscope, for what good it does. Consumption damages lungs.

We don't need to cut open my chest to know that."

Although he had to wonder how she knew without use of the equipment, but he was focused on a more important topic. "You were speaking of a laboratory?" He tentatively drew another breath. The pain was less. Perhaps having a beautiful woman caressing him drew his blood downward and relieved the pressure.

Suddenly looking brittle enough to break, she focused her attention on polishing glass. "Yes, if I am to help the ill, I need a laboratory to test and perfect my medicines, understand how and why they work," she said in a voice that sounded as if she tried to convince herself.

"Now that my pharmacopeia is almost finished," she continued, gaining momentum, "my need for a true laboratory is the reason I'm eager to finally claim my inheritance. A distant cousin of mine has just married. Her new husband owns an old abbey near Harrogate where she means to establish a school for midwives. There are buildings on the grounds suitable for an infirmary, and she wants to establish her own clinic for dispensing her *potions*." Her tone mocked his earlier scorn. "She said there is enough room for me to establish a laboratory if I'm willing to aid her in preparing and dispensing medicines."

Dare pushed himself into a sitting position. Had she been a snake oil dispenser, he would have scorned her herbal quackery. But playing with botany had once been an acceptable lady's pastime. She didn't seem intent on poisoning him with it. Yet. "Harrogate?" he asked warily.

"Yes," she said, setting the expensive glass down with care. "I know nothing of mineral waters, but your mother indicated they were of interest to you. That is one of the reasons I am here."

"I've been attempting to separate the various minerals in spa water, looking for the curative properties," he admitted. "Harrogate's waters are particularly potent."

He hadn't forgotten the earlier part of her speech, and he continued with caution. "Once you marry, you will inherit an estate near Harrogate and this abbey?"

She nodded. Her velvet-lashed, purple eyes got wider, if that was at all possible.

Despite all her exterior composure, she was nervous, Dare realized. He was a huge brute, lying here like a bull in a field. She was a delicate lady, with a very odd mind, but that didn't change the fact that she was a gently bred female and should not be here at all.

Which was when his lust-weakened brain comprehended the whole—*she knew he was dying*. She had come to him with a *proposition*. She needed a husband. He needed funds. But her courage had failed at the sticking point. He almost fell off the chaise in his haste to show he wasn't a complete dunderhead.

Dare regained his feet, set aside the glass she was cleaning, and took her ungloved hand. Her bones were little more than twigs.

She hastily snatched her hand back, which made his next gesture awkward. Cautiously leaning on the table, because his strength frequently failed him these days, he got down on one knee.

"Miss McDowell, would you do me the delight and pleasure of becoming my wife?"

She burst into tears and sobbed, "Yes, of course, please."

And then she grabbed her gloves and began pulling them back on.

Two

EMILIA HATED CRYING. But she'd been so overwrought, and Lord Dare had seemed so unreasonable, and she'd feared all was lost, and now. . . *He was on his knees*! She'd not expected that at all. She had only thought of this as a business proposition! She did not need romance. Really, she'd be happy to simply sign papers and be done.

Hands shaking, she felt foolish struggling with her gloves after his romantic gesture. But she was still weak from laying her hands on him earlier. She had hoped she'd overcome her fatal compulsion to touch the ill, but not *touching* was how she came to be unmarried all these years.

And now that he'd actually proposed. . . How could she tell him to keep his hands off her when he was trying so hard to do the right thing?

But when he did not immediately stand after her barely whispered *Yes*, she could do no less than hold out her newly gloved hand and help him up. Raising all that great height was apparently a difficult procedure. She reluctantly lent him what strength she had.

Even through the gloves she felt prickles of warning traveling up her arm, and oddly, to her midsection as well as her lungs. She resisted her instinctive need to heal his pain. There was no point suffering with him. Consumption could not be cured.

She wanted to cry again that such an imposing gentleman should be doomed by such a hideously debilitating disease. As soon as he lurched to his feet again, she pulled her hand away.

"You honor me," Lord Dare said, pressing a dry kiss to her cheek.

The brief touch of his lips did not hurt, she realized with relief, but his proximity was frightening in its. . . She didn't have a word for what she felt.

She'd never met a man who held her interest for more than the ten minutes it took to speak with him. But this insanely impetuous man had understood everything she hadn't said and instead of scorning her—he'd acquiesced! In a few minutes, he'd analyzed all the pluses and minuses that she'd spent countless restless nights debating and made his decision without hesitation. Perhaps *astonishment* was the word she looked for.

"No more so than you honor me," she muttered. "I cannot believe you haven't called me mad or simple-minded or simply shocking."

"Oh, well, we are both a little of all that," Dare said cheerfully, attempting to tuck in his shirt and button his waistcoat. "But let us say we are pragmatic. I'm not at all certain I want to hear what romantic delusion caused you to turn your back on all the gentlemen who would gladly take you up on your offer."

"I am twenty-six years of age. I've had quite enough time to inspect all the available bachelors, and they've all come up short, sometimes literally," she admitted with a deprecating laugh, stepping away from him so he did not loom quite so much over her.

"We have only met once and briefly," he reminded her. "You cannot have met *all* of society."

She grimaced. "I think I have a better notion of who is available than you. You are much like my Ives cousins-in-law. You spend your time in male circles, intent on your own interests, which means you are seldom available in ballrooms and parlors for me to study, as most other gentlemen are. And you can scarcely say you know *me* or my family or you would understand why my choices are limited."

He glanced around, locating his frock coat over a bust of some ancient Greek. She watched in fascination as he pulled on the coat. She'd never really seen a gentleman dress before. Which made her wonder—would he expect to *live* with her? Would she have to become used to this familiarity? Her throat clenched at the possibility. Surely not. He was a man of a wide variety of interests, all of them city related. She should be safe enough in the Yorkshire countryside.

This would be a marriage in name only, mere names upon a license and the legal settlements.

"You are saying there is something about you and your family that makes gentlemen decline a fortune? That must be a very large *something*." Buttoning his coat, he glanced down at her, looking quite ridiculous with his smudged face and white eyes.

Despite being of a very fine cloth and tailoring, the coat fit loosely on him—one more sign of his illness. Sadness enveloped her as Emilia recognized how sharp the viscount's mind was. Had she only met the gentleman sooner. . . They would have despised each other. From all reports, he was very much a masculine sort with little interest in society ladies. He even treated the females of his family with appalling disregard.

"I am a Malcolm." She waited for recognition of this flaw. He looked at her blankly. He really did not go about in society much. A little more of her confidence returned now that she held his interest. "My family is said to be descended from the *witches* you scorned earlier. We have eccentric beliefs—one of which is that what belongs to the females of the line, stays with them. Trusts were established long ago to lock up our fortunes so our husbands cannot spend or gamble them away."

He stopped fastening his coat and stared at her from beneath singed eyebrows. Honestly, the man looked little better than a chimney sweep. Well, maybe three or four chimney sweeps all packed together.

"I cannot touch your inheritance once we marry?" he asked warily.

"Smart man." She opened the study door, knowing his mother was waiting anxiously not far away. "If you do not hesitate at my obvious flaw of being unfeminine and unladylike, you may argue the settlements with my great-grandfather's executor and my father's solicitor. They are both eager to have me off their hands, and they will approve of you. I'm sure the arrangements for the funds you need will be satisfactory."

He looked relieved to know that funds would be forthcoming, establishing the basis of this marriage as one of convenience, thank goodness. She had no romantic notions. This bargain would achieve what she wanted more than anything else in the world—and that wasn't a husband.

Lord Dare's brilliant brain evidently kicked in, and he bowed gallantly. "Unfeminine? Never. In my eyes, you are Venus. Never say you are less." He kissed the back of her glove, apparently recognizing the need for gentlemanly flattery at a moment like this.

She waited for the shudder or the prickles, but as with his earlier kiss, her gift didn't react. It wasn't as if she had much experience at kissing of any sort.

Even in his illness, Montague Dare was a dashingly handsome gentleman. Had she been any other female, she might have swooned at his attentions. Unfortunately, she had more sense than that. She removed her hand to avert any potential pain, delicately laid her glove on his filthy coat sleeve, and allowed him to lead her to the drawing room, where Lady Dare and two girls barely out of the schoolroom studied them with worlds of hope in their eyes. Emilia had sisters of that age, excitedly anticipating their coming-outs in a few years, full of the expectation of youth. She almost wept at their optimism that all would be well.

No matter how terrified she was of what she'd just agreed to do, she must remember that her purpose was to help others. Nervously, she clung to Lord Dare's sleeve as he made his announcement of their betrothal.

The girls cried out in excitement and flung themselves at their brother, despite his dirt. To Emilia's dismay, the demonstrative Lady Dare hugged her. She stiffened against the onslaught of prickles, but if the older lady harbored any real pain, it was swept away on the tide of her joy and relief.

"You will never regret this, my dear," the viscountess declared happily. "God has sent you our way, and we will take care of you as our own precious treasure."

Seeing Emilia's discomfort, Lord Dare lifted his mother and handed her back to his sisters. They all wiped tears, and then Lady Dare flung her short arms around his broad chest, smearing herself with soot. "You have no idea how happy you've made me!" she cried.

Apparently, Emilia's dreams weren't the only ones achieved today.

Over his mother's head, her betrothed crooked an eyebrow as if to ask *Are you sure this is what you want?*

Well, no, she wasn't sure at all. She simply had no other choice.

"YOU'VE DONE WHAT?" Lady McDowell asked in horror that evening, as Emilia presented her betrothal as a *fait accompli*. Her broad face paled against the dusky gloom of the family parlor.

"You are the one who told me about Lord Dare." Emilia did not generally fritter her time in the parlor, but even as independent as she was, she knew she needed the help of her family to forge this next step in her life. "He was a perfect gentleman, and his family is thrilled."

"I should imagine they are," her mother said grimly. "But you might have consulted me and your father first. I swear, Emilia, there isn't a feminine instinct in your entire body. You actually went to his *house*?"

"Of course. I needed to speak with him alone. We have agreed that it should only take a week to arrange the marriage settlements and obtain a special license."

The obstinate man had also insisted that he could not continue living in his mother's house once they were wedded. They'd had their first argument when Lord Dare had declared that he was perfectly capable of journeying all the way to her inherited estate in Yorkshire.

That had not been her plan at all, and the argument had left her more than a little uncomfortable. She was apprehensive about his expectations of married life, but she had not anticipated the argument and had not prepared a speech about a proper marriage of convenience. Surely he understood the terms of their arrangement.

Even she had been forced to agree that he could not stay with his weeping mother and sisters. Her grandfather's cottage was large enough to house both of them in their own suites. She didn't think Dare would like rural life much, but Harrogate was nearby. He could probably rent an inexpensive flat there once he grew bored in the village. He had a manservant to look after him, after all.

"I would like the ceremony to be held at our home in Cambridge, if possible," Emilia told her mother. "That will nicely break Lord Dare's journey so he has time to rest before we depart for Alder." At least this way, if they left together after the ceremony, it would look like a true marriage. Not being under the eye of all society would be an immense relief.

Lady McDowell hastily wiped at her eye. "My eldest daughter, the first to be married. I have dreamed of this moment for years, and I cannot even prepare a sumptuous celebration? It's *August*. There is no one about anywhere!"

Emilia had only seen her mother cry once, long, long ago. She had no wish ever to see her weep again. That was half the reason she was doing this. Awkwardly, she leaned over to pat her mother's hand. "Please, Mama, for Lydia and all the other children who can be saved, I *must* do this. You know I must. I was never meant for a real marriage. And Lord Dare understands as I cannot expect any other man to do."

Her mother dabbed at her eyes with her handkerchief. "He and his family are so *traditional.* I had hoped. . . Your cousins found nice Ives men who understand their gifts. . ."

Emilia shook her head. "You know for yourself how disorienting and painful it is for me to be touched. Now that I've found a way to heal with herbs, it's much less dangerous than using my hands. And the benefit of healing with herbs is that anyone can do it. Lydia is breathing easier now, isn't she? She doesn't need me?"

Lady McDowell took a deep breath that lifted her ample bosom. "You are right, of course. I do not know how you knew to mix your herbs with steam so her asthma has almost disappeared. After we almost lost her. . ." She picked up her notes and turned a page. "I will send a note to the staff in Cambridge to set the house to rights. Another to my sisters who can send the word out. We *will* have a celebration, if it's the last thing I do."

"I certainly hope it won't come to that," Emilia said in amusement, relieved to have the discussion over. She had known that her mother, of all people, would understand.

Daughter of an earl, wife of a viscount, Lady Daphne McDowell was the mother of six oddly-gifted children. She had to be disciplined and organized and *understanding.*

Emilia would do anything for her family, including die, which she had almost done once already. The pharmacopeia was a far better solution than dying.

AS HIS BETROTHED had predicted, the marriage settlements hadn't taken long, Dare acknowledged. He had spent the better part of a week learning all the parameters of the lady's trust and dowry. He was so pleased with the result, that he was even tolerant of his new bride's eccentric family wedding rituals.

Standing beside Miss McDowell before the vicar, he gazed with interest over the small crowd of guests on the lawns of her family's ancestral home in Cambridge. None of them seemed concerned about the peculiar additions of cape and thorny crowns Lady McDowell had insisted he and his intended wear. He'd been a bit taken aback by the vows they'd just exchanged—where had they found a vicar willing to accept promises to *love, honor, and take thee in equality?* But his bride's intense expression held Dare transfixed. He would have agreed to anything to make her smile at him. She didn't, but under the circumstances, he couldn't argue with her need for independence. She could be a widow within the year. He bent to kiss her icy pale cheek, and she squeezed his coat sleeve.

At the end of the service, he shook the pigeon cack off his new top hat and watched leniently as the newly-released birds flew into the park's trees.

They'd both been caught up in the *business* of marriage this past week. There hadn't been time to talk, but he'd had a lot of time to dream of his fiancée—and their marriage bed. These past months living with his mother and sisters had been frustrating beyond all patience. He wasn't dead *yet.*

He supposed, though, he should have asked the lady how she'd imagined this marriage of convenience would work. Since he seldom had difficulty talking women into bed, he'd not given it much thought until now, when this one was almost within his reach.

While his own family wept with joy, his new family surged around them, shaking his hand, and hugging his bride, who didn't seem to appreciate the embraces.

In the week leading up to their wedding, he'd done no more than kiss the new Lady Dare on her cheek. Although no one knew the cause of consumption, his reading of medical journals made him wary of contagion. Kissing seemed dangerous. His bride hadn't complained about the lack of affection, which had him wondering about her willingness to consummate their marriage.

Dare never turned aside a good challenge.

Although he'd like to punch the one approaching now.

His cousin Peter did not look like a person one wished to punch. Slender, fashionably-dressed, an expensive beaver covering his honey-colored hair, he was a short man with an attitude behind his affable smile.

"Who invited you?" Dare asked grumpily.

"Your mother, of course." Peter's smile slipped as he turned his back on the crowd. "I'm your heir, if you'll remember. She's all that's polite."

Dare's damned mother was all that and more. "You are talking of the woman you intend to put out of her home, you'll remember." Feeling a coughing fit coming on, he clenched his fists to hold it back.

"Your sisters will marry, and she can live with them," Peter said with a dismissive wave of his gloved hand. "The elderly do not need the space a young family does. Rather nasty of you to marry just to make your bride a widow, though, isn't it?"

Dare glanced at his bride, currently enveloped in the embraces of his sisters and looking uncomfortable. An unexpected surge of hope braced him sufficiently to hold back his cough and to smile malevolently at his cousin. "My wife is a paragon of female virtue. Her family is very prolific. Just look around you. This is a very small portion of her relations. My advice is not to count your hens before they're hatched, dear cousin."

Feeling happier than he had in months, he strode toward his bride, leaving Peter stewing in his own evil juices.

For the morning ceremony, his new wife had worn a white muslin gown and matching wide-brimmed hat adorned in white and black roses. He despised those hats that hid her face and kept him at a distance. But in the August humidity, she looked cooler than he did. Still he noticed she surreptitiously removed the silly rowan crown they'd both worn according to family tradition. He handed his to her mother, along with the ridiculous cape, now that the ceremony was over.

"Do you need more horehound?" his bride whispered, touching his coat sleeve with her gloved hand and leaning close between hugs and excited chatter.

Dare gestured at his pocket where he'd stored the honey-lemon-flavored candies she'd given him. They had a bitter aftertaste but suppressed his cough. "I have a few more. But we need to leave soon if we're to make the first stop of our journey before dark."

He had to concede that the challenge ahead wasn't just his new wife, but his own damned weakness. His head pounded, and he had the strength of a limp noodle, but he wasn't about to mention weakness to his stunning bride.

He regretted that he wasn't the man he'd once been, but he was still a man. And Emilia was all woman, smelling of lavender, looking like a virginal Venus, and causing what was left of his blood to race. He wanted strength for his husbandly duties tonight—if only they could escape soon.

Lord Theo Ives emerged from the crowd of well-wishers to pound Dare on the back. "Welcome to the exotic world of Malcolm marriage, old boy. You'll never be bored again."

Lady Aster, Lord Theo's wife, released her husband's arm to take Emilia's. "Come along, I need to speak with the dowager Lady Dare about the details of your husband's birth so I may draw his astrological chart."

Emilia sent him a pleading look, but Dare figured it would be a very short conversation and a very short chart given his fate, so he let her go. Besides, he needed to discuss investments with Theo.

"Did you talk with the rest of the railroad committee?" Dare asked, leading Theo toward a grove of trees, away from the wedding party. "Has the Crown agreed to sell that final stretch of land that we need to finish the tracks?"

Theo rubbed his nose, and Dare experienced a sinking feeling. Theo wasn't much of a talker, but his rubbing his nose meant he didn't *want* to talk.

"You won't like this." Theo finally found his words. "In an amazing piece of bad luck, my uncle and his new wife now own the entire property. Rather than sell the single strip we need, the Crown bestowed *all* of Alder Abbey on Pascoe. We've missed our opportunity."

"How is that bad luck?" Dare asked. "We've not been able to pry the plot out of the Crown's hands, but your uncle has somehow managed to put it back in circulation. We just need to pay him instead of the king. Or we could make him an investor. He should be happy to be rid of that worthless stretch."

Theo shoved his hand in his pockets and rocked back on his heels. "One would think that would be the easiest solution, but you haven't had time to grasp the intricacies of being married to a Malcolm. They look so fragile and lovely, don't they?" He glanced at the sea of frilly hats and delicate fabrics blowing gracefully in a breeze as the women gathered around the bride.

Women were *supposed* to be fragile and lovely. Dare noticed his bride stood taller than all the rest, but that didn't make her any stronger. She was already sending him another pleading look. He swelled with pride that she turned to him. He nodded to her, then regarded Theo without understanding. "What do our wives have to do with anything?"

Theo held up his fingers and began counting them off. "One, Malcolms probably own half of England. Two, the women are all married to some of the most powerful men in the kingdom. Three, they control as much of the wealth as their husbands. Four, they are the most intransigent, whimsical, irrational flight of moon-touched pigeons as you can imagine. You have no notion of what you've let yourself in for."

Whimsical women, he understood. Powerful ones—that was a rather quelling notion, but even if such a creature existed, Dare didn't see how it applied. "What does this have to do with your uncle and his land?"

"Pascoe is married to another Malcolm, the same cousin who has invited Emilia to build her laboratory and clinic in *Alder Abbey*. It is the reason your bride is finally eager to marry and take over her grandfather's estate. Do you really think they will give up that land for a railroad?"

Dare refused to believe two reasonable men couldn't sit down and negotiate a contract. "If we don't connect the properties on either side of the abbey land, the railroad can't go through. We'll lose everything. I'll talk with him."

Theo nodded, not looking optimistic. "I don't have much invested, but the rest of you. . ." He made a helpless gesture. "You may be our only hope."

"I'll talk to your uncle," was all Dare said, saving his breath to fight the urge to cough. "Men are rational, and the land is his."

"Probably not now," Theo said with a sigh. "He would have put part of it up as a dower for his bride and offspring. Looks like my brother's berlin has arrived to haul you to your fate. Sorry to set you off on your wedding journey on a sour note. Maybe once you're there, you can find alternatives."

Dare hoped so. His marriage settlement provided the wherewithal to see his family properly housed, but his investments must pay for their future. He didn't want to leave his mother in penury, as his father had. He'd worked hard and long to be better than that.

RECENTLY TAILORED, Lord Dare's wedding clothes fit his manly shoulders and narrow hips to perfection. Emilia had scarcely been able to pry her gaze from her new husband all morning. Now that she clutched his coat sleeve in preparation for departing, she was relieved to confirm that the layers of fabric prevented her from sensing whatever pain he suffered. Or her nervousness did.

She was about to leave behind her family and embark on a journey to her new future. She had a right to be nervous.

Dare led her toward the grandiose coach the marquess of Ashford had generously sent down for their use. Here was their first test of disorder at the way things ought to be. Men were supposed to hand ladies in, but she stepped aside. "You will have to climb in first," she nervously informed him.

He shot her a look of surprise, then intelligently, peered inside. His eyebrows rose. "Where are our legs supposed to go?"

"It's a mattress, so you may rest," she said, clasping and unclasping her gloved hands. "But it needed to go on the far side so we can climb in and out. The plank can be removed and the mattress rolled up, if you prefer, but we've stored your valise and a box beneath it. I have rather a lot of. . . books. I was trying to think of what you might need," she whispered. "I am not very good at it."

In fact, she was very bad at thinking of others. She'd never really needed to do so—unless they were ill.

"I am not an invalid yet," he growled, glaring down at her.

Oh, dear, she had so hoped. . . She raised her chin as she had learned to do when arguing with gentlemen. "You will be an invalid much sooner if you do not take care of yourself."

"I will take care of me," he insisted. "I do not want posies or soup or *mattresses*. Men take care of women, not the other way around."

She thought her eyebrows might fly off her head. "That is the most absurd notion I've ever had the displeasure of hearing. Women take care of men from birth. You'd be incapable of feeding yourselves otherwise. You may remove the mattress, if that is your desire, but I will refrain from carrying you out of the carriage if you pass out before we reach our destination."

She was shivering with temper—on her wedding day! She had tried so hard to think of a way to please him. . .

He turned his glower back to the unusual arrangement across the seats. "I detest being reminded that I am ill."

"I detest being told I am female and thus weak," she retorted.

"Women *are* weak," he insisted. "I should know, I've lived with them all my life." Rather than argue or posture more, her groom climbed in to test the strength of the plank. Apparently satisfied, he reached down for her hand and lifted her in. "But I appreciate that you thought of my comfort."

He did not say it in a tone of mollification, but at least he'd accepted the arrangement.

"If. . . if we are to learn to live together. . ." Taking a seat, Emilia twisted her gloved hands as she nervously sought words. The footman shut the door, enclosing her in the dim interior with the imposing gentleman attempting to situate himself on a mattress far too short for his length. She took a breath and tried again. "We need to learn more about each other's likes and dislikes. I had thought this might be similar to the settee in your study."

She pushed a pillow behind his back to give him more support.

Dare flung his tall hat over the toe of his shoe and loosened his cravat. Without warning, he found her hat pin, removed it, and flung her hat on the far seat as well. "If you really wish to learn my preferences, I prefer to see your face."

She ducked her head to look at her hands. "As I prefer to conceal it," she countered, feeling the heat rise in her cheeks. She despised that blush with all her heart and soul.

She really had not thought it through when he'd insisted that he journey with her to Yorkshire. But how could she have denied him? He was ill. For better or worse, he was her husband now.

Dare coughed, fought with a reply, then leaned back against the pillows in disgust while he fumbled for his handkerchief. Emilia opened her reticule and removed a paper of horehound drops.

"I wish these did more than suppress the cough," she murmured.

"Safer than opium," he gasped between bouts. "Can you reach the valise?"

Normally, she would have questioned. But this transition from being herself into being part of a couple was awkward. If they were to share the same house for a while, she would like him to be comfortable with her. He was helping her achieve her dream, after all, and even in her self-absorption, she recognized that a dying man ought to be given what made him happy. But she heartily disapproved of patent medicine, which is what she feared he had in his valise.

She tugged the bag out anyway and set it in the small space between them, opening the latch so he needn't struggle to sit up more.

He rummaged with one hand until he pulled out a clear bottle that appeared to be no more than water. "Mineral water," he said, as if understanding her curiosity. "It can't hurt to try."

She smiled in relief and returned the valise to the floorboards. "People have been drinking it for centuries. I don't think it's killed anyone yet, although I doubt that it has cured them either."

He swallowed the water, then took one of her lozenges. "We have no way of knowing what it does. We need more scientific means of experimenting, which requires comparison between groups using the waters and those who don't. And even then, every person and every disease is different, so it would take very large groups for the experiment to be effective."

This was the kind of conversation she understood, and she was delighted that he didn't think her too feeble-witted to comprehend. "If we only understood the source of the disease, it might be easier to experiment with than with people. It is one of the reasons I've wished for a microscope, but the university will not allow me to use theirs, and they're too expensive for my budget."

With the coughing halted, he folded up his handkerchief, set aside his bottle, and angled himself so he could see her. "I'm surprised you know anything about microscopes and experimentation. Most women simply nod knowingly and talk about their modiste when I mention them."

Emilia tried very hard not to shoot him a look of icy disgust. He seemed teachable. She would be patient. "Most women aren't given the education I have." Or the incentive to learn what she needed. Unfortunately, she thought telling him of her healing ability would push his credulity if he didn't even believe she had a brain.

He nodded, looked doubtful, and apparently tested her by saying, "I have the most recent Dolland instrument, but lighting is still a problem. Chemical methods are more successful in separating the elements of water."

"I was fortunate enough to be allowed to look into a Dolland at the university. It could be most useful in my research, but I am not interested in chemicals and elements," she replied, proving she knew as much as he. "I am interested in living organisms.

Microscopes are revealing that plants and animals have a cellular structure. What causes those structures to become diseased?"

He frowned, then closed his eyes. "An interesting approach. Let me think on it. The rocking of the coach is a better soporific than laudanum."

"It's been a rather long day, and it's only half over," she agreed, castigating herself for exhausting him with her need to defend her research. She'd spent this past week reading all she could on consumption. Rest was essential, which was why she'd had the mattress installed.

Once he closed his eyes, she found the latest scientific journal she'd been reading, removed her gloves, and settled into her corner. She had considered changing into a travel gown rather than cover her wedding gown in road dust, but had decided being cool was more important. Besides, this first part of the journey was along well paved roads, and would merely take them a distance outside the city. Tomorrow would be more daunting.

Despite her immense concentration, she couldn't read. The big man beside her seemed to fall almost comatose. She had to keep checking to see if he breathed. Did she dare. . . ?

She contemplated the rise and fall of her husband's shirt front. He'd managed to unfasten coat and waistcoat again. The man obviously did not like confinement. His neckcloth was still loosely tied but fell to one side. Did she dare. . . ?

She'd used her gift on him earlier. She thought it had helped. At the time, her fear and nervousness had made it easier to detach the physical connection that her gift demanded. Healing was far more difficult with children, when every instinct demanded that she *cure* them, to her own detriment.

She didn't mind suffering with her patient if she knew she was healing him. The real problem was when she didn't let go in time. She hadn't fully tested her abilities when she connected with a patient, but the problem seemed to be that the healing itself deprived her of the life energy she needed to breathe.

Herbs were far safer.

She wasn't foolish enough to believe she could cure consumption, of course, but if she could prove to herself that she actually helped. . .

She either tried now or must give up all hope of ever using her daunting gift. Delicately, she laid her fingers on Dare's shirtfront. He didn't stir.

With a little more confidence, she flattened her palm against a hard wall of muscle. Her new husband was a tall man, well-built, but lean. She wished she dared open his shirt, but that was a step she couldn't take. Instead, she focused on his breathing, the way his lungs moved beneath her hand, the harsh raking of air against damaged tissue... Prickles crept up her arm, forming a raging current straight to her own lungs, creating a deep angry ache...

She lost herself in the energy, the exchange of pain and heat. If only she knew more...

He jolted awake, sitting up with a start. "What the—?"

Startled, Emilia yanked back her hand. Trembling at how far she'd gone, she pretended nothing had happened. Weak and not a little dizzy, she flipped a page of her journal. "You're awake. Did the nap help?"

Healing always drained her. She ached in all the places he must, and she still had no means of knowing if she'd helped.

Dare rubbed absently at his chest and peered around the window curtains. "I've been better. We should be arriving before long. I'm a bit peckish for a change. I don't think you ate much of the wedding breakfast. Shall we dine early?"

Emilia hid a smile of triumph. If he was hungry, she'd helped heal him a little, she was sure—because her gift drained her, and she was now exhausted and had no interest whatsoever in food.

Three

DARE WAS DISGUSTED with himself for sleeping through the hours he'd thought to use seducing his bride. Climbing out of the coach, reinvigorated from his nap, he watched his calm and collected wife stand to one side while servants clambered and bustled about, handling the luggage and horses. She'd donned her hat again, so he couldn't read her eyes.

Despite the heat, the dust, and the sweltering journey, she appeared detached from her surroundings. She clung to the heavy valise she'd insisted on removing from beneath the plank under his mattress. Books, she had said. She was taking books to their bridal chamber.

He didn't even know what to call her. The formality of *Lady Dare* didn't suit her—that was his mother, devil take it. But they had scarcely reached the intimacy of using her given name either.

She took his arm when he offered, dipping her blasted hat in acknowledgment of his support. Only when he led her to the stairs in the innkeeper's wake did Dare realize she clutched his arm as if he were her anchor. Did the night ahead make her that nervous? He regretted having to release her when she lifted her skirt to follow in single file up the narrow stairs.

The inn had been chosen because it catered to aristocratic clientele, and their room had been arranged in advance. Their host led them to a large chamber with a wide bed and a small dining table. A door connected to a smaller room with two cot-sized beds, for children and servants—or a reluctant bride.

"Would you prefer to rest before dinner?" Dare asked, discarding his hat as the last of the servants departed. He regarded his seemingly composed bride with fascination.

She removed the garden of roses on her head. Rays from the setting sun accented ebony tresses with an almost blue-black sheen. A lovely hint of pink colored her high cheek bones.

"If you would not mind. . ." She hesitated.

"Let us understand each other from the start," he said

impatiently. "I will not fall into a sulk if you do not wish to do what I want. I will not strike you if you outright object. I will not break if you have a better idea. I am impatient, irascible, and tediously single-minded, but I still manage to be a gentleman. I have only a short time left in this world to learn your preferences. Speak your thoughts without fear."

Without her hat in the way, he could see the weariness of her reluctant smile. "Then I should like nothing more than to wash and lie down, please. I will leave you to the larger bed. I believe the wagon with our servants and the rest of our baggage means to continue further down the road to arrive ahead of us. If I need aid, I'll call on an inn maid. Thank you for understanding."

Dare wanted to roar objection. All week he'd been planning for this evening! Admittedly, the inability to kiss her had a hampering effect, but he must have some kind of mental deficiency to let her escape without so much as a hug or semblance of regard. He could argue that the servants would gossip about their lack of conjugal rapport. . . but he had stupidly promised that she could have whatever she liked.

He would be an outright cad to object after she had seen to his comfort on their journey. The irony was that she had been right. He now felt invigorated enough to have the wedding night he'd planned. Tomorrow, he might not be able to say the same.

It was a delicate situation, but one he hoped he could manage with some degree of finesse. After all, he'd dealt with his all-female family for years without having them take off his head.

Clenching his jaw against protest, Dare bowed. "Your wish is my command, my lady."

She nodded, picked up her satchel, and slipped into the smaller room, closing the door behind her.

Now what the devil did he do with himself and all the restless energy he'd never been able to contain until he'd been struck down by disease?

Not daring to take a bracing ride across the countryside and risk stirring his cough, he stomped down to the tavern to look for food and a good card game to join.

EMILIA WAS PERFECTLY capable of removing her own clothes. Her modiste understood her needs and designed everything to perfection so no other person need touch her. It helped that she was so skinny that she really didn't need much of a corset. Her life had become much simpler once she'd dispensed with busybody servants tattling about the hours and company she kept.

She hung her lovely wedding gown on a hook and covered it with her gossamer hat. She untied the laces of her corset and shimmied out of it. She hadn't suffered this exhaustion since she'd tried to save her infant sister from a severe asthma attack and had almost died herself. Caution had come not just with age, but with genuine fear of dying.

She tucked her precious satchel into the wardrobe. Wearing her shift, she slipped between the covers, listening as her new husband let himself out of the room next door. She couldn't regret that he seemed healthier for her exertions.

But lying awake, wondering what a vigorous man like Devil Dare might be doing in an inn full of temptation, she had to admit to conflicting emotions. She had planned this marriage thinking they'd each go their separate ways—but she'd rather thought his way would be lying helplessly in bed. Foolish of her, she realized now.

She had known from an early age that marriage and carnal relations would never be for one with her unpredictable gift. A dying man had appeared to be an ideal solution. . . unless her need to heal him killed her first.

Lord Dare seemed like a reasonable man. Perhaps she could explain her dilemma about touching and pain. Tomorrow. Or after they reached Harrogate. Sometime soon, when she was certain he wouldn't scorn her. Secure with that decision, she dozed.

She heard him return sometime later. The room was dark, but she didn't know the hour. He bumped against furniture—looking for the lamp? She couldn't decide whether to be fascinated with this new aspect of her life or frightened.

He started coughing at the same time as she realized she'd missed dinner and was hungry. Normally, she would call for Bessie, who was more companion than maid. But the servants had gone ahead to prepare the house for their arrival while the newlyweds were theoretically. . . newly-wedding.

She got up, lit a lamp, and pulled a robe from her valise. Wrapping it around her, she rummaged for more horehound. She wished she had a better palliative, but opium was a final stage option. As her new husband cursed, fumbled around, and coughed in the other room, she summoned her courage.

She heard him groan and cast up his accounts, and she panicked. Was he drunk?

How could she have forgotten that he was known as *Devil* Dare? A pleasant afternoon while he napped, a few brief conversations, and she thought he'd changed?

Should she pretend she didn't hear him? Except, he was ill. She was constitutionally incapable of ignoring the ill.

Knocking briskly on the connecting door, she opened it without waiting for him to reply. The hot August heat made the room uncomfortable. He'd lit a lamp, so she could see to cross the room. He splashed water in the basin behind the dressing screen while she opened the window to let in what small breeze there was.

Dare emerged dressed only in shirtsleeves and trousers, looking a little pale but not drunk. She swallowed hard at all that broad male chest covered only in thin linen. Her husband was amazingly muscular for an ill man. And she shouldn't be studying his physique.

Silently, she handed him the horehound. He grimaced and rummaged in the drawer in the stand beside the bed, producing a bottle. Thinking he was taking his mineral water, Emilia waited. Only when he'd swigged and coughed some more did she see the label.

She grabbed it before he could return it to the drawer. "Fowler's Solution?" She carried the bottle closer to the lamp to read the label. "It says nothing of the contents. Do you have any idea what is in this?"

He snatched the bag of horehound from her hand and helped himself to one. With the cough under control, he began to breathe without the frightening choking sound. "I told you, my physician recommended that I test it."

"You've said yourself that you need more subjects before a *test* is a true experiment. You can't take both mineral water and patent medicine and expect to know which cures you." Instinct told her to fling it far, far away, but she had to respect his decisions if she expected him to respect hers. She returned the bottle to the table.

"Neither will cure me," he said with a fatalistic shrug. "But Fowlers calms the cough when nothing else does."

"Which means it could contain codeine," she warned. "It's addictive."

Perhaps the heat she felt at his lingering look was simply an effect of the room's closeness.

"I know better than that. I tested it chemically. Formaldehyde and sulfuric acid detects opium derivatives." He rudely sprawled out on the bed and eyed her dishabille with lascivious interest. "Are you rested now?" he asked with a degree of hope in his voice.

Ah, there was the devil he could be. A thrill raced through her at the way his eyelids lowered to study her with masculine curiosity. She was unaccustomed to this sort of attention, so of course she preened a little. Just a little.

"How do you know what detects opium? I've never heard of such a test." Despite her effort to see her husband as helpless, Emilia had to force her attention to their argument and away from the interesting sprawl of his long legs. . . and other parts. . . on the bed.

"I invented the test. Don't have much better to do these days. If I thought it was of any use, I might write a paper on it some time, but I doubt anyone else cares what's in their quack medicine." He watched her in the same way a cat watched a mouse.

"I care," she said defiantly, refusing to be intimidated. "Apothecaries hand out dangerous chemicals without having any notion of what they do to our bodies. Good food and sunshine can cure ills without quackery."

His eyes danced with the laughter that had probably helped earn him his nickname. "Ah, now I see, you're irritable when you're peckish. I've been selfish. I should have brought something up for you. Let me call the innkeeper. They probably have some of their tasty meat pie left over."

"How do you know I'm hungry?" she asked peevishly, looking away from his knowing gaze.

"Because my sisters become cross if they're not fed regularly." He sat up and reached for the bell pull. "I should prove myself useful in some manner."

Within minutes, he'd summoned food and drink and ordered hot water for both of them.

She wanted to be spiteful and disagree, but he was right—she needed food. And she was the one being unreasonable because she didn't like him taking charge when she should have been able to do so herself. Grudgingly, she took the chair he pulled out. The meat pie smelled wonderful.

"I am not accustomed to traveling without my maid to deal with servants," she said stiffly.

"But you are accustomed to making business propositions to strange men?" he asked, settling back on his bed rather than sit across from her. "I'm surmising you simply forget to eat."

"Well, that, too," she admitted after swallowing the first delicious bite. It was very mean-spirited of her to object to her husband being attentive. "I have had to fight with men for every bit of advanced education I've acquired, so a business proposition isn't new. Traveling without a retinue is. My family is very large, and there is always someone to go with me."

"What kind of education must you fight for?" he asked with interest. "It's not as if any of the universities will allow females."

"My family is not poor. I have pin money that allows me to hire students and professors who need a supplemental income." She tasted the ale he'd provided and wrinkled her nose at it.

"You have half a dozen lovely sisters with dowries, and the students were all panting on your doorstep, eager to do anything you asked," he corrected.

She shrugged. "As I said, I have copious knowledge of available men. Most of them are utterly useless, spineless, or misogynistic beyond all use." Which was rather why she resented his not being any of these or what she expected at all.

"But a few of my tutors understood the wisdom of introducing me to their textbooks and lecture notes," she continued in between bites. "Those truly interested in botany helped me with my experimentation techniques. Unfortunately, I have reached the limits of their knowledge. I need a laboratory, a microscope, gardens, and a conservatory that my father can't provide."

"Do you know how to create a laboratory?" he asked, only raising his eyebrows slightly at her expensive list of demands.

"I've read Antoine Lavoisier's articles, and pamphlets written by other scientists since then. They are mostly chemistry related," she said, scowling again at his apparent doubt of her knowledge. "I've made lists of what I'll need."

"Is your grandfather's house large enough for this or will you be using your. . . cousin, didn't you say? Her grounds?"

"Lady Pascoe-Ives is a distant cousin who recently acted as midwife for two of my close cousins. She's an herbalist and female physician as well, so we've been corresponding. She claims there is adequate room for a laboratory once she raises funds to rebuild the original infirmary." Emilia finished her pie. After her nap, she felt rejuvenated, but glancing at her husband, she could tell he was half-asleep. He looked much like a satisfied male cat sprawled across the covers.

"I should leave you to rest. Thank you for thinking of my dinner." She rose.

He held out his hand. "If we are to live under the same roof, we should learn some physical means of expressing regard for each other. It's a good way of defusing arguments."

She felt that odd thrill again, the one that *wanted* to bend over and kiss his cheek, as a wife was entitled to do. "I am not an affectionate person," she argued.

But he looked so tired and drawn that she risked the painful prickles of skin against skin, and took his hand. Then daringly, she leaned over to brush his cheek with her lips. She noticed his fever more than the tingling up her arm. When he attempted to pull her closer, she held a hand to his brow. "I will bring you some willow bark tea."

"I do not want a nurse," he said between clenched teeth.

"You want a money tree," she said pragmatically, patting his hand and letting it go. "You can drink the tea or not. It's no matter to me."

"I would like a wife," he stated unequivocally.

Emilia froze in her tracks. "A wife?"

"I am still a man," he growled, holding her gaze.

She could hear her pulse pounding in her ears. "There is no question about that," she whispered.

"We will start work on marriage tomorrow, shall we?"

The devil was definitely in his eyes. She'd thought them gray earlier, but in this light, they were a seductively pale green. His lips bent in a sensual curve that drew her gaze, and she swallowed. "Tea," she said senselessly, before fleeing in utter terror.

Four

DARE DAMNED HIS COUGH, his weak chest, and his disease as he waited for his lady wife to emerge from her chamber the next morning. They'd breakfasted in their separate rooms, but he'd hoped she might need help with her fastenings, and that he could make his first overtures then. But while he cast up his accounts again, she emerged fully clothed, carrying her valise, and already wearing her frivolous hat. This time, the hat was adorned with purple flowers to match her purple gown, he noted, hastily rinsing his mouth and pretending to straighten his neckcloth as he stepped away from the dressing screen.

The physician had warned the medicine might be as bad as the disease, but it lengthened his life just a little, he'd have to live with it.

Dare supposed his wife's gown was purple. His sisters would have insisted that it was violet or mauve or lavender. All he knew was that his bride looked stunning in it. It was made of a fabric sturdier than the muslin she'd worn yesterday, so he assumed it was some sort of travel gown. But it clung to her slender waist and narrow hips. Embellished with ruffles and a short cape, it created hourglass curves where he was fairly certain there were none. He enjoyed the effect. She'd even tilted the hat back enough that he could see the color rising in her fair cheeks as he continued to stare.

"Did I miss a button?" she inquired with hesitation.

"I would like it if you missed a button or three," he admitted salaciously. "You could miss the whole cape, and I would be a happy man. How did your former suitors keep their tongues in their heads around you?"

He offered his arm before he said anything else ridiculous. Perhaps the disease ate at his brain. He took her heavy valise, and it almost wrenched his arm from his socket. Books, she'd said. She'd brought books to bed.

Her cheeks brightened to rose, but she slipped her gloved fingers into the crook of his elbow. "I am sure I do not know," she said with just a touch of acid. "I would think loose tongues would lead to unpleasant drooling. I should be forced to consider rabies."

He couldn't stop a chuckle. "Only my brilliant wife would call me rabid. I think I like it."

"I am still new to this. . . intimacy of saying what I like, as you do," she said, not as stiffly as before. "No one has ever insulted me in quite such a manner before."

Dare laughed. Feeling in charity with the world again, he almost clattered down the narrow stairs as was his usual wont, but he was aware that she had to lift her skirts and go slowly. He wouldn't have her breaking her neck, so he walked sedately and caught her arm again once they reached the common room.

"I'll have you know that wasn't an insult, my lady," he said in mocking offense. "I normally do not pant over ladies and wish their clothes to the devil. But you, my lovely wife, are a confection beyond any man's wildest dreams. I still cannot fathom why someone with more to offer hasn't snatched you up before me, although I am eternally grateful that they did not."

He would say many things to worm his way into her bed, but he honestly meant these.

She tilted her hat down so he couldn't see the color rise in her cheeks, but now that he knew he could make her blush, he was relentless. Even if he could only touch her with words, it added spice to the long ride ahead.

"I did not wish to be *snatched* by just any man," she replied as a footman opened the carriage door. "But as far as I am aware, no man has ever shown interest in snatching me."

Dare leaned under her hat to kiss her cheek before tucking her valise back in its hiding place and climbing into his bed. He despised being treated as an invalid, but he decided to accept the notion of a rolling bed as long as there was any chance that his bride might join him. He waited until she was inside the carriage with the door closed before removing his gloves and pulling at her hat pins.

"Then I declare every man in London to be deaf, dumb, and blind. You are so far beyond exquisite that perhaps your beauty blinded them." He flung her hat to the far seat with his gloves.

Instead of berating him, she sat still for a moment. He feared he'd gone too far and that she would switch to sitting at his feet rather than be near him.

Finally, she spoke without looking up. "Is flattery your idea of seduction?"

Ah, she remembered what he'd told her last night—he wanted a real marriage, or at least the bed part.

Dare leaned back against the pillows and admired his polished boot toes while he considered the question. "Actually, I don't think so. I flatter my mother and sisters outrageously, and I'm pretty certain it's not to seduce them. They're pretty, and they go to great lengths to look so, and they deserve recognition of their efforts."

She turned her head so he could see her large purple eyes and pink cheeks. "I have a modiste who tells me what is fashionable. The only effort I make is to braid my hair when my maid is unavailable. I will tell Madame Durand that you appreciate her efforts, thank you."

Dare laughed, then coughed. She instantly rummaged for the horehound, and he took one without argument. They were nasty but effective, and he wanted to talk since there was little else they could do. He took a sip of the mineral water she offered when the cough calmed down.

"Thank you." He returned the container to her. "I am apparently out of practice in flattery as well as seduction. One does not have to flatter glass beakers to get what one wants."

She smiled with more assurance at that bit of nonsense. "Precisely. I am not very good at expressing admiration for a gentleman's hand with horses or the quality of his boot polish or whatever it is that ladies say to suitors to flatter them. But I'll happily admire your extensive collection of glassware. Do you have someone in particular who creates it for you?"

"Come here and let me whisper sweet beakers in your ear." He held up his arm and reached for her shoulders.

She glanced warily at his arm, then shifted ever so slightly closer so that he might rest it on the useless cape covering her bodice. He reached around and found the bow and pulled the ribbon. "It's a hot summer day. You don't need this."

"My shoulders will be nearly bare without the pelerine," she protested. "And my neck is much too long for the style otherwise."

"Tell that to your modiste, not to the husband who wishes to admire your beautiful shoulders and neck." He removed the purple monstrosity and flung it to join the hat.

The ruffled neckline of her gown hid her bosom, although he

was already aware she wasn't voluptuous. That scarcely mattered when he was nearly drooling over lovely, supple shoulders the palest shade of alabaster. Her skin was so fine, he could see the pale blue vein in her throat. He traced his finger along it, enjoying the texture of her silken, lavender-scented skin.

She instantly stiffened. He waited, his finger lingering just over her pulse. "I cannot believe I am so fortunate as to have a wife as beautiful as you. I'm not sure what I've done to deserve it."

She gave an exaggerated sigh and shifted away again. "My beauty or lack thereof is irrelevant. I am far more interested in the source of your glassware."

"And here I thought I was single-minded! Do you find me repulsive?" he asked with curiosity. Ladies generally did not dismiss his attentions. Gauging from the heat in her cheeks, he was reasonably certain that she might be minimally interested.

She sent him what he assumed to be a shocked glance. "Repulsive? Why would I find you repulsive? Because of your cough? That hardly reflects on who you are. From all I've ascertained, you are a generous gentleman who takes care of his family, and an intelligent man who knows about laboratories and chemicals, even if you do tend to blow them up. If I'd found you repulsive, I would not have presented my proposition."

Dare angled himself to better study her. Her attitude of cool elegance appeared a little more vibrant than usual, and she actually seemed to be regarding him with attentiveness. "You find my *intelligence* attractive? I do not believe you live in the same world as the rest of us, my dear."

He shrugged out of his coat as he spoke. "I'm fairly certain you're no otherworldly angel or you wouldn't be sitting in the same carriage with me. Have you no curiosity about fleshly pursuits? Have you never kissed in the shrubbery with an admirer, if only to see what it is like?"

Dare didn't see any alarm in her expression as she watched him struggle out of the prison of his coat. Her detached scientific inspection would make him feel like a botanical specimen if it weren't for the rose circles high on her cheeks.

"I may have tried kissing once when I was very young. I didn't like it much. You will understand that I spend the majority of my time in my studies. I've not had much opportunity to be exposed to rakes who kiss in the shrubbery."

His beam of delight should have terrified her, but she only widened her eyes.

"Then let me be your first rake. I don't consider seducing innocents a wise investment in my time, but since you are my wife, we'll both learn something new." He reached for her lovely, almost-bare shoulders and encouraged her to shift closer again. He could swear she flinched—and he halted.

She was a grown woman—surely she had some notion of what marriage was about?

"Are you sure seduction is a wise idea?" she asked with doubt, using her gloved hand to move his fingers from her skin. "You have said kissing may be contagious. And I would think any exertion would return your cough. You do not need to exert yourself for my sake."

Ah, she was just nervous. Laughing, Dare stroked the underside of her delicate chin with his less-than-delicate hand, then lifted it so he might kiss the pink on her cheekbone. "I think I can manage the kind of exertion I have in mind, and I don't think kissing your lovely cheek will hurt. A beautiful woman should be offered tokens of appreciation for her efforts to improve the view."

"That's flummery," she said in disgust, but this time, she did not move away.

EMILIA CLASPED HER HANDS tensely while her husband stroked her throat with his *bare* hand.

He touched her—and she did not feel his pain.

Perhaps the excitement he stirred in her breast overrode the perception of pain. She needed to experiment with what made her more aware of him than herself.

Breathlessly, she waited as he toyed with her hair. Still, no pain, and her heart began to pound in anticipation. The heavy braided chignon looked dreadful on her. Until now, she hadn't cared. The big hand tugging loose her pins produced interesting shivers and made her think she should care.

If she thought of hair, she didn't have to think about how her flesh had unexpectedly developed an urge to be caressed, or how her insides knotted with longing when her husband pressed kisses along

her cheek. Her senses were too overwhelmed to encourage the
dangerous connection of her gift. She was aware of the shaving soap
smell just inches from her face and the sudden need to know how
hard a square chin might be, or if she could feel the whiskers
beneath his skin.

Until now, she had avoided male proximity and stifled any
curiosity to touch and sniff.

Her husband didn't *want* her to stifle her urges. Even as an
invalid, his big body sprawled across the large carriage with the
muscled tension and power of a lean panther, and she wanted more
than anything to stroke the sleek planes of muscle.

This was supposed to be a marriage of *convenience*, not a visit
to the Garden of Eden. Shaken, she couldn't force her formidable
mind to think this through. She simply wanted the boldness to kiss
his cheek as he did hers.

But then she would want to touch his chest. Her unpredictable
mind/body connection would take over. He'd panic and push away,
demanding explanations, and she simply couldn't bear it. . . .

He resolved her dilemma by taking her hand and placing it
against his shirt, as if he knew what she wanted. "I'd like for you to
touch me," he murmured, kissing her nape. "It's been far too long
since a woman has touched me."

He deliberately drew on her sympathy, she knew, but how could
she resist? She needed to touch, and he wanted to be touched. With
appalling fascination, she waited for the pain, for the insensible, too
sensitive connection.

Tell him, a little voice whispered. But she couldn't, not yet. She
would hate it if he laughed. Or looked at her with horror. It was not
as if he was the most understanding of men. But he was her
husband. If he didn't mind her touching, surely she should be
allowed to, just a little.

Swallowing hard, she splayed her fingers across his linen, which
ought to be safer than bare flesh. In relief and delight, she felt his
heart beat and his lungs gasp for air without absorbing his pain. She
wished she knew more of consumption and how his lungs *ought* to
feel.

But his kisses provided a satisfactory distraction from her
medical curiosity. Captivated by the wonder of his mouth on hers,
she stroked his hard chest simply for pleasure.

His bare hand slid beneath the neckline of her gown, at her shoulder, not far from her breast. The traveling gown was meant to be worn with the pelerine he'd so casually tossed. It had been too hot to add a chemisette. She gasped as his lips pressed against the rise of her breast.

"We will be stopping soon," she warned in a whisper, but her hand couldn't retreat from his chest. His waistcoat was open, as usual. She could unknot his neckcloth. . . but they would be almost disrobed when it came time to change the horses.

And she really hadn't thought any of this through. She was simply delighting in pain-free *touching*.

Lord Dare lifted his head enough for her to see his heavy-lidded eyes and the direction of their gaze. Emilia felt the heat rise in her breast, mottling her too-fair skin, another reason she preferred to be fully covered. Her nipples hardened, and she feared she was just as silly as any other foolish female he looked upon.

"I'll not take you for the first time in a coach," he murmured. "But there are so many other pleasant ways to pass the time."

Unable quite yet to pull her hand away from his chest, she stroked just a little lower, only a little, until she felt a *wrongness*. Did consumption also attack lower than the lungs? She hastily yanked her fingers away before the prickles started, and she forgot to be cautious.

He caught her misbehaving hand and pressed a kiss to the back of it. "I know seduction wasn't part of our agreement, but you do not seem to object. Am I correct? Or are you simply being polite by not slapping me out the window?"

She could hardly catch her breath much less consider a proper answer. She yanked her hand away and folded it in her lap. "Men generally do not show interest in me, so I did not give seduction any thought," she said honestly. "I'm anxious to start on the laboratory and to check on my grandfather's herb garden, and there was so much to do with the wedding and packing and. . . I just did not *think*."

"And you considered me too ill to make demands," he finished for her with a deprecating laugh. "I may be in a few months, when winter closes in. But in the meantime, if there's any chance that you might wish to be a wife in truth. . ."

Now, now, tell him now. But she couldn't, not any more than she could deny a dying man his wish or deny her own curiosity. If he had only a few months, why let her lack of knowledge stand between them? She had always feared that physical intimacy would cause the same dangerous connection as healing, but if she wasn't falling into the vortex of her gift now. . .

She swallowed hard and looked up to meet the shadows in his lovely gray-green eyes. She saw the sadness and the heat and the hope. . .

"You are hoping for an heir, are you not?" she answered, understanding more than he would say.

Looking disgruntled, he rumpled his hair and sat back. "It's not likely," he pointed out. "And if you do not wish to be left alone with a child, there are ways to prevent conception. My first thought was simply of how much I want you."

He said that as if he honestly meant it. She'd heard the rumors. Her husband was accustomed to having women in his bed. That he'd been deprived these last months of illness and living with his mother meant he would seek any woman handy. And she was *convenient*. There was the reason he was abandoning the city and its pursuits for rural boredom and took an interest in a bean pole like her.

She could feel his longing deep in her center, but rather than act on the pooling heat, she contemplated his statement with interest. "You really mean that, don't you? But now that I have mentioned an heir?" A child. . . She had really never given one a thought. Hers wasn't a maternal nature.

His disgruntlement slowly melted into a grin, then spread to dance in his eyes in a manner that made her heart go pitter-patter. He was a handsome, conniving male animal and almost nearly irresistible when he smiled like that.

"I would want to come back as a ghost to see Cousin Peter's face if you delivered a boy. He is planning the wallpaper for the townhouse already. He's told me he plans to install his childless wife in the rotting hunting box that we laughingly call my estate, and install his mistress and children in my mother's Mayfair home. He wants to bring his bastards up like ladies and gentlemen."

"The children aren't at fault for the iniquities of their parents, but he cannot be a very sympathetic man if he's telling you his plans for your death!"

"Exactly so," he murmured, sliding his fingers a little further beneath her bodice.

Her new husband had the devil's way about him, of a certainty. But miraculously, he still wasn't causing her any of the pain she feared. She held her breath and waited to see what he would do next.

Five

DARE HAD SEDUCED his fair share of women over the years, but he felt like a green youth when it came to his own bride. His prick rose to the occasion with no more provocation than a scent of lavender and a hint of soft skin as she leaned into him. They were in a carriage, deuce take it!

But it had been such a damned long time. . . Closing his eyes and indulging in sensation, he nibbled on the shell of her ear and felt her quiver delightfully. Still, she did not turn toward him. What would it take to stir white-hot passion in his bluestocking wife? Her corset offered no hindrance—

The hunt was on. He undid the tidy corset bow beneath her bodice, and his lady inhaled sharply.

Just that slight inhalation heightened his lust to feverish. Either that, or he was actually fevered. He was a sad, pathetic excuse for a man, but her newly-aroused excitement intensified his enjoyment of the experiment. With satisfaction, he knew he could now determine just how much bosom his bride possessed.

He ran kisses down her cheek and throat while he maneuvered his hand beneath her bodice and corset chemise, cupping a sweet peach of a breast. The nipple was already at full peak, and her moan as he tweaked it nearly crippled him. He needed to yank all that fabric out of the way and taste. . .

The driver shouted at the team and the carriage slowed.

Mentally cursing, Dare rested his forehead against the silk of her hair, regretfully stroked a furled nipple, and removed his hand. "I know waiting enhances the anticipation, but I fear I may collapse in a swamp of need before this journey ends."

She didn't immediately right herself but clenched her gloved hands in her lap and continued leaning against him, head bent. "I. . . I am at a loss as to what to say, as usual. Should we stay in the carriage?"

Tempted, but aware of the constraints of travel, Dare wound a loosened tendril around his finger and kissed her ear again. "The next stop will not be as nice an inn as this one. We'll only change horses there, so it's best to use the facilities here." He forced his legs over the side of his makeshift bed and secured her garden hat, returning it to her. Sighing with regret as he gave her fair bosom one last glance, Dare refastened her silly purple cape over her shoulders. "I'll have no other man admire what is mine. I'm feeling oddly possessive today."

Which struck him almost as hard as his lust. His mistress could have taken a dozen lovers, and he wouldn't have cared so long as she made time for him. But this woman. . . This one was *his* and his alone. Somehow, that made a difference. Perhaps because all that mattered to him had been inherited—except his horse. He had gained Emilia of his own accord, and she was a precious asset he must nurture, as his father had never tended the wealth of resources he'd been given.

The footman handed Emilia out. Dare had to adjust his trousers and don his coat before he was even remotely decent. Grabbing the door frame and using the steps instead of leaping out as he had once used to do reduced his ardor somewhat. He was only half the man he'd been. He'd do well to remember that.

"We should arrive in Alder this evening, shouldn't we?" she asked in a low voice before they entered the inn.

"Barring lame horses and broken axles, yes," he said with fervency, taking her hand on his arm and leading her to an inn maid who would see to her needs.

He'd been a selfish idiot to believe they could travel without her personal maid. He still didn't regret the rose in her cheeks when she threw him a thoughtful glance over her shoulder, before she was led away down a dark corridor. *Tonight, they could share a bed.*

He arranged a luncheon basket so they could return to the road immediately. Then he availed himself of the facilities, felt no need to cast up what remained of his breakfast, and forewent the medicine bottle.

His lady returned with her hair properly rearranged, looking as modest as was possible in that fashionable outfit, by the time a fresh team had been harnessed.

He climbed in, helped her up, took the lunch basket and set it on the floor, and signaled that they were prepared to proceed. As the door shut and he returned to his damned bed, he watched in satisfaction as her hat landed on the far seat. She deliberately untied her cape and flung it to join the hat, conveying her surrender.

A surge of joy and lust energized him.

They had an hour or more before the next stop. Dare tugged his bride until she tumbled across his lap.

EMILIA GASPED at suddenly being enveloped in big, warm male. She, who barely hugged her own family, was now shoulder to thigh with a near stranger, with his strong arms surrounding her. She could feel his limbs through her layers of clothing.

And it was. . . interesting. *Exciting* even, if she could recover from her attack of nerves. If only she could think clearly. . . She couldn't, but it seemed their mutual lust diverted the healing connection that began with prickles warning of pain and energy depletion to follow. She might suffer later but it was worth the risk. This contact was too new and marvelous to forego.

"We have at least an hour to play, more, if we leave the curtains drawn," he whispered in a deep voice low in his throat. He returned to fiddling with her bodice fastening.

She'd been the one to wantonly cast aside her pelerine. She could not complain if he took full advantage of her loose behavior. She did not want to complain. She had not been able to think of anything else the whole time they were separated. She wanted his hand on her breast again. That had been the most amazing. . .

She gasped as he located the bodice hook beneath the ruffle.

"I will double your modiste's wages," Lord Dare said in admiration, easily unhooking her. "A front-opening bodice is nothing short of brilliant."

It had been Celeste's idea, actually. Her new cousin was a seamstress with very practical notions. But Emilia was incapable of discussion while her husband systematically worked her fastenings and his bare fingers came closer to her aching flesh. The prickles were always worse when flesh touched flesh. She held her breath, praying. . .

"And the corset, too!" he covered her face in kisses, distracting her from what his agile fingers were accomplishing—until his big hot hand had covered her breast.

She almost melted. Instead of noticing pain, she became

excruciatingly aware that she was sitting across his thighs, and there was a long, hard. . . movement. . . beneath her bottom.

"It's too much," she gasped, clutching his waistcoat and dislodging his encroaching hand.

He arranged her more comfortably across one hard thigh but returned his hand to her breast. "Your turn, then. What would you like to do next?"

She was in serious danger of expiring from sensation and could scarcely pull two words together. "I. . . I do not know."

But she did. She wanted to touch his bare chest, except his waistcoat was fastened for a change. And his shirt was tucked into his trousers. And of course, touching bare skin was likely to. . . She settled on untying the black cravat around his neckcloth.

He shrugged out of his coat while she pried at the knot she'd unfortunately made with trembling fingers. He nuzzled her throat, reducing her thoughts to oatmeal. By the time she had the knot undone and started on his wilted linen, he was rucking up her skirt and petticoat.

"What. . . what are you doing?" she whispered as the heat of his hand caressed her stockinged limb. She didn't know if the rush of sensation was lust or his pain or her imagination.

"Wishing there was a respectable inn at the next stop," he said fervently. "You have legs a mile long, and I want to feel them wrapped around me."

Just the notion of wrapping her legs around him. . . Her mind flew out the window.

Then he ran his hand up to her garter, his finger brushed her bare thigh, and Emilia nearly elevated off his lap. Tension and excitement pooled in her lower parts. "This is. . . I think. . . Perhaps we should wait."

But she didn't want to wait. She wanted his hand to keep doing what it was doing and more.

He chuckled, bent his head, and nuzzled her exposed breast, and she couldn't have fought him if she'd wanted.

She was sitting in a carriage with her bodice open and her skirts up to her waist like a wanton! He really was the devil!

And then this tongue lapped her nipple, and she came apart, shaking and trembling and turning to liquid inside. His finger brushed her nether lips, and she almost cried her need.

"You are as hungry as I am," he said in satisfaction. "Let me thank you for offering your business proposition."

And he pushed his finger inside her, rubbed a magic spot, and sent her over the brink.

SURROUNDED BY THE delicious scent of sex and lavender, enrapt in the moans of the innocent he seduced, blanketed by soft feminine flesh, Dare held back his cough for as long as he could. He was so immensely grateful for this moment he'd never hoped to know again, that he didn't even regret his inability to achieve his own satisfaction. His arousal wilted as he struggled with his cough and the searing pain in his belly. He fumbled for his handkerchief, and his satiated wife immediately unburied her face from his shoulder.

He had to help her return to her seat from the awkward position he'd put her in. As he coughed up his lungs, he noticed she didn't even take time to fasten her bodice while she rummaged through their bags for lozenges and water.

Admiring her white breasts eased him past the embarrassment of his ridiculous illness. Pert pink cherries capped plump vanilla confections. He wanted to lick them all over.

"I've heard the sun and fresh air can ease the congestion," she offered, holding the water bottle while he sucked on the lozenges. "We'll set up a chair outside where you can rest when the sun is out."

"I have too much to do to lie about," Dare declared with a firmness that brooked no argument. "Once I've separated the minerals in the water, I need to test their properties as restoratives. Bath's water is high in magnesium, for instance. I thought I'd see how that reacts with sputum."

His bride curled her lip in disgust. "Ugh. Spitting into a beaker sounds most unhealthy. My grandfather had a workshop where he made his medicines. You can probably set your equipment up there. It won't hurt for you to sit in the sun and read and write occasionally outside the shop."

Dare regarded her with fascination. He'd just given her what he would swear was her first sexual encounter, and now his bride sat there like a prim miss, fastening her underclothes, and discussing workshops. How had he managed to marry the one woman in all the kingdom with brains?

She sent him a sideways glance that said he'd been silent too long. He took the water, swallowed, and was at a loss as to how to reply. His formidable mind had shut down beneath the conflicting messages she sent.

When he said nothing, she finished fastening her bodice and sighed. "I am no good at small talk. Was I supposed to thank you for teaching me carnal lust?"

Dare choked and coughed, more in surprise than because his lungs demanded it. He pulled her close again, leaned back on his pillows, and closed his eyes.

"I suspect this is what is called the honeymoon period, where we are in constant awe and admiration of the creature we have brilliantly chosen to marry. In another month or so, you will be yelling at me for ignoring you, and I will be locked up in my room, exploding things, and the honeymoon will end. Until then, accept that I adore everything about you, including and specifically your lack of frivolous speech."

"You *adore* me? That is a trifle far-fetched." She settled her head against his shoulders, though, relaxing at his silly declaration. "I have a great many peculiarities, so the shouting should be of firework quality."

He laughed. "Shouting takes too much breath. I might just torch your draperies in frustration."

"I wouldn't do that, if I were you," she said sweetly. "I have a dozen recipes for purgatives, some especially designed for the spleenish."

"Spleenish!" he sputtered, relaxing with soft woman in his arms. "Don't turn silly on me now. I'll give you nights to remember."

After he was gone went unsaid. Perhaps he ought to drive her mad and make her glad to see the end of him. It didn't seem right to leave her mourning his worthless carcass.

Six

EMILIA READ RESTLESSLY while her husband napped. She wasn't a silly miss. She was a Malcolm, after all. She had access to her family journals. She knew women enjoyed carnal relations. Her fear of pain had led her to believe she wouldn't enjoy them so much.

Instead, she sat here wanting more—much, much more, when she ought to be considering consequences.

Her entire existence had been predicated on the notion that she could not safely have a fulfilling marriage. What if she had been wrong? Had she thrown away her chance for love?

She cast her napping husband a glance. Although his color was healthy, and his broad chest rose and fell normally, she feared she had exhausted him with just that little bit of exertion. Or had her gift connected without her being aware, due to her. . . mindlessness? Should she refrain from indulging in sexual congress for the sake of their mutual health?

He had touched her more than any other person since her childhood, and his pain had been swallowed by her hunger and excitement. She wasn't feeling exhausted, either, so maybe desire disconnected her healing gift. Witless lust was entirely new to her experience.

The whole downfall of having inexplicable gifts was that they were just that. . . inexplicable.

Lord Dare woke at the next stop but didn't seem inclined to climb out and stretch, so she offered him their lunch basket. They ate and talked with none of their earlier seductive exchange. Instead, he picked her brain for the little bit she knew about her great-grandfather's property and the abbey where she hoped to set up her experiments.

At the next stop, she needed to use the facilities. Lord Dare approved of this inn and climbed out after her. As they approached the door, a familiar groom raced up.

"My lord, the wagon has broken a spoke."

In moments, all the servants they'd sent ahead had anxiously clustered around them. Deciding there was little she could do about a broken wheel, Emilia asked her maid to accompany her to the facilities, letting Bessie tell her all about the day's exciting events. Only a little younger than Emilia, she seemed more a mousy, excitable child than an efficient lady's maid. But she had been trained to be exactly what Emilia needed.

"And his lordship's man, James, he helped push us out of the ditch, but it was no use. We had to walk here. He carried my bag! He's quite handsome, although a little short. Isn't this a fancy inn? I've never quite seen the like."

Bessie's chatter reminded her of home, and her younger sisters all nattering at once, and Emilia almost smiled, even though the news wasn't good. She'd been dreaming of sharing a bed with her new husband, in their new home this evening. Now it looked as if they must delay their journey.

When she returned to the common room, she found Dare talking with the innkeeper, a frown creasing his handsome brow. He glanced up and smiled at her, making her heart dance just a little, but the smile faded as the innkeeper insistently shook his head.

"We are in a bit of a pickle, my dear," her husband said. "It seems the wagon has lost a wheel and it will take a day to replace it, so even if we go on to our new home, it will have to be without our trunks and servants. I've asked if we might take rooms here, but our host says they are all spoken for due to a prizefight in Leeds. He can put up the grooms in the stable, but I don't think you'll find that satisfactory."

Emilia wrinkled her nose. "So there will be no other inn between here and Harrogate for us?"

"Not even Harrogate, I fear, my lady," the innkeeper said. "They hold a horse fair this time of year, which is why there's a fight scheduled in Leeds. It's all of a piece."

"To catch the purses of traveling gentlemen, he means," Dare said. "They'll stop on their way up from London to see the fight, and if they have any coins left, will continue on to buy their horses. We could throw ourselves on the mercy of the clientele and beg that someone give up a room, I suppose, but I'd rather go on and leave the wagon behind."

Emilia nodded agreement. "My grandfather had several elderly retainers who should still be looking after the place. I don't see a problem. We might try to fit Bessie and James into the carriage with us, though. I don't know if Mrs. Wiggs and Mr. Barton can manage the stairs these days."

That meant no more instructions in the art of lovemaking until they were in the privacy of their chambers. And Bessie's chatter was likely to drive them both into walking. But she had to offer the suggestion. The grooms might be happy to sleep in the stable, but a lady's maid and valet were accustomed to better.

"All right, then we shall journey on," he said. "Perhaps it would be best to take bread and cheese with us, and a jug of lemonade. We might be arriving late."

With Bessie settled in the narrow slice of rear-facing bench that the mattress did not occupy, and James riding with the driver, the carriage set off, leaving their main baggage behind. It would only be another day, Emilia reassured herself. It wasn't as if she were a clotheshorse needing fancy gowns three times a day. Her traveling gown and the changes of clothing in her valise should be sufficient.

Dare napped the better part of the afternoon. With Bessie watching, Emilia didn't venture to feel his chest to see if he breathed any easier. His coughing was less when he slept, which she thought might be a good thing. She read and Bessie mended. As predicted, the remainder of the drive was long, and even though it was summer in the north, the shadows were lengthening by the time they arrived in the village of Alder Abbey.

Emilia strained to see how much had changed since her youth, but in the gloom, she could see no more than familiar shops and cottages. Her grandfather's house was a mile or so north of the village, she believed, on a rather large property. Many of the hedgerows along the lane after they left the village belonged to her. Or Lord Dare. She didn't understand the complexities of marriage trusts.

As they turned down an overgrown drive, she could see no lights anywhere in the modest three-story country house. Emilia knew word had been sent ahead to prepare for their arrival. She'd expected to dodge Mrs. Wiggs' hugs and had looked forward to Mr. Barton's dry commentary on the state of good help these days. Although, she supposed, now that she was a married lady, they might not treat her as the child she had been.

She and Bessie stepped into the twilight. Dare followed.

Frowning at the drive's state of abandonment, he went with the groom to see if there was a sound stable for the team.

The footman the marquess of Ashford had sent with the carriage rapped the door knocker while Emilia glanced around in bewilderment at the overgrown shrubbery and unmown lawn. No one answered.

They waited for Dare to return with the keys.

"I'm quite certain Father said the estate was paying to keep the help on," she murmured as he fished in his coat pocket for a key ring.

"I was told the place would be ready when we arrived. I hope everyone hasn't gone to the fair or the fight." He said this last with a chuckle as he located a key and handed it over to the footman.

"Grandfather was proud of his roses and lawn. He would never have allowed them to reach this state. I know he's been gone for years now, but still. . ." She glanced around in dismay. Even in the dusk, she knew the neglect wasn't right.

Ashford's footman inserted the key, jiggled the lock, and finally shoved the door open. It creaked on its hinges.

"We'll set things to rights in the morning," Dare said with masculine assurance, draping his arm over her shoulders and steering her away from the unkempt lawn.

James, Dare's short but muscular valet, removed a carriage lantern to light their way. As the servants lit tapers and hunted for lamps to illuminate the interior, Emilia sagged in weariness at the disarray revealed.

"I should have set up housekeeping here years ago," she murmured in dismay at the ghostly shapes of Holland linen draped over all the furniture.

"Unmarried maidens cannot set up housekeeping on their own," Dare admonished, squeezing her shoulder. "I doubt your father or the estate executor would have allowed it, in any case. I will, however, have a sharp word with whomever is responsible for this abandonment. I *saw* the expenses of upkeep. I asked for them particularly when I discussed the settlements with your father."

"If I did not remember this place so well, I would think we'd mistaken the property. But there is grandfather's secretary desk." She yanked the covers off the parlor chairs, sending a storm of dust into the air. "These are the same chairs I used to sit on to read." She held up the lantern. "That is an oil painting of my grandmother behind those cobwebs. What can have happened to Mrs. Wiggs and Mr. Barton?'

Dare gestured at his valet and the footman. "Search upstairs and down, if you please. Find out if anyone appears to be in residence."

Even Bessie was silent and wide-eyed in the gloom of a parlor shrouded in linen and layers of grime.

Unable to tolerate waiting, Emilia led the way from the parlor to investigate the remaining rooms on the ground floor. The once well-waxed mahogany chairs and dining table remained arranged as if awaiting the next meal. A layer of dust coated the polish.

The butler's pantry that led down to the kitchen showed no indication of intrusion. The silver tea set was tarnished but still stood in its position of honor. The china and crystal inside the windowed buffet were less dusty, if not exactly gleaming.

"It doesn't appear as if the staff robbed you and ran away." Dare said what she was thinking.

"Mrs. Wiggs and Mr. Barton were elderly. I suppose they could have taken ill or gone home to family. But they would have left someone in charge." Emilia led the way to the all-purpose room at the rear where her grandfather had a habit of depositing anything he didn't know what to do with. The assorted equipment, books, and boxes appeared undisturbed.

"The dust and cobwebs aren't overly thick." Dare ran his finger through a layer of grime on the table. "Your grandfather has been dead for how long?"

"About five years, this winter. I am no expert on dust accumulation, however," Emilia said, running her gloves over a bookshelf. "Besides Mrs. Wiggs and Mr. Barton, he used to have a footman and a housemaid and a cook. He did not entertain, so he had little need for more. The lesser servants might have been let go when he died."

James clattered up from the kitchen. "No sign of break-ins, my lord. No food in the pantry. Linens still on the beds in the chambers below stairs. No obvious sign of mice or other vermin. Shall I begin carrying in bags?"

Dare lifted his eyebrows in question, leaving the decision to her.

"We have the linen in my travel trunk and the mattress in the carriage to sleep on if you're concerned about vermin. We'd best check the state of the beds upstairs, though," she said, knowing they had little choice.

"Would you rather call on your friends at the abbey and see if they will put us up?" he asked.

She shook her head. "It's late, and they are newly married and still sorting out their household. It would be an imposition. If there is no sign of intruders upstairs, we should see what we can manage here for the night."

Robert, the tall footman who had accompanied their borrowed berlin, met them at the foot of the stairs. "Servants quarters in the attic and main chambers haven't been occupied in a while, my lady," he reported. "Covers over everything. Attic shows no leaks. I opened windows to cool off the rooms."

"They knew they were leaving," Dare said grimly. "The executor definitely has some explaining to do."

Emilia gestured toward the kitchen stairs. "Robert, perhaps you and James would prefer the cooler rooms below for tonight. Bessie can have one of the smaller chambers upstairs near us." She glanced at her tall husband, who looked both angry and weary. "Do you think the driver will be all right in the stable? Shall we ask?"

With a curt nod, he sent Robert out to discuss the situation with the marquess's driver. Bessie and James followed to fetch the feather mattress and baggage.

"I might not be the bargain you'd hoped to gain, my lord," she said in a low voice as they climbed the stairs to inspect the chambers for themselves.

Her husband's grip tightened on her shoulders. "Call me, Dare, please. And no, I am not unhappy about the prize I have won. I don't much care where or how I live so long as I have a roof over my head. The people under that roof are what matter to me."

He pressed a kiss to her hair to reassure her. Emilia wasn't reassured. She wasn't born yesterday and knew he was practiced at using words to flatter and soothe.

She had never lived without a full complement of servants. She didn't even know how to hire one. Her honeymoon was not the time to discover that she had been woefully sheltered from reality.

They chose the wide suite of rooms overlooking the front lawn. Emilia remembered her grandfather sleeping in a smaller chamber near the stairs. He'd always called this larger one the Queen's Chamber and let Emilia sleep there when she came to visit.

Dare opened the casement windows so James could shake out the mattresses to be used for the night. Bessie made up the beds when they were done. Emilia used a rag for a dust cloth and rubbed away some of the dust, although it filled the air and set her husband to coughing again.

"We need hot water for washing," Bessie insisted once the big bed was made.

"I believe there is a pump in the kitchen," Emilia said without confidence. "But I have no idea if the chimneys will allow a fire."

"I'll take a look," the valet offered. "The pump will need priming."

Immensely grateful that they'd brought their personal servants, wondering what they would have done had they arrived without any, Emilia suggested that the remainder of the luncheon basket contents be distributed among them.

Once everyone had scattered to their tasks, she winced as her husband opened the bottle of patent medicine. She could hardly blame him for seeking relief. He had to be exhausted.

She had initially thought he would stay in London and leave her to sleep here alone. When he'd insisted on traveling with her, she'd debated what room to put him in. And now, it seemed the matter was settled without discussion. The servants expected them to share a bed. Dare expected it. She. . . really ought to think about it, but she couldn't push past the need to learn more of lust. Foolish of her.

Nervously, she studied the old bed with its high square posts. The extra mattress hadn't added much height, but it was a tall bed. And not terribly wide. Her travel trunk, valise, and book satchel had been carried into the dressing room next door. There was no cot there for Bessie, so her maid had chosen a small chamber beyond that.

Emilia was alone with her husband, with no good reason not to indulge in sexual congress. But now that weariness had set in, and she was faced with reality, she was having doubts.

Lord Dare shrugged out of his coat without waiting for the return of his valet. Should she do the same? Bessie knew Emilia usually undressed herself in the late hours when she returned from her studies. She never came unless called.

Emilia swallowed and gazed longingly at the dressing room. He had *said* she must be honest and direct. She never knew what to say. So she said nothing. She simply left the main chamber to change in the smaller one—promptly bumping her nose on a wardrobe in the darkness.

She knew she was blessed with above-average intelligence, but sometimes she had the sense of an earwig. Without light, she had to fumble to find a lamp and return to the big chamber to light it.

Dare had stripped to his shirtsleeves and was unfastening the flap of his trousers. When she reappeared, he stopped to fill and light the lamp for her.

"It's a good thing they left oil and clean wicks," he muttered. "I cannot fault the staff. It is your executor who will feel the brunt of my wrath."

"I think we should ask around in the village first, see if we can locate any of the staff. My father would never have allowed an incompetent executor to manage my inheritance, I'm sure." Her husband's masculine proximity acutely reminded her of what they had done earlier. Beneath his linen, his shoulder muscles bulged most interestingly, and she was over-curious about what waited behind the placket of his trousers. The lust haze obscured rationality again.

"At least we have decent accommodations," he said, glancing at the freshened bed as if following her thoughts. He tipped her chin up and kissed her cheek. "Sleep, first, I think. We both need our strength."

Emilia felt the annoying heat rising in her cheeks. She nodded briskly and retreated to the dressing room.

She'd gone into this marriage as a business proposition, in order for Dare to buy his family a house and for her to acquire this property and set up her laboratory. Men seldom noticed her, so she had expected her husband to do the same. She had fully anticipated that they would go their own separate ways.

She had never considered being a wife and *mother*. She'd given more thought to the nomenclature of a new variety of *kalmia polifolia* than she had to motherhood. She'd better start thinking about it now.

Seven

DARE HATED NIGHTSHIRTS. He would wake up sweating if he wore one.

The terrified look on his bride's face as she'd caught him unfastening his fall warned him that nakedness might send her running.

Damn, this marriage business was awkward. Or perhaps it was this *mortality* concern that made him more aware than usual. He'd never worried about bedding a woman before. He prided himself on being rather accomplished at it.

His gut gnawed with more than unease. Feeling his breath coming in shorter gasps, he tried to stave off a spasm with more mineral water and the last of the horehound. He'd make his bride a widow too soon, he feared. He should try to create half-way decent memories so she wouldn't spend the rest of her life regretting their marriage. How the devil did he do that?

He left on his shirt, turned off all but one lamp and dimmed it, and climbed between the fresh linens his wife had brilliantly thought to pack. He'd traveled far and wide, never paying attention to what he slept on unless it crawled, but he had to admit, scented sheets were preferable.

Anticipation had him partially aroused before she even slipped back into the room. In the lamp's light, her silhouette inside a high-necked nightdress revealed slim hips and small bosom, but he'd already discovered them. It was her long-legged walk and the curve of her tiny waist that held his fascination now. He feared he could snap her in two, or that his rutting lust would terrify her. She turned off the one remaining lamp and became a shadow in the darkness.

He lifted the covers and she slid in, staying safely some distance away. Dare knew all wild creatures, especially women, required gentling until accustomed to confinement. He meant to start where they'd left off earlier, but perhaps he should go slower.

He wrapped his arm around that delectable waist, pulled her closer and pressed a kiss to her nape. "Sweet dreams, my lady wife."

She lay perfectly still but didn't pull away. "Good-night, my. . . Dare."

He loved the sound of his name on her tongue. He'd sleep well this night.

HE DIDN'T WAKE SO WELL. A rooster crowed so loudly that Dare swore it sat on his aching head. His quick intake of breath at the pain brought a fresh round of coughing. And as his bride attempted to slip from his reach, a scream and a shout from outside destroyed any possibility of lovemaking for the nonce.

Dare reached for his travel pistol on the bedside table. His fetching bride dashed for the window. She'd braided her long black hair, and it swung down her slender back to a nicely rounded posterior. He was almost distracted from his weapon.

She shoved open the window and leaned out. "Bessie, it's a rooster! Go back inside, and it will quiet." She leaned out further, presumably peering past the overgrown roses on the wall. "Robert, is that you? Do you think there might still be hens in the hen house? Eggs?"

Having lived most of his life in town, Dare sighed and set his gun down. He automatically reached for his medicine bottle, but the coughing had stopped. Perhaps he needed a good shock to keep breathing. "Eggs?" he inquired with interest, feeling hungrier than usual. "Do you know how to cook them?"

"Absolutely no notion," she admitted, pulling her head back inside. She hesitated at sight of the weapon on the table. "A pistol? Why?"

He felt a fool in a nightshirt with his hairy legs sticking out, but his bride didn't shrink in horror. In fact, she regarded him with interest, which had the expected result. But realizing now wasn't exactly the time to express his ardor, Dare reached into the wardrobe. "It's best to be prepared when traveling, and I'm not much of a swordsman."

"Do all gentlemen carry weapons?" she asked with what distinctly sounded like worry. "I cannot remember my father doing so."

"If he doesn't keep one on him or under his carriage seat, then his driver or footman might carry one. It's always best to be armed."

He held his clothes to his waist when he turned back to face her.

His blushing bride was staring at the pistol as if it were a puzzle to be pondered. He'd love to know what went on behind her high, intelligent brow, but he had a notion he wouldn't be finding out today. More accustomed to action than quizzing the females of his family, he set the clothes down and began unfastening his nightshirt. "Shall I call your maid for you?" he suggested.

She glanced up, noted what he was doing with alarm, and hastily departed. Not one for small talk was his bride, Dare noted with amusement.

Fortunately for all concerned, the hens were still about. Someone must be taking care of them. Bessie found eggs, and James knew how to cook them. Robert, the marquess's well-trained footman, had already run into the village to procure bread, butter, and tea. No one had thought to ask for sugar, so they drank their tea bitter and ate as if starved.

Dare was accustomed to eating with his manservant when traveling and didn't mind a shared meal in the kitchen. Apparently Emilia's maid was more co-conspirator than servant and didn't protest their informal dining either. She also didn't shut up and didn't wash dishes. Since he had as yet to see Bessie help his wife dress or undress, he wondered what exactly the maid did do.

They'd included the footman and driver in their informal repast, if only to save carrying hot food out to the stable.

"Robert, did the marquess give you a time for returning the carriage?" Dare asked, leaving his dish in the metal sink while the driver fetched more water from the pump.

"He's up north with his lady wife, awaiting the birth of his heir, m'lord. He'll not be needing me or the carriage for a while, and said it would be convenient if we kept it here so Lady Pascoe-Ives might use it when the time comes."

"The midwife," Dare confirmed, checking with Emilia. "Do you have any notion how soon she will need to travel north?"

The Pascoe-Ives were the occupants of the abbey he needed to visit. He had to figure out if they'd be willing to sell a portion of the abbey land to the railroad. He hadn't been there when the surveyors plotted the track. He needed to look at the maps and see which properties they crossed and where.

"I believe Lady Ashford is due next month," Emilia said. "That's all I know. We need to pay a call on the Pascoe-Ives, but I'd rather visit the village and ask after my grandfather's servants first."

"That was my thought. I need to post a letter to your father about the state of neglect here so he can look into it from his end. And while I'm at it, I'll set up accounts with the merchants. I can ask after the servants as well, if you wish to stay and see things to rights here."

She gave him a look that would have withered weeds. "I know as much about housekeeping as you do about dishwashing. I'll go into Alder with you. A few of the merchants may remember me, and I'll need to establish a source of pens and paper, as well as pots for my plants."

Well, he had told her to be honest.

Fighting a cough and the gnawing in his gut, Dare acknowledged her demand with a curt nod. He could scarcely complain of his bride's unfeminine lack of interest in the household when he'd married her as a business proposition. "Can you be ready within a half hour?"

She gave a commanding nod at the driver instead of replying. The man got up from the bench where he'd taken his meal, deposited his plate in the pan, and with a tug of his forelock, left to prepare the horses.

Dare tried not to splutter around his cough. "Who elected you queen?" he muttered, offering her his arm as he rose from the table.

"Queen?" she asked in genuine puzzlement, shaking out her skirt.

Today, she wore some pinkish-red thing without the enormous fashionable sleeves. Dare found himself abnormally fascinated with her attire, perhaps because he kept trying to see beneath whatever folderol she covered her bosom with.

He coughed into his handkerchief without answering.

"I'll need the equipment from the wagon before I can make more horehound," she said regretfully. "I do hope they arrive soon."

That was probably a safer topic than explaining that he was accustomed to women waiting for *him* to take charge. If she was to live as a widow after he was gone, it was no doubt a good thing that she knew how to command the male servants.

"I can buy horehound in the village," he said as they entered their shared chambers.

"Not medicinal horehound." She picked up her skirts and departed for the dressing chamber.

Medicinal horehound? She complained about his perfectly legitimate prescribed medicine and fed him doctored candy?

It finally dawned on him, *his wife was a quack.*

"GOOD MORNING, Mr. Thornbull. I don't know if you remember me, Sir Harry's great-granddaughter?" Emilia lay a packet of writing papers on the counter, along with the rest of her shopping list.

Mr. Thornbull was a stout man just past middle-age, with thinning hair, spectacles, and a round face. He peered over the top of the glasses. "Miss McDowell, as I live and breathe. We thought you had forgotten us."

"Of course not." She removed one of her gloves so she might count out coins for the paper. "I have only just married. We came directly after the service was said. I had hoped to find Mrs. Wiggs and Mr. Barton still with us. I should like to visit them if they're nearby."

He looked suspicious, but the coins and the shopping list opened the path of communication, as she'd hoped. She might not be good at small talk, but she understood negotiation. She wasn't entirely certain why he should regard her with suspicion, however.

"Mr. Barton fell last winter and broke his hip," the merchant said grumpily. "He felt he wasn't capable of his duties and went to live with his daughter in town."

Town presumably meant Harrogate, not London. Not wanting to stem the flow of information, Emilia figured she could inquire elsewhere if she needed his direction. "Oh my, no one told me! Did Mr. Crenshaw send someone to help Mrs. Wiggs then?" Crenshaw was the name Dare had found in the books, the one who received the monies to be dispensed to the staff.

"If he did, I know naught about it," the stationer declared. "She said as she was afraid to stay about the place alone, she'd rather stay with her sister."

"That is most odd. We were told the house would be ready, and I'd so hoped to see the staff again. I should visit Mrs. Wiggs and see how she fares. Her sister is out toward Willow Lane, isn't she?" Emilia made that up. She remembered the name of one of the village lanes but knew almost nothing about the housekeeper's sister.

"Other direction," Mr. Thornbull corrected curtly. "Aster Cottage, as you come into the green."

"I thank you most kindly, sir. Should my husband come looking for me, tell him I've gone to Aster Cottage, if you would. And if you know of anyone seeking employment, please send them to us."

They parted on a slightly better basis than upon her entrance, Emilia decided as she strolled to the green in search of Aster Cottage. Her mother and sisters had always done the shopping, but Emilia was comfortable with stationers. Her family was never short of servants since Lady McDowell saved women from the streets and workhouses and sent them to Emilia's cousin Aster for training. Emilia knew at least partially-trained staff could arrive in weeks, if she asked.

But she wanted to know what had happened to her grandfather's staff.

Ashford's enormous berlin occupied nearly one whole side of the small village green. They really needed a gig, but there had been none in the stable, and she couldn't ask Dare to walk any distance.

She debated stopping to ask directions, but she thought she'd look for asters first. They wouldn't be blooming yet, but plants, she understood better than people.

The task was easier than expected—Mrs. Wiggs was sitting in the yard by the time Emilia walked down the street. The stout housekeeper's hair had turned completely white over the years, and she'd gained weight, but her hug was as strong as ever. Emilia felt pinpricks from every ache the woman suffered before she could break the connection.

"You look that much like Sir Harry in his youth that I would have known you anywhere," Mrs. Wiggs exclaimed, looking Emilia up and down. "And you're all grown up and married! Come in, come in, have a sip of tea. My sister is out. We can have a good coze."

Emilia recalled her great-grandfather as gray-haired, brown from the sun, wrinkled and speckled with sun spots. But Mrs. Wiggs had been with him since they were both young, so she tried not to wince at the comparison.

After pleasantries were exchanged, Emilia brought the conversation around to her purpose. "Lord Dare and I were led to believe that you and Mr. Barton were still in the house. I was disappointed to find you had moved on. Do you know who was appointed in your place?"

Mrs. Wiggs looked puzzled. "We weren't told of no one. We understood the old place was to be sold for the new railroad. I left everything ready to be packed up and moved."

"Railroad?" Emilia asked in horror. "I know nothing of a railroad. I mean to continue grandfather's gardens. Who told you this?"

The housekeeper looked puzzled. "I don't know precisely. There were some gentlemen about last winter, about the time Mr. Barton took his fall. Then Mr. Crenshaw said as we weren't needed anymore. When we heard the rumors about the railroad, with you never coming back, we decided the rumors were true. The village has been talking of naught else since. What do we need with a railroad, I ask you?"

Emilia had no better idea than Mrs. Wiggs about railroads. She'd never even seen one. After ascertaining that her housekeeper was willing to return a few days a week to train staff, she left in search of Dare.

She found him swilling his wretched medicine and leaning against the carriage as if he were exhausted. He straightened those broad shoulders she'd glimpsed last night and put on his most charming smile at her approach, but she could tell simply by touching his arm that he ached in too many places for her to discern one from the other, rather like Mrs. Wiggs.

It was disconcerting to realize that such a wide strong chest could conceal such damage. She pressed one palm against his shirt front, enduring the warning prickles up her arm while attempting to send a spurt of healing energy. He covered her hand with one of his and leaned down to kiss her cheek. She was coming to enjoy those little gestures of affection, even though she knew he meant nothing by them.

"Mrs. Wiggs will be out to the house tomorrow," Emilia told him once he settled on the seat beside her. "She will bring maids, but Cook has found another position."

"Supplies will be delivered this afternoon, and I've made arrangements for hay and grain for the stable. It is the mysterious Mr. Crenshaw who was supposed to pay staff who eludes me. His name is on the books, but no here knows of him. The funds were deposited at a bank in Harrogate, so I suppose I must go there next."

"Not while the fair is in session," she warned. "Rest a bit before making another journey. Perhaps something will turn up. Mrs. Wiggs told me that she heard the house was to be sold for a *railroad*," Emilia said in indignation. "Wherever would that lie have started?"

She glanced up when her husband said nothing. He reddened and started to cough.

Eight

THE CARRIAGE was pulling up their drive before Dare recovered from his cough. Emilia wished she had the courage to press her hand against his chest again. But she preferred to experiment when he was asleep. She really didn't want her dashing new husband looking at her as if she were demented.

She was actually starting to think like a *wife*! Knowing a bit of Dare's history, she knew that couldn't be good.

Awaiting them in the yard was a very large personage garbed in black muslin, in the slender fashion of a decade ago, but wearing an enormous bonnet adorned with. . . peacock feathers? Emilia tried hard not to stare as the woman crossed her arms beneath her generous bosom and dangled a shiny reticule over her belly.

"Is this your Mrs. Wiggs?" Dare inquired as the carriage halted, and he studied the apparition through the window.

"No. I don't believe I've ever met this person in my life," Emilia whispered back. "But I did ask Mr. Thornbull to spread word that we needed staff. I had just hoped Mrs. Wiggs would be here before we started hiring. She knows everyone."

"Perhaps this is simply a neighbor come to call." The laughter in his eyes put the lie to that belief as he clambered down and held out his hand to help her out.

How had she come to trust this impossible man so easily? "This is not London," she whispered indignantly. "She *could* be our neighbor. Stop laughing."

"M'lord, m'lady." The woman performed an awkward curtsy. "Forgive my forwardness, but I heard you had need of staff and came right over. I am Mrs. Peacock."

Holding Dare's arm, Emilia could almost feel laughter rumbling in his chest at this explanation of the peacock-feathered hat. At least he wasn't coughing. Not daring to look at him, she wondered what was expected of her. Did she invite the woman in for an interview? She had a hard time not staring at the exceedingly long and iridescent feather.

"How do you do, Mrs. Peacock?" Dare said in a gravelly voice that hid his laughter. "We had hoped to have Mrs. Wiggs interview staff."

The woman drew herself up to her full imposing height. "Mary Wiggs and I have known each other since childhood. She will vouch for my abilities, even though I've never hired out before. My dear John passed away last winter, and I've been at sixes and sevens ever since. When I heard you were in need of a cook, I thought to myself, *self*, here's a chance to see a bit more of the world. I'm that used to cooking for others, but not so much on my own."

A bit more of the world. . . Their kitchen? Tongue-tied at her best, Emilia didn't know how to proceed. It didn't seem to matter. Mrs. Peacock proceeded for her.

"I'm sure m'lord has better to do than question me, but if her ladyship would grant me a few minutes, I can show you a menu I've prepared." She bobbed another curtsy. The feather bobbed with her.

"A trial run perhaps," Dare murmured. "What staff we have will rebel if they must eat eggs all day, every day."

Emilia took a deep breath and tried to nod regally as her mother was wont to do. "Of course, Mrs. Peacock. So very kind of you to think of us. Won't you come in? We're not prepared for visitors yet, so you will excuse the disarray."

"Never having been in service, I wasn't sure of the etiquette," the would-be cook said in her roundest accents, following as they climbed the steps. "But I'm not one to miss an opportunity when it beckons. I am most grateful for your understanding."

The front parlor looked little better than it had the previous night. The covers had been left where they'd been dropped. In the morning light, the cobwebs on the ceiling and windows were visible. Emilia debated if interviewing in the formal parlor or her grandfather's cluttered study would be preferable.

His noble lordship decided the matter for her. "I'll leave you two here, shall I? I need to find a room for my work before the wagon arrives with our trunks." Dare pressed a kiss to her cheek and ambled off as if he expected her to know how to interview cooks.

The prickles his kiss caused were rather. . . enticing. They stirred pleasure more than pain.

Setting her chin, determined to learn her new status as householder, Emilia chose a delicate chair for herself and gestured for Mrs. Peacock to take a seat. The cook chose a stout sofa dating back a century or two.

Mrs. Peacock rummaged in her reticule. "A gentleman likes his beef, he does. I understand that." She removed a neatly folded paper. "But ladies like more genteel fare. I've been cooking for my family for forty years, so I have lots more recipes where these come from."

Emily studied the long list written in an elegant copperplate she hadn't expected from an uneducated servant. Written communication, she understood. "This is quite an extensive menu, Mrs. Peacock. I fear you may be bored with just me and my husband to serve. We do not anticipate many visitors."

Mrs. Peacock's feathers dipped in understanding. "A young couple, understandable. But that will let me learn what you like. Family and visitors will come in time. You just mark off what you don't want, and leave me to see to what you need."

Emilia desperately wanted someone other than herself in charge of the kitchen and meals. She'd never really met any cooks, except as a child. Mrs. Peacock seemed far above any servant of her station. Remembering Dare's suggestion, she hesitantly offered, "Why don't we agree to test each other for a week? Let us see if we suit."

Mrs. Peacock beamed. "That's fine then. Shall I start now? I'll make a list of supplies."

Thinking of the ancient kitchen, Emilia tried not to wince. "Sir Harry lived simply. We will need to order more than food. But you are welcome to study the situation and let us know what you require."

She had no bell to summon a servant, not that Bessie or John was likely to perform the duty of a housekeeper. She assumed the task herself, leading the way to the butler's pantry. Indicating the kitchen door, she prayed Mrs. Peacock wasn't a silver thief. "Mrs. Wiggs will be along tomorrow. The food deliveries should arrive this afternoon. You are welcome to look around, although I fear there is not much you can do yet."

"Don't you worry, m'lady. I'll have the place in hand in no time. It will be a pleasure to see other than my own four walls of a change." Mrs. Peacock sailed down the steps like a captain entering his ship without mentioning what her compensation might be, should the week be successful.

Remarkable. She'd just hired her first staff. Almost.

At a loss as to what to do next without her notes and equipment, Emilia set out in search of her husband. She found him in her grandfather's cluttered study, leaning one shoulder against the wall, arms crossed, and examining the jumble. She had to admit that Devil Dare was a fine figure of a man. She couldn't help a small thrill at the ridiculously proprietary notion that she had been the one to capture him, and he was all hers.

"Is there an attic to carry this to?" he asked, gesturing at old saddles and boxes of dusty tomes. "This probably ought to be the office we use for interviewing staff and keeping the books."

We. She had never been part of a *we.* It was a trifle scary. He might be strong and handsome now, but learning to rely on him would be a mistake. Still, he had earned the right to carve a place for himself—in her house and her life, but not her *heart.* She had to shield her softer impulses if she were to survive her gift.

"There's an attic," she said, "but I suggest we sort what needs to be thrown out first and wait until we have a footman to carry up the rest."

"Our funds aren't unlimited," he warned. "Once they are used to purchase my mother's house, the investments will produce significantly less income than they do now, so we should economize while we can. How much will your cook cost us?"

Emilia wrinkled her nose. She wasn't used to thinking of *cost,* except when it came to buying her equipment from her allowance. "I have no notion. We didn't discuss it. If she lives in the cook's quarters, that should be part of her compensation, I think, but if not. . ." She sighed. "She will undoubtedly want utensils we do not possess. But we cannot go on without a footman and a maid."

He surveyed the clutter and looked grim. "If I thought I could live just two more years, my own investments would be complete and productive," he said. "But there is a great deal of work to be done between now and then, and I fear failure. I hate to leave you on limited funds."

That was honesty. Emilia swallowed and tried to summon her own courage to be equally blunt. She needed to tell him that she might possibly extend his life. "If you will allow me to help. . . I cannot make promises but—"

Dare straightened and made a dismissive gesture. "I cannot

allow you to do more than you have. I'll take a look at the outbuildings, see if one will be suitable for my workshop."

He walked away, leaving her hard-to-find words to sputter and die. There was a reason she had never married—men never listened. If he'd only let her try. . . She still couldn't promise that he'd live two years.

STEPPING OUT the back door, Dare fought the grinding in his gut which the ugly conversation with his bride had exacerbated. He hated talking about his imminent demise, but he had to make Emilia understand her diminished circumstances. She didn't seem much inclined toward financial matters, so it would be up to him to set boundaries.

He hated that too. He would shower her in roses and beakers, if he could, but he was not a wealthy man. His father had seen to that. In a few years, with the railroad running and his other ventures turning a profit. . . then he might buy anything she liked. Time was running out, however.

Not one to dwell on regrets, Dare rattled the locked door to a long, low shed he'd been eyeing as possible work space. He'd have to go back to the house and find the keys. Turning to leave, he noticed a garden gnome leaning over the stone fence around what was presumably the kitchen garden. Wearing a nondescript coat, baggy trousers, and a grimy cap, the gnome presented a toothless, withered crabapple face as Dare approached.

"Shame to let 'at garden go," the creature said through missing front teeth. "Taters and onions still growin'. Summat 'em herbs the lady likes under ta weeds. Reckon you need a gardener?" he asked with little hope in his voice.

A gardener. Emilia wanted gardens. He had a blasted estate now which needed tending. Watching coins fly out the window, Dane leaned his hip against the wall and tried to see food in the overgrown greenery. He wouldn't know a potato from an onion. "Were you Sir Harry's gardener?"

The gnome bobbed his head. "Name's Artur. I'm old, but I can do ta work."

"You were let go when Sir Harry died?" One more task on his list—find out what the hell had happened here.

"Not a'til dey said ta place was bein' torn down. Sorry I was to see such a grand place go, but I hear tat's changed now?"

Finally realizing the old gent couldn't pronounce *th*, and that his name was probably *Arthur*, Dane nodded. "We have no intention of tearing it down. Do you know where to find the fellow who told you otherwise?"

Arthur ducked his head and looked at his feet. "Railroad swell, I reckon. I got paid my wages for ta half year's work I'd done and told I warn't needed more. Didn't seem right, but times change."

Dare's gut ground more, but he couldn't believe anyone in his consortium would have done this. "Should you see the gentleman again, let us know. We paid to keep staff on, not let you go."

The old man turned rheumy eyes toward him. "You mean I can have my place back?"

"If my wife approves. The garden is hers." He certainly wanted no part of it anyway.

Arthur beamed with relief. "I'll just start here. Her ladyship can let me know when she's ready. Good to have you here, m'lord."

Whistling through the gaps in his few remaining teeth, the gnome hobbled down to the kitchen gate.

Dare realized he was now responsible for a great peacock and an antiquated gnome, as well as their personal servants, one of whom was never around. What next? Circus ponies? Invisible men?

Maybe he should consider making everyone happy before he died and leave them to figure out their own security later.

As his father had.

Dane found a bush in which to cast up the contents of his churning stomach.

AS THE MARQUESS'S borrowed berlin rolled down a narrow lane between stone walls in the direction of Alder Abbey, Emilia primly folded her gloved hands in her lap while her husband closed his eyes and rested his head against the seat back. He'd refused the lunch Mrs. Peacock had conjured from nothing and had taken a nap instead. Emilia hadn't dared touch him for fear he'd notice.

She was terrified. She was so far out of her normal milieu that she feared she'd never feel secure again. She had a dying husband who really ought to be saved if possible, but she didn't know how to approach him about the odd abilities he wouldn't believe. Worse, she didn't know if she'd shorten her own life even if he did allow her to try. And she was supposed to manage a household while continuing her experiments and producing the pharmacopeia that had occupied most of her adult life. That seemed to be the small tip of the iceberg in the ocean of responsibilities she was about to drown in.

The carriage turned up an even narrower drive into a jungle of neglect worse than her own lawn. She couldn't decide if that was good or bad. She had thought the Pascoe-Ives had money, but then, a deteriorating abbey was a great deal of work, and they'd only been married a month or so.

The ivy-covered, L-shaped building and long low cloister walls loomed into view. The aging stone and medieval arches were picturesque. Emilia hoped they were sound.

Dare sat up as the horses slowed. He whistled as he studied the ancient stone walls. "They will need a king's fortune to restore that place."

"I understand the main portion was comfortably occupied until a few decades ago." Emilia strained to see through the window. "It is beyond the cloister that most concerns me. The abbey would once have had an infirmary and a medicinal garden outside the walls. We are hoping we can raise funds to restore them."

A tall, dark-haired Ives, who Emilia recognized from her cousin Aster's mad household, trotted around the corner with a toddler perched on his shoulder. He chased after another toddler of approximately the same age as the first. The boy on foot raced up to the enormous carriage horses, shouting in delight. Grinning broadly, the man set down his daughter and waited for the footman to lower the steps, then held out his hand to assist Emilia down. "Lady Dare, welcome! Bridey has been dying to meet you. Aster sends her regards and says to send her a list of needed staff when you're ready."

"If you call my cousin by her name, you know we are informal. You must call me Emilia, sir. We are all family. I am still the annoyingly lofty creature your nephews complain about, when they notice my existence at all."

"Surely not," Dare said, swinging down from the carriage, the picture of health, as if he had not been pale and weak moments before. "Theo isn't such a nod-cock as to complain about a lovely lady in the house."

He stuck out his hand to shake Pascoe's. "We met at Iveston, when I was consulting with Theo on microscope glass."

"Devil Dare, yes, I believe I've heard the tales," Sir Pascoe acknowledged. "I doubt you'll appreciate the risk of *this* venture, but come in. Let us show you around—after I gather up my rascals."

Their host scooped up the two laughing toddlers and handed them over to a harassed-looking nursemaid, who had just run around the corner in apparent pursuit of her charges. Emilia thought the curly-haired cherubs were adorable, but then, she didn't have to run after them.

Could they afford nursemaids should she have a child? *She* certainly couldn't take care of a babe! Aside from being paralyzed with fear about holding a babe, she simply didn't have time or knowledge.

The impressive medieval doors opened onto an equally impressive hall of stained glass and a soaring cathedral ceiling. To either side of the hall, however, were more modern chambers.

Emilia caught only a brief glimpse of the salons as Sir Pascoe led them deeper into the interior. She knew he had earned his title and this property for aiding the king with vital national issues. She had met him as an intense diplomat in fashionable clothing, looking very much the black-haired imposing Ives that he was. But today, he was casually dressed in rural tweeds and leather and laughing as he gestured at gargoyles and saints carved into the walls and ceilings.

"My bride and I argue the benefits of renovation over restoration," Pascoe said as he led the way down still another rambling corridor. "I think we should leave the gargoyles to frighten off the vultures who will inevitably descend to pick our bones. Bridey says we must dress as monks and nuns to do that."

"Vultures?" Dare asked. "You're expecting trouble?"

"I love trouble," Pascoe said with relish. "I'm *hoping* for it." He shoved open a door that led into an arched walkway.

Dare glanced down at Emilia with questions in his eyes.

"We're women," she whispered in explanation. "Medical practitioners do not want women treating women. It is all very foolish. I cannot believe anything will come of it."

"Says the scholar who knows nothing of the extreme arrogance of men. Bridey should be in here." Pascoe pushed open another door into a wide, stone-floored room smelling of drying herbs. An auburn-haired woman as tall as Emilia, but better proportioned, looked up from a table at their entrance.

"Emilia, at last," the woman exclaimed, wiping her hands on her apron. "And Lord Dare, how good to meet you. We did not know whether to interrupt your honeymoon idyll so soon."

As they exchanged pleasantries, Emilia could sense her husband's tension. Assuming he was fighting off a cough, she studied the array of herbs Bridey had accumulated.

"Would you mind if I helped myself to some of your horehound and a bit of that sage?" she asked, finding the herbs in the drying leaves overhead. "Our wagon broke a wheel and my supplies haven't arrived."

"If we are to work together, you must consider this room as your own," Bridey declared. "I have much to learn from you. I'm eager to see this pharmacopeia you've described." She reached for the requested leaves.

Delighted to have someone who understood the properties of herbs almost as well as she did, Emilia happily delved into a familiar environment, leaving Dare to occupy himself. While she conferred over cough recipes, Dare and Pascoe wandered to the door in a discussion of their own.

Only when Sir Pascoe shouted "Railroad!" did unease knot her stomach.

Her husband looked pale but determined. Sir Pascoe merely looked livid.

Emilia exchanged a glance with Bridey, and as one, they wiped off their hands and left their work on the table.

Nine

"RAILROADS ARE the country's future," Dare insisted as he sipped the bitter herbal tea his wife had forced upon him. "In war time, they will speed the transportation of coal, iron, and wood to our ports for the navy."

Only slightly older than Dare but more experienced in the ways of governance, Pascoe waved a dismissive hand. "I understand their importance. I had hoped to find a consortium in which to invest. But the task of land acquisition is monumental and expensive. The tracks need to be laid through wasteland, not crop-bearing fields."

"Fine for freight, but what about transporting people? Imagine taking the train from London to Edinburgh in hours instead of days!" Dare had yet to mention the needed land for track already planned for Alder. He'd fallen asleep before he'd had a chance to examine the survey maps.

He was afraid just his casual broaching of the subject was leading toward disaster. His family's future relied on his ability to talk people into what he wanted. If the disease was attacking his brain and his ability, he was in trouble. He clenched his teeth and listened rather than offer protest.

"We can't have noisy, coal-spewing monsters near towns until we know they're reliable," Pascoe said, reaching for a crumpet. "For one thing, they'll terrify horses."

The beautiful wife Dare wished to seduce was watching them with consternation. He was accustomed to taking risks. Emilia was not. He fought his cough and changed the subject until he had more information. "Tell me more about the vultures that threaten this school my bride wishes to work in."

Lady Pascoe—Bridey—spoke up. "It is nothing yet. Pascoe cynically expects the worse. For now, we're only setting up the infirmary and schoolrooms. Aster and Emilia's mother will help us find a few select women to be trained as midwives. Women have performed that task for *centuries*. This insistence that only a male physician can treat a woman's body is utter idiocy."

Dare frowned. "You have the skills and training of a licensed physician?"

"As much as I have the skills of an apothecary," Emilia said in that stiff polite voice she sometimes used. "No man will teach us or allow us to work as their assistants, an education required by law—laws passed by men, you will remember. We are self-taught for the most part."

By Jove, she might not talk much, but when she did, she packed a punch. Before Dare could take adamant exception to his wife working as an apothecary, Bridey interceded.

"My grandfather was a physician. He taught me. I have learned more from experience, just as any good physician must if he is to be of any use. We do not mean to interfere where there are proper physicians and hospitals and wealth enough to pay for them. What we want to do is help women who do not have access to medical care."

Dare lifted a questioning eyebrow to his wealthy city wife who had never been deprived of anything in her life. She met his gaze with defiance.

"I have done the research and study that most apothecaries have not," she insisted. "I have read everything available, tested, experimented, and know what works and what does not. I am trying to learn *why* things work and better ways of administering medicines, which is why I need a laboratory. If I had been trained by a male apothecary, I would simply have been taught how to measure and mix ingredients according to whatever recipe book he uses. And most of those are so outdated as to be laughable."

Outdated Dare understood. Horses and wagons and herbal medicines were *outdated*. The future was in steam engines and minerals. But he knew when he was outnumbered. With a determined interest in sharing his bedchamber with a willing wife, he sipped his tea and just listened to their audacious plans. He prayed Emilia did not mean to invest her funds in this losing proposition, but he knew better than to mention that as well.

In fact, he might choke on all the things he wasn't saying. But his bride had an uncanny way of knowing when he was losing his strength. She rose and offered their farewells, welcoming their new friends to visit their hovel soon so they could make plans.

"I am turning into an old curmudgeon," Dare grumbled as he

handed her into the carriage and pulled himself in like a weakling.

"Is it illness that turns people into curmudgeons, not age?" she asked distractedly. "Sir Harry would grumble and carp and poke fun at the servants, but I thought it was because he was older and wiser than everyone else."

"Illness and wisdom," he decided, dropping into the cushions with relief. "I think I should be allowed to spend my final months pointing out the fallacies of everyone around me."

She snickered. His lady wife *snickered*. Dare turned a cynically lifted brow in her direction. "You laugh. I am very wise. I married you, did I not?"

That brought an outright chuckle. He removed her confounded hat so he could see her smile. "You don't smile enough," he told her. "See, there's my curmudgeonly wisdom for today."

"I think I would like it very much if we could be *foolish* for the rest of the day instead of wise. I feel as if I'm carrying the weight of the world on my shoulders. Normally, I like feeling worthy, but today, I want to laugh and feel joy. What does your wisdom make of that, my Lord Curmudgeon?"

"That my lady needs kissing." Which he proceeded to do, dragging her against his side and planting kisses all over her cheek and down her swan-like throat until she squealed.

At least he still knew how to woo a woman.

THE WAGON WITH their boxes had arrived while they were gone. Their one footman and two drivers had unloaded everything into the cobwebbed parlor, among the discarded linens and spiders. Emilia studied the disarray in exhaustion. She had never fully realized how much she had relied on her mother's efficient staff.

Her husband wrapped his arm around her waist and surveyed the dusty stacks with a chuckle. She didn't feel any fever pouring off of him. She really needed to study why Dare's disease didn't pain her by touching as others did.

When she wasn't consumed by lust, however, she could sense his weariness, if not his pain. He shouldn't be worrying about carting heavy boxes about. She really needed to take notes about how the consumption affected him. His symptoms didn't seem to quite match what she'd read—which wasn't unusual. Medical science was imprecise at best, and her understanding leaned toward herbs and not anatomy.

"Do we open the crates methodically one at a time, or just rip them open willy-nilly in search of what we need at the moment?" he asked.

"We do neither right now," she said. "We will dress for dinner and see what our new cook has prepared for us out of thin air, although I do hope our pantry supplies have also arrived."

He tugged one of the straying strands of hair she hadn't adequately pinned. "Dress for dinner? In this hovel? Why?"

"Because that is what one does?" she asked, never having thought about it.

"This one doesn't," he declared. "Why should we not start off as we mean to carry on?"

As *she* meant to carry on, since he wouldn't necessarily be here to support her in this outrageousness in a year from now. The notion of dealing with all this by herself was suddenly overwhelming, and a little more heart-breaking than she'd envisaged.

She had always assumed once she married, she'd simply move into her great-grandfather's familiar home with everything being exactly the same. She had not really even worked a husband into the picture, assuming he'd go his own way. But these past days had shattered that fantasy. She hadn't wanted to rely on Dare, but she had been, because she was so accustomed to having family with her. Once he was gone... She would have to carve an entirely new existence all on her own. She took a deep breath to suppress her panic and organize her thoughts.

"Since my clothes are somewhere among all those trunks," she decided, "I suppose I can wear the same gown this evening. But we do have to maintain a level of civilization once we are in a position to expect company. And I still really must wash and straighten up before dinner." She turned pointedly toward the stairs, walking away from his... unsettling... arm.

"Shouldn't your maid be down here sorting through all this, looking for your trunks?" Dare asked, following on her heels, emanating masculine energy and disturbing her mind.

"Bessie? She will if I tell her to. But she has more important tasks."

"Does she sew your clothing, then? I thought you had a modiste for that."

Emilia stopped in the upper corridor to examine him

quizzically. "Does it matter what Bessie does? I am not asking what your James does all day."

Dare flashed her one of his charming grins, but it didn't seem to quite reach his eyes. Her husband was a man of many layers.

"My clothing trunks weren't in that jumble down there," he informed her. "While your Bessie was twiddling her thumbs, James has probably filled all the wardrobes in the suite with my attire. You'll have to fight for shelf space. I daresay he has hot water heating and my evening clothes pressed and laid out, although he knows by now not to expect me to actually wear them."

Emilia glared. "I do not need anyone to wash and dress me, and until now, my clothes were always in my wardrobe exactly where I want them. Bessie has better uses." She turned in the opposite direction of their suite, her husband still on her heels. She'd swear he radiated curiosity.

She opened the door on the chamber her grandfather had once used as his private office. Bessie glanced up from her work, and left an ink smudge on her brow as she brushed a wisp of hair out of her face. "M'lady? Do you need me?"

Dare leaned his shoulder against the jamb and studied the dusty bookshelves and old-fashioned walnut secretary desk. "Are those botanical prints?" He nodded at the frames studding the walls.

"Pressed leaves with inscriptions," Emilia replied curtly. "They were my first herbals. I learned from the books on that wall."

She crossed to examine the pages Bessie worked on. "You are a wonder, thank you. You should probably rest your eyes and hands for a while. It's almost time for dinner."

"Yes, ma'am, m'lady. Let me finish up this sketch, and I'll be right with you." She picked up the watercolor brush resting in a glass swirling with colored water.

Dare loomed over Emilia's shoulder, studying the pages Bessie worked on. "She's your secretary?" He glanced over at the valise she'd carried in the coach with them. "This is your pharmacopeia?"

Emilia nodded, swung on her heel, and walked out. "I have only the one complete draft besides my notes. Bessie is creating a final copy for the printer." The printer she would have to pay herself because no male publisher believed the book worth the paper it was written on. She seethed with irritation, but it was an old story. One she had learned to overcome—with money.

"One copy?" he asked in disbelief. "One copy could be lost in fire, to thieves, flood, anything!"

"You think I have not thought of that?" She marched back to their suite. "Do you have any idea how long it took to find someone to make a fair copy? Finding a reasonably competent artist took forever and then I had to train Bessie after Aster found her. It's taken a *year* to reach this stage. I made the first draft from my notes, staying up in the evenings to do so when everyone else was attending balls and the theater. I could not spend additional years making a second copy. I've learned so much more. . . I really need to be editing this edition."

All her frustration, anger, and hopes were tied up in that office with Bessie. She didn't know how to express them to her new husband without pounding him and the walls with her fists. She'd certainly pounded enough desks over the past year.

The moment their door closed and they were alone, Dare pulled her into his arms and hugged her. Briefly, she risked resting her head against his wide shoulder. His embrace had a way of depleting her temper. She'd never allowed anyone to hold her because she hadn't been able to deal with the. . . connection. . . established. It wasn't just the prickles and pain, but an elemental drain of energy she could not quite describe.

But oddly, Dare blunted the pain that others exacted. And her own emotions wrapped her in a hot blanket akin to steam—almost painful but also relaxing and comforting. She sank into his embrace as she would never venture to do with any other.

"I apologize for thinking your work was no more than my mother's foolish embroidery," he said into her hair. "Ladies have to occupy their time and minds, I know, but I had no notion. . ." He hugged her tighter and kissed her ear. "I wish I had you and Bessie to organize my chaos of notes. It has not once occurred to me to hire someone to do so, much less train anyone!"

She relaxed even more and nodded against him. "I can help with hiring and training. But I suspect you'll have to keep your own notes. Most secretaries do not wish to be blown to bits."

"Are you laughing at me?" he asked, setting her back to study her expression, grinning lopsidedly as he did so. "I'll admit my methods aren't orderly, but my few attempts at articles have been accepted in scientific journals."

"While you ride about investing in railroads and steam engines and microscope glass and things my father refrained from telling me about," she replied, stepping away from his aches and his warmth. "Do not think I walked blindly into this marriage. Whereas I approach all change with caution, you, sir, are a risk taker."

"I am." He crossed his arms and accepted her accusation. "And I have wrecked my health as a consequence, I know. But it had to be done."

She lifted a quizzical eyebrow. "Someone held you at gunpoint and said kill yourself?"

"My father, essentially." He shrugged. "He ran us to the brink of ruin, then rode off a cliff one drunken evening, leaving me to deal with the consequences. I had to come home from Oxford not just to console my mother and sisters, but to keep the creditors from carrying off every stick of furniture. One cannot overcome obstacles that high without taking risks."

She stared at him, wide-eyed. He stood there looking authoritative and gentlemanly, as if he'd just asked which party she would like to attend that evening. He must have been no more than a boy. . . "*That*, my father did not tell me," she said in a whisper of awe.

"It is not something we let get about," he admitted. "It is a truth universally acknowledged that wealth attracts wealth."

She chuckled at his paraphrase from a popular novel. "So you pretended to still have a nice income, put off the creditors, and gambled on what?"

"Waterloo, essentially. I wagered Wellington would win and soon bring home his men. I invested borrowed money in horses and ships, hoping there would be hundreds of soldiers needing good transportation. It was lucky timing."

"The timing was there for anyone to see. You're the one with the confidence to use it," she corrected. "And knowing what I do of you, I assume you burned the midnight oil racing about the countryside in all sorts of weather to gather the funds, the horses, and the ships."

"But my days of juggling a dozen balls have run out." He shrugged out of his coat and began unfastening his linen. "What time did you tell Mrs. Peacock to serve dinner?"

She wanted to linger and watch him undress. He had apparently realized that arriving at the table covered in road dust was not polite. But people waited on them. Now was not the time to indulge in her womanly curiosity. She glanced at her pocket watch. "In another half hour. If you would prefer to rest, I can have dinner sent up."

He shook his head, sending a gold-dusted lock tumbling over his brow. "Abandon my bride for our first meal together in our new home? Not likely. I am not entirely an invalid yet."

She wanted to explain that she might help extend his life a few months by laying her hands on him, using her gift, but perhaps giving him that hope was not a good idea. If she failed. . . he might hate her. Sometimes, she was very slow thinking through human reactions.

Daringly, she stood on her toes and kissed his whiskery cheek. "You are more man than most," she murmured, darting out of his reach before he could grab her, and retreating to the dressing room.

She really needed to think about tonight, and the expectation of a man who was not entirely an invalid yet.

DARE HADN'T BEEN really *hungry* in longer than he could remember, but apparently country air was good for him. Or Mrs. Peacock's light broth, meltingly delicious bread, fancy greens, and thin slices of ham sat easier on his stomach than richer fare. He was afraid to eat too much. Nausea was a poor companion to lust. But he felt remarkably satisfied as they departed the table.

"Did you help Mrs. Peacock choose the menu?" he asked his bride as they faced the parlor jumble together after dinner.

"Not at all. She had an enormous list. I suggested she make do with what had arrived. Dinner was the result. Was that enough for you? I fear she's trying to please me by assuming I eat lightly."

"A meal designed for ladies and invalids, no doubt. Word spreads quickly among the servants, and James knows I do not eat." Dare lifted boxes he recognized as his and shifted them to one corner. He didn't want to wear out his renewed energy before bedtime.

"If so, Mrs. Peacock did well. You ate everything set before you. That trunk is books. Do not think to move it," she warned.

The reminder of his weakness irritated him. Once upon a time, he would have taken it as a challenge. With a grumble, he realized illness had taught him caution, a little late. He said nothing but sorted out other trunks he knew weren't his. "Which of these will you need on the morrow?"

"The two smaller ones should suffice. I'll stay home and help Mrs. Wiggs organize and interview, I suppose. I cannot move my equipment to the abbey until a room is prepared."

She sounded so sad, he wanted to hug her again. Instead, Dare lifted one of her small trunks to his shoulder, and offered his other arm to her. "We'll have the marquess's footman for a while longer. We may as well keep him employed. James has cleared the worst of our suite. Let us repair to our private parlor."

Where he could divest his beautiful bride of all her clothing was the thought primarily on his mind. Her bold kiss earlier had stirred him more than his lust. Lust was for interchangeable women who offered physical release. His intriguing wife stirred him in possessive, proud ways he'd never experienced—and aroused his need to explore.

As Emilia took his elbow and lifted her skirts to go up the stairs, she sent him an admiring glance. The look sizzled his innards, and Dare realized he'd never suffered even a calf love for any woman. He'd never had time. In his youth, he had sought the favors of young ladies whose fathers he wooed for business reasons. Once he had access to the right clubs, he'd discarded that approach. She was right—he'd been living in an all-male society of his own making.

Surrounded by his mother and sisters, he'd never noticed the lack of feminine company. Lust could be quenched by women he saw in bedchambers and nowhere else. They weren't exactly conversationalists—but then, neither was Emilia. Yet her company captivated him as others did not.

Perhaps it was just his perverse desire to prevent his cousin Peter from inheriting, as slim as that chance might be. It was the kind of gamble he enjoyed.

Dare set the trunk down in the dressing room while she examined the wardrobe and dressers. "Did James leave you any space?"

"He very neatly divided everything in half," she said with one of those rare smiles he craved because they made him feel special. "I'll have Bessie clear the wardrobe in the smaller chamber for my gowns. I have a great many, I fear, even if I do not wear them often."

"There is so much I'd like to learn about you." Knowing it was early yet and that she probably had a list of tasks as long as his, Dare traced his finger down her peach-soft cheek. A blush rewarded him. "Have you given any thought to our discussion about an heir?"

She blushed deeper. "Is there. . . I mean, I know it's unlikely, but. . ." She looked frustrated at her inability to phrase the question.

"Would you like to write out your query as a botanical theory?" he asked in amusement. "I can explain birds and bees, but not plants so much."

"Birds and bees spread plant pollen," she said crossly. "It's a nonsensical phrase referring to pollination. It is not at all the same for people."

Dare had a hard time not laughing. *Intellectual* discussions caused his bride no problem in speaking. "Is there a logistical problem I should be aware of?" he asked, doing his best to use impersonal phrases.

"Several," she said with a heavy sigh. "I had not really anticipated. . . Well, men usually aren't interested in me."

There was an opening he could use. Dare tugged at the fine muslin chemisette adorning the neckline of her bodice. "I believe we have already established that I am not just any man. I am a man of rare perception with the ability to see past your shyness to the intelligent, beautiful woman you conceal."

"I am not shy," she said irritably, but she didn't stop his marauding fingers. "I simply have no patience with flapping eyelashes and coy titters."

"A fact I admire more and more," he said with relish, leaning over to kiss her heated cheek, while whisking off the muslin, leaving her shoulders bare. "Wind gusts from flapping lashes send me fleeing every time."

She laughed a little and bless all that was holy, began toying with his neckcloth. Just her proximity had his cock primed. Her touch would soon turn him into a drooling imbecile. When he was more coherent, he would write into his will that he wished to be buried with her scent of lavender.

"Nursemaids," she muttered insensibly, unknotting his linen. "Are they costly?"

Nursemaids—babies—conjugal rights: he worked backward to determine her meaning. "I will indenture my sisters, if you would be so kind as to bear my child."

She poked his chest to show she understood he jested, then set to work on his waistcoat. "Did no one warn you that Malcolm women seldom bear sons? I did not think to say since I did not think as far as sharing a bed."

"Whereas, that's all I thought about," he said fervently, finding the fastenings of her gown. Hope slammed against his ribs. He was ready, if she was willing. "And right now, I cannot say that infants are on my mind at all."

She untied his shirt and pressed a kiss to his chest that had his heart galloping.

"If I may have nursemaids and you do not mind about an heir. . ." She took a deep breath, stepped back, and met his gaze with determination. "Then I see no reason why we should not be truly man and wife."

Ten

EMILIA DID NOT know what to expect of her agreement to share Dare's bed. Her husband had seemed very calm and pragmatic in discussing her concerns. He'd made her believe that he wanted *her*— not an easy task given her experience.

To her astonishment, at her agreement to share his bed, Dare hooted—literally *hooted*—with joy and lifted her into the air as if she were a mere wisp.

His reckless joy wiped away all her *thinking*. It was as if he cast aside the heavy burden of her gift, dispelled all her fears, making her feel lighter and more carefree than she could ever remember being. He encouraged her ecstatic buoyancy by swinging her in a circle, then carrying her out of the dressing room and back to their bedchamber, fervently covering her face and hair with kisses.

"I need to put a dozen years of lovemaking into every night," he declared.

She didn't warn him that his lungs were already overworked, and this exercise had exacerbated the problem—that was the fear talking. Instead, she daringly held her hand to his chest and experienced the warning prickles, then the hot shock of energy transferring from deep inside herself to him. Her excitement buffered the pain, creating a risk that she wouldn't cut off the healing connection in time. But sometimes the desire to heal was so magnetic, it was hard to stop—rather like kissing.

Wrapped up in his lust, Dare didn't even seem to notice. While she clung to his linen, he set her feet back on the floor and eagerly dragged her bodice off her shoulders. He kissed her breast above her corset—creating a hot river from her breast to her womb. That sufficiently distracted her enough to break the connection.

All the blood left her brain, and she nearly passed out from sensation. She grabbed his arms, whispering, "Slower, please. It is hard. . . I can feel. . ." That had always been the problem—she *felt* too much. How could she explain?

"Slower, it is." He ran his hand into her hair and pins clattered against the plank floor.

Light-headed, she almost giggled. "That is not slower."

"How am I to give you a hundred nights in one if I do not ravish you immediately?" he asked with perfect logic, spreading her waist-length hair across her shoulders. "By all that's holy, this glory should be woven into gossamer fabric. Men pay fortunes to dress their women in black silk. You need only wear your hair down."

The cascade of hair over her bare breasts stimulated a flush of desire, and Emilia knew she was turning pink. "Hair is a nuisance that takes too much work. I shall cut it off and ask a weaver to make a shirt of it for you to pet." Since he was unfastening her bodice, she was not at all certain what she was saying. Her breasts felt tight and swollen, eager for his caress.

"It is not your hair I wish to make love to," he murmured, nipping at her throat, pressing soothing kisses to her skin as he pushed her bodice to her waist. "Your mane is magnificent, but these. . ." He released her breasts from her corset and pushed them up so cool air blew over the heated crests. "These are triumphs of beauty."

"That is ridiculous," she tried to say, but she wasn't entirely certain her tangled tongue released the words. The erotic sensation of a man's hands holding her breasts deprived her of all thought.

Dare loomed over her in all his glorious muscular masculinity, and she needed to *touch*. She tried to tug his shirt free, but his trousers were too tight.

"A dying man is allowed to say whatever he wishes," he insisted, before lifting her so he could suckle at her breast.

Emilia smothered a shriek and grabbed his shoulders for support. Her spine turned to water and her legs instinctively wrapped around his hips, seeking solace for the ache between them. "Specious argument," she protested breathlessly. "You are obviously not dying yet."

"I am dying of lust," he asserted, holding her with one arm while unfastening his trouser buttons with his other hand.

"Plants in a weakened condition often produce more seeds than usual to ensure propagation of a new generation," she rattled mindlessly. He dropped her on the bed to wrestle off his shirt and to gaze lasciviously on her wanton state of undress. He cocked a wry eyebrow at her inane utterance.

The day was still light enough that she could admire the contours of his lean muscled chest when he flung the shirt at the floor. A stream of gold-tipped hair ran between his flat male nipples, tapering to a rivulet above his unfastened trousers. Once her gaze fell to his hips, she could not raise it. Intellectually, she knew men were made differently. But he might as well have imprisoned a live python in there.

"Propagation is exactly what I have in mind," he assured her, dropping down beside her to untangle the ties of her skirt that she had been too stunned stupid to undo. "I had no notion that propagation would add such zest to the pollination process."

She almost laughed outright. Except he was exactly right. Just the thought of the miracle they might create tonight terrified and excited her beyond all the boring staid experiences of her boring staid life.

She lifted her hips so he might yank off her skirt and petticoat and did not protest as they landed in a heap with his shirt. Her corset, under-chemise, and stockings were her only cover. She waited for modesty to make her flush, but she could only watch in fascination as her husband peeled off his trousers. The python pressed demandingly at his drawers.

"Damn, you smell good," he murmured, leaning over to brand searing kisses from her ear to the top of her breasts.

All the hard temptation of his chest loomed over her, and she could scarcely register anything else.

"I want to smell you, lick you, and frig you all at the same time," he murmured, tasting her nipple again.

She thought to protest his crudity, but she made the mistake of laying her palm flat against his *bare* chest first. The jolt of electricity nearly left her paralyzed.

She absorbed the prickles, the heat, and the rush of his blood and his breath and the pain in his center all in one blow. The sensations mixed with those of her own intense desire, as if they were all one creature. The ache between her legs became a tension so exquisite, she didn't know how to handle herself.

Fortunately, Dare did. He slid his fingers into the nest of her lower hair, and she almost rose off the bed.

"Yes," he hissed in satisfaction. "Your blood boils as mine does."

Without further warning, he stripped off her corset and chemise and swooped down to suckle her breasts while his fingers played their magic between her thighs. There was no chance of forming any healing connection while he cast her into the throes of lust.

"Dare," she whispered urgently, feeling as if she might come apart from the pressure and the dangerous mix of sensations. "Please. I cannot bear—"

He used his thumb to press while his fingers spread her. The tension reached new pinnacles, her inner muscles clenched, and Emilia arched into his hand, biting back screams. He took full advantage to delve deeper. The quakes, when they came, cast her into another realm, one of nothing but sheer physical pleasure, shaking her very existence. How could just a touch cause such immense revelations? And all these years, she'd *feared* touching?

Limply, she was barely aware when Dare tugged off his drawers.

"Propagation, my sweet," he murmured in laughter as he covered her helpless body with his powerful one. "Think gurgling adorable infants."

And he eased his python into the slippery channel between her legs. Except the stiff, thick—very thick—velvet-covered iron was no wiggly soft snake. Emilia gasped as he pushed into her.

"Infants for the betterment of the world," he whispered encouragingly in her ear as her body resisted the invasion. He covered her nipple with his mouth and licked it.

Whatever he did worked. Emilia opened for him, blossomed, allowed his rod into her pistil and deeper. He tore her open, and she cried out, but his shoulders were right there to grasp, and her sheath was wet and ready, and he slid deep, filling her past all her flower parts and beyond.

Her books had not explained *this*.

DARE FELT THE congestion in his lungs threatening his breathing, but the pent-up need for physical release was too great to stop and gasp now. He pulled out of the tightness of his wife's body for a moment, giving Emilia time to adjust. She was his first virgin, and he wasn't entirely certain what to expect, but at least he had started by giving her pleasure. He hoped that would mean she would be receptive to more nights like this one, even though he seemed to be hurting her now.

She was so damned *tight*. She whimpered a protest as he eased into her again, but her slim hips rose urgently, asking for more. Blessed be the mismatched stars that had brought this woman into his life. . .

He accepted her invitation and drove deeper, higher, desperate for relief. She quivered, and he feared he'd hurt her more. Before he could pull back, her inner muscles clamped around him, and she cried out with another quake of pleasure.

Her enjoyment was all it took. Pain and ecstasy slammed through him. Dare buried his own groans in her hair as he pumped deep inside her, flooding her with all the seed he'd not spilled in months.

The sweet scent of heaven wrapped around him, and he nearly passed out from lack of breath. Drained, he still wanted, needed more, but he could scarcely gasp for air.

Rolling over, he carried Emilia with him, holding her beautifully rounded bottom and staying buried within her. He didn't want her to escape while he slept.

She pressed a palm to his chest and heat seeped deep inside him. If he'd killed himself this time, he'd die happy, hoping he'd at least created an heir with his last breath.

EMILIA WOKE TO an unfamiliar woman's voice chiding the crowing rooster and to a solid male arm and leg wrapped around her. Her face was buried in a muscled shoulder that smelled of raw male flesh, and she inhaled the sweaty saltiness with delight. Who knew it would feel so good to be close to another person?

With trepidation, she examined how she felt. The pleasant soreness between her legs wasn't as unsettling as having a big male body sprawled up and down her, touching her everywhere. She waited for the prickles that warned of pain to follow but didn't sense any. Beneath her excitement and the warmth and weight of him she sensed the dull ache with which he must live, but whatever they'd done last night had neutralized actual pain. She wanted to send him energy—but she wasn't compelled to do so. Yet.

She must have squirmed. Dare shifted more of his weight to his side so she could escape if necessary. His python was erect and hard already. It would be simpler if he was more the size of a bird beak.

She wasn't entirely certain her pistil was prepared for another assault.

A knock on the door reminded them that they were never truly alone.

"Hot water, m'lord," a male voice called through the panel.

An irritated growl filled her ear. She covered Dare's mouth before he said anything irascible. Feeling very daring, she called, "One moment, please."

She slid out from beneath his hold and hurried to the dressing room in search of a robe.

"That's why one has maids," he called after her.

"And separate chambers," she called back, tying her robe. "Shall I look into that?" My, she was feeling feisty this morning.

His reply was a thump on the floorboards. She peered around the door to watch her magnificently naked husband stalk to a dressing screen before shouting, "You may enter."

"My lady?" Bessie called from the corridor. "Shall I take your water to the other chamber?"

One of these days, she supposed they would sort out all this newness. Emilia peered into the smaller bedchamber she had only glanced at yesterday. As she remembered, it was filled with aged wardrobes, a small bed, and an ancient dressing table. Not exactly welcoming, but it had a separate door to the hall, unlike this in-between dressing chamber.

"Please do, Bessie." The tweenies had always carried up her wash water at home. Bessie was usually at work at her desk. What had brought about this miracle of thoughtfulness?

Her secretary maid scurried in, setting an old ceramic pitcher on the wash table, then looking around for the trunk with toiletries. "James carried up an entire pail of water," she whispered in awe as she rummaged through the trunk's contents for soap. "Shall I see if this place has a tub?"

Ah, enlightenment—Bessie had wanted to impress the valet. Perhaps she'd name this place Birds and Bees Cottage. "Not this morning. There is too much to do. The tub used to be stored in the kitchen. There's a little room down there grandfather used for bathing. We'll have to come up with something more modern."

Dare loomed in the doorway, looking tall and rumpled in a maroon robe. "Like servants?" he asked in a low growl. "We're supposed to bathe in the kitchen?"

"You are the one who said we should not hire too many people," she retorted. "I told you Grandfather got by with only a few. And the manservant was elderly when I was little. Mr. Butler mostly polished silver beside the fire. If you wish to bathe in comfort, we will need more help."

Bessie laid out a gown and scurried out of the room.

Dare rubbed his heavy stubble, coughed, and screwed up his brow in thought. "A steam engine to pump water upstairs, perhaps. We could sell the patent if we made it work." Coughing harder, he retreated to his own room.

Emilia trailed after him, frowning as he dosed himself from the medicine bottle. She had been mindless last night, lost in so many sensations that she had not felt his pain so much as her joy. But she remembered the *unrightness* in his gut. Consumption occasionally affected other parts of the body like bones or kidneys, but she didn't remember reading anything about the digestive organs.

"Or we could catch rain water on the roof and pipe it down," he continued, his brain outracing his weakening body. "That would be cheaper, although it's an old idea, and we can't sell it."

"You are quite mad, but it's a happy mad." She watched where he stowed the bottle while her own ideas mulled about in her brain. "If you are to use Grandfather's workshop for blowing up things, I'll use his growing house for my herbs. But I'll need a place to mix and store them. The abbey is too far away for regular use."

Dare kissed her hair. "We'll look after we break our fast. For some reason, I am unreasonably hungry this morning."

She hoped and prayed that meant she was helping. Consumption often went into remission, she knew. If her healing energy and fresh country air could make that happen. . . They could have *years*.

Not knowing exactly how she felt about that, she hurried off to dress. She had never particularly wanted to marry, had not seen the need for a demanding male in her life, but now. . . She could see the advantage of sharing the burdens of running the estate. And now that there was no question about whether or not she could endure carnal relations, she could definitely see the benefit of having a husband in bed.

The magical Mrs. Peacock had prepared rashers of bacon, boiled eggs with a savory sauce, and tomatoes cooked with herbs so delicious that Emilia could have eaten them all. The toast arrived hot and buttered. There was even coffee for Dare, and she enjoyed it simply for the effect it had on her husband. Instead of grumbling and poking at his food, he looked blissful, cleaning off every platter placed in front of them after she'd helped herself.

"We are definitely keeping Mrs. Peacock," he said, putting his linen back on the table and shoving back his chair.

"Then you had best discover how much she wishes to be paid, and if she wants to take up residence in the house. I believe she stayed overnight, but she has a place of her own."

"I'd better calculate budgets or I'll be putting my family into the street just so we can pay staff. Will you do the interviews with Mrs. Wiggs?" He stood and offered his hand to help her up.

"I expect she'll arrive with an army, and I'll have no say in the matter. Perhaps you had best calculate budgets first so I can tell her when she exceeds it. And I'll poke around and look for a place for my work."

She had an ulterior motive in sending Dare off to play with numbers. As soon as she knew he was ensconced in the downstairs study, Emilia hurried up to their shared bedchamber. James had already straightened it up and vanished on his lengthy list of duties. She hurried to the dressing table where Dare had stored his foul Fowler's Solution. He had several bottles. She borrowed one, tucked it in the apron she wore when she worked, and hurried out to the old glass-roofed house her grandfather had once used for his plant experiments.

The glass was broken in places and covered in ivy. The bedding tables were bare and filthy. One day, she might have it repaired so she could experiment in growing exotic herbs. But for now, it was private, and it had tables, and no one would question if she carried her herbs back here and mixed them.

It wasn't sanitary enough for making pills. All her reading had convinced her that clean conditions were absolutely necessary, and Bridey agreed with this theory. Emilia knew she had to wait for facilities at the abbey that she could keep sterile. But for now, she could scrub a table, cover it in fresh linen, and set up her mortar and pestle. She poured some of the foul medicine into a cup and sniffed it. There was an old pharmacopeia in the study where Bessie worked, but she didn't need to consult medicine lists for what she wanted to do. She simply needed to duplicate smell and viscosity. There was a faint odor of lavender. She dipped her finger in the liquid and licked it. There was a vaguely salty taste. She just needed to disguise the flavor of her healing herbs and his healthy mineral water, create a slight oily thickness, and Dare would never notice the difference.

It was an experiment, she told herself. If he actually worsened for drinking her healthy concoction, she'd throw it away, and he could go back to his foul solution.

If her medicine couldn't help Dare, she'd have to question everything she'd learned and believed about herbs. Her life work would have been a waste.

She couldn't let that happen. She'd make a perfectly dreadful housewife.

Eleven

"THERE IS A dreadful stench coming from that shed," Bessie said breathlessly, having run past Dare's workshop to reach Emilia's glass shed. "And Mrs. Wiggs is here with half the village."

Satisfied that she'd done the best she could to create an imitation but *healthy* Fowler's solution, Emilia looked around for a place to pour out the foul medicine. All she had was the shallow bowl she'd carried her herbs in. She poured the rest of the Fowler's in there, refilled the empty bottle from a beaker of her herbal solution, and tucked the refilled bottle back in her apron pocket.

"I assume the stench means Lord Dare has finished his budget and is now preparing to blow up more glass," she said distractedly, glancing around at the disorder she was leaving behind. She was accustomed to leaving her worktable neat and tidy. Perhaps, once they'd hired servants, she'd have more time. "Tell Mrs. Wiggs I'll be right there."

She stopped at the shed, knocked, then leaned in. The stench of sulfur was overpowering. "Are you there? Mrs. Wiggs has arrived, and I need numbers to dash her dreams." The dim light from a single window did little to illuminate the gloom and smoke. She could see Dare peering into the microscope she coveted with all her heart and soul. He'd directed lamp light to mirrors in an attempt to make it work better. Wearing the adorable half glasses she'd only seen him wear the day he'd asked her to marry him, he glanced up impatiently, named a sum, then returned to work.

Emilia had no idea if it was a generous amount or not. She'd never paid any servant but Bessie.

Hoping maids would be less expensive than secretaries, she hurried into the house.

Mrs. Wiggs waited in the crowded parlor beaming happily. "There you are, m'lady. I've brought the best the village has to offer."

Behind her waited half a dozen young girls, all looking expectant and eager. Short ones, tall ones, wide ones. . . Emilia's eyes narrowed as she noticed a thin one almost cringing at the back of the pack. She wasn't much older than Emilia's younger sisters. The girl's expression was tight with hope and fear, but her eyes were flat with despair. And silhouetted against the light from the dirty parlor windows, she showed a belly rounder than her thin build should carry.

Oh, dear, this would be much harder than she'd imagined, and she'd imagined a hurdle higher than she was tall. "Why don't you come back to the office, Mrs. Wiggs? Give me a list of whom you wish to hire for what, and what wages they'll expect." She steered the former housekeeper from the parlor and down the corridor.

"I don't think you can get by on fewer girls," Mrs. Wiggs protested as Emilia closed the doors after them. "Mrs. Peacock will leave without a scullion and a kitchen maid. You'll probably need a pot boy as well, but Tess can handle his duties until I find someone suitable. We'll need at least one upper and one lower housemaid, a laundress, a butler, and two footmen, but I started with the womenfolk today."

"Tess?" Emilia asked faintly, matching this formidable list to the staff in her father's house and realizing Mrs. Wiggs was understating the total.

"My grand-niece," the housekeeper said, twisting her hands together. "She's young, but she's a good girl, and needs some training. She knows her way around the kitchen and has helped Mrs. Peacock before."

Emilia kneaded the bridge of her nose, looking for the words that were so hard to find. "Would Tess be the thin one at the back of the parlor?"

"She's a good girl," Mrs. Wiggs insisted again. "The best student in the school. Writes a fine copperplate and reads like a scholar. But she'll be happy washing and chopping and whatever is needed down below."

Down below, out of sight, as her belly grew. "And her husband?" Emilia asked desperately. "Will he not object? Or will he be asking for a place as well?"

The stout old lady almost wilted in dejection. "The lout ran away without marrying her. She made a mistake, but she's learned a hard lesson. She's a good worker."

"And the babe?" Emilia knew it was possible for women to work while carrying a child, but the work of a kitchen maid required long hours and carrying heavy burdens. Malcolm women were accustomed to pampering unborn children—because they were wealthy and could afford to. How did other women do it? She rubbed her brow some more, trying to work her way through this dilemma.

"I have another grand-niece in Harrogate who wants a child more than anything in the world," Mrs. Wiggs said anxiously. "She's said she'll take the babe. But Tess's father has thrown her out, and she needs to learn an occupation. She'll take nothing if you'll house her until the babe is born. I'd take her myself, but I live with my sister, and there's no room."

Emilia knew this was what her mother and Aster did—rescued women, taught them, gave them security so they didn't end up on the streets, at the mercy of any man who came along. But her family was wealthy, and she was not, not after making her bargain with Dare.

Still, it was impossible to throw the child out. "I can't have her carrying pails of coal and boiling water," she protested faintly. "And in a few months, even running up and down stairs will be dangerous for her. I already have a secretary, and it's probably best if she does not undertake the task of my husband's secretary. What position can she perform that will not harm her or the babe?"

"Mrs. Peacock will look after her," the housekeeper said, looking hopeful. "There's cutting and rolling pastry and bits like that she can learn to do. And then after, she'll work twice as hard, I promise. She's smart enough that someday, she can take my place."

Vowing to consult with Bridey before putting that skinny child to heavy work, Emilia nodded and began the task of going through the other applicants and their skills and cost.

She had yet to ask Mrs. Peacock how much *she* expected. She feared a cook that good would ask twice what she paid all the other staff put together. But her husband needed to eat properly to keep up his strength.

DARE WIPED a bead of sweat from his brow, jotted a note on the level of sulfur in the Bath water he was testing, and was wondering how he might acquire Harrogate spa water when Emilia tapped on the workshop door again.

This time, he was happy to see her. Tired and ready to sit down, he wiped his hands off on a rag and hoped for a kiss or two. Or more.

Her expression deterred that thought. "Problems?" he asked.

"Nothing someone with more experience might handle," she said wearily, glancing around at the dark interior.

The workshop was purely utilitarian. There had already been a scarred and battered plank table and sagging shelves. His up-ended trunk served as a seat and his traveling desk served as table for his notes. There was nowhere for her to sit.

Offering his arm, he suggested, "Perhaps we should go back to the house. There are likely rats and spiders out here."

"Or worse." She shivered and accepted his arm. "Everywhere I turn, I miss items I'm used to having around me, and I despair of keeping expenses in control. I need a horse," she said flatly.

"So do I. And a gig. And all the accompanying expense of keeping animals, including grooms and hay and repairing the stable," he acknowledged. "If you go riding alone, you will need a groom to accompany you."

"The area is rural. I don't need a man to follow me about," she protested. "But it seems foolish to take out an enormous carriage and team if I simply wish to visit the abbey. Where will you be taking a gig?"

"To Harrogate to buy the horses," he said, trying to sound cheerful. "And to purchase spa water. Taking an expensive berlin to the horse fair to purchase cheap riding hacks is not a good way to get the best price."

"There is a hot spring on the grounds," she said, gesturing toward the fields. "I need to see if my grandfather's experimental mosses and liverwort still survive in that hollow. The area is littered with springs, apparently. You can bottle your own."

That perked him up. "Our very own spa? Convenient! But I still need a way to go to town. I daresay I can borrow a hack, but I'm not at all certain I'll have the strength to ride home with a string of animals afterward. And I'd really rather sleep with you than in a crowded inn with a dozen other fellows."

That Dare admitted his weakness showed his trust in her, she thought, or his level of discouragement. She wished she understood people as well as she did plants. "Has the horse fair started? Should I go with you?"

He shook his head. "There is too much to do here, and the town will be crowded with men. Accommodations are likely to be a stable if I'm forced to stay overnight. We sent your father's wagon back too soon. I'll have to walk into the village and see if I can rent one. How did the servant interviews go?"

"That is why I need a horse," she said with a sigh. "I really need to consult with Bridey. I think I have just hired an unwed mother for a kitchen maid who ought to be teaching school."

He looked at her blankly. "Do I want to question that?"

She chuckled. "Best not. I'll let you hire the male servants, shall I? Except if you'll not be here tomorrow, I will have to curb Mrs. Wiggs' enthusiasm for hiring the entire village until you are home again."

"Our budget will allow male servants?" he asked dubiously. "They cost twice the amount."

"Not in our household they won't," she warned. "If they want a position, their pay will be commensurate with their work, not how pretty they look. And they'll be carrying the coal and water and sharing their fair share of the hard labor."

"Ah, you don't *want* to hire male servants," he said in amusement. "That makes my hiring task easier. I'll tell them the wage and the chores, and they'll all leave rather than do women's work."

She shot him a glance to be certain he teased. Satisfied, she explained what Mrs. Wiggs had told her. "These will be untrained farm boys hoping to learn a position. Younger sons, mostly, who won't inherit the farm and would rather not work for their families. They're accustomed to hauling and chopping. They might not last long on what we can pay them, but they won't know that what we require of them is unusual. If you agree with her choices, we'll stay under budget."

"And your Mrs. Wiggs plans to train them all without a butler or steward?"

She nodded. "Saving the wages of a butler opens the budget for the additional staff. I've convinced Mrs. Wiggs that we're not a grand household and won't be entertaining on any scale. We simply need people to take care of the house while we work on our projects. If I had been the housewifely sort, we probably wouldn't need half the staff. But I have no intention of changing," she said with an air of defiance.

At the top of the stairs, he kissed her cheek. "And I don't wish you to wear yourself out on menial tasks during the day, when I have much more interesting ones prepared for you at night. We have only just begun to fulfill our marital duties, my little hedgehog."

The thrill of desire shot straight through her, until Dare ambled off to wash, and she remembered the false bottle of Fowler's she'd put into his dressing table earlier.

Please, let it ease the wrongness that was causing him such pain, or she'd start doubting her gift as well as her medicines.

Twelve

WISHING HE hadn't been so tightfisted as to reject taking the comfortable berlin into Harrogate, Dare tried not to topple from the farm wagon in exhaustion at the end of the day. He found it difficult to believe he'd built the foundation of his wealth by haggling with horse traders and had once loved the challenge.

Still, he was confident he'd purchased two respectable nags and their tack today. He had also accomplished a more interesting objective—he'd learned the direction of the elusive Mr. Crenshaw.

While the farmer who'd allowed him to accompany him into town urged his spindly nags around a sheep flock, Dare took a swallow of the Fowler's solution. With luck, it would give him enough energy to prevent him from crawling in among the boxes in the wagon and falling asleep. The farmer beside him looked at him askance but refrained from commenting.

"Know anything of a Frederick Crenshaw over Hadenton way?" Dare asked, turning to check on the string of animals tied to the wagon bed.

The farmer shoved his cap up to scratch his scalp. "Reckon I heard of him. Don't know him."

The banker had said Crenshaw was a respectable gentleman with an estate. Thieves weren't gentlemen in Dare's book.

Once the wagon reached the house, Dare let Ashford's driver and groom handle the new horses while he loped inside, eager for a glimpse of his bride. He didn't know why just the sight of Emilia lifted his spirits, but she was more refreshing than any tonic water.

He nearly stumbled over an ornate carpet in the narrow foyer. He stopped his hasty entrance to examine his surroundings. A hall table had been set up near the door with a dish for calling cards and a bouquet of roses. He peered into the once-filthy salon that had been stacked with trunks yesterday. The ancient furniture now glowed with polish, and another carpet graced the newly-waxed floor. The filth-covered paintings had been removed, but he saw no light squares where they'd hung, so he assumed the farmhouse-plain walls had been washed as well. Miracles happened!

He had a suspicion that Mrs. Wiggs was the miracle worker though. Maybe he should have married *her*. Dare grinned, imagining Emilia's reaction if he said that. He'd have to try it.

A mob-capped maid hurried to meet him. She bobbed a curtsy and stared at the floor. "Shall I take your hat, m'lord?"

Too astonished to do anything else, Dare handed over the old tweed cap he'd worn to blend in. "Where is my lady, do you know?" It was late, so he assumed she would be dressing for dinner.

He was about to take the stairs to look for her when the maid replied, "She just went out to her workshop, I believe, m'lord."

Drat. Since when did Emilia have a workshop? The growing shed, did she mean? Determined to tell his bride about his day, Dare loped through the house and out the back door. He was tired and hungry but he had to admit to curiosity about what his intrepid wife did with her time.

A shriek from the crumbling glass house sent him running. Emilia barely spoke much less shrieked. Removing his pistol from his pocket, Dare tore open the rickety door prepared to shoot at wolves or thieves.

He discovered his wife standing on a barrel and pointing at a twitching mouse on the floor.

In disgust, rather than waste shot, he lifted his boot, prepared to put the creature out of whatever misery it was in, until Emilia shrieked again. "No, don't kill it!"

He stared at her in incredulity. "Shall I find a nice house for it? Feed it mincemeat?"

"I apologize for scaring you," she said stiffly, looking for a way down from her awkward position.

Dare caught her waist and hauled her off the barrel. She felt so good, he held her there, burying his nose in her lavender-scented tresses and enjoying the press of her breasts against his waistcoat. "Why can't I put it out of its misery?"

She pressed a hasty peck on his whiskery cheek—at least she was learning to express affection, however meager.

"Come, look." She stepped back, took his hand, and led him to a table that was no more than planks on sawhorses covered by table linen. She pointed at a low pottery saucer.

"Nice saucer?" he asked in confusion.

Her exasperated glance warned he'd answered wrong. Dare studied the table. Puddles of water had pooled on it, but that was to be expected given the holes in the glass roof. Cockroaches floated upside-down in one puddle. Something hairy and equally dead floated in the saucer. He curled his lip in disgust. "You need better facilities."

"That," she pointed at the bug-infested puddles and spoke with horror, "is not water. It's your medicine."

He was usually not slow on comprehension, but for the life of him, he couldn't work out how his medicine could be out here killing bugs. *Killing bugs.* He stuck his finger in the puddle and sniffed it.

She slapped his hand before he could bring it to his mouth and taste it. "There is something very wrong with your medicine. I *felt* it. And now I've proven it."

She *felt* his medicine was wrong? One did not *feel* medicine, except by sticking a finger in it, and that didn't prove anything. Perhaps he was the one who lacked understanding.

"Those bugs *died* in your foul solution." She pointed at the mouse on the floor, which seemed to be staggering to its feet. "That mouse probably drank it."

"We don't know that. You are jumping to conclusions. The bugs could have just drowned." But intrigued, he removed a grain scoop hung from the wall to slide under the staggering mouse and looked for a safe place to deposit it. "And why would my medicine be pouring through the roof anyway?"

She snickered a little but offered him a large planting pot and a saucer for lid. "Raining Fowler's? We might all die. I was experimenting."

"You were experimenting with my medicine?" He didn't know whether to be outraged or curious. Since he really wanted another glorious night in her bed, he chose to be curious. He still thought he needed to end the mouse's misery.

"Give it some cheese. That sometimes negates the effect of mild poisons," she suggested, ignoring his question.

"You want me to carry a mouse into the kitchen and ask for cheese?" He handed the pot to her. "You do it. I'll watch."

The laughter gurgling from her luscious lips restored some of his humor.

"Put that way. . . I don't suppose the grooms have apples for the horses? Oh, perhaps there are potatoes in the garden!" She lifted her skirt and hurried into the growing twilight, leaving him with a potted mouse.

Life with Emilia at least wouldn't be boring. Dare bent over to sniff the puddle. It did smell like his medicine. What if he looked at the bugs under a microscope? Could he tell how they died? He doubted it, but now that he understood she wasn't jesting, he was shaken. His medicine killed bugs?

He was studying the bottle in his pocket when she hurried back in.

"The bottle you took this morning is not Fowlers," she told him. "It's a few mild anti-congestives and digestives mixed in your mineral water. I doubt it will kill bugs, although you can try."

She used a knife from her worktable to slice thin bits of a withered old potato. She winced when she looked at the mouse, then dropped the potato in. Dare leaned over her to watch the vermin sniff the vegetable.

"He'll need water," he reminded her. "Or do we feed him my medicine to see what happens?"

"I cannot bear to deliberately poison a living creature." She actually sounded mournful. "It is a pity. Dissection might reveal what happened."

"I doubt it, but I can try on the cockroaches. I assume you don't mind killing them?"

Her mouth fell open as she looked up at him, but nothing came out. Dare spent the moment admiring the way her violet eyes darkened to midnight purple. She might not be beautiful in the common way, but she was so striking that his mind blurred when she was around.

"I've not given thought to killing bugs," she finally said in dismay.

"Then don't give it thought. I'll come out and clean up later. Let us go in now and prepare for dinner and I'll tell you all about my successful haggling and your new horse."

She smiled in relief and took his arm. "Yes, please. Are they fine horses?"

"They won't win any races, but they'll go for hours without dropping, so I think they're very fine."

They chattered about normal, mundane household matters, but Dare knew his wife's versatile mind was pondering medicine and croaked cockroaches just as his was.

He had been drinking *poison*?

DINNER WAS another glorious meal of tasty light fare, although Mrs. Peacock added a nice cut of lamb to the menu this time. Emilia approved of the addition of salad greens and promised herself that on the morrow, she'd venture to the kitchen garden. Her brief foray for the potato told her someone had taken the garden in hand, but she needed to see it in daylight. And then, she really needed to look into the more extensive herb gardens.

But for right now, her husband's health took precedence. She'd never believed she could save a dying man. Now. . .

Consumption wasn't curable. The medicine might have been making Dare sicker than he needed to be, but nothing would kill the tubercles growing in his lungs. But if she could slow their growth. . .

It crushed her to watch him consume everything on his plate like the healthy man he should be and to know that a year from now, he could be confined to bed, living on broth, and coughing up his lungs. She didn't often cry, but she wept inside at this horrid waste of a courageous man who had done all within his power to pay his father's debts and save his family from humiliation.

Now that he wasn't taking the Fowler's, could she persuade him to take healthier drinks—if she could create some?

She really needed to set up her own workshop. She couldn't ride over to the abbey every time she needed to mix a solution. The servants had stored her equipment in the glass house until it could be transported to the abbey. Perhaps she should unpack a few things. . .

She glanced at Dare, who was frowning at his plate—or in thought. She was beginning to see two sides to her husband: the charming Devil Dare he presented to the world, and the studious scholar who blew up glass in his efforts to harness the earth's elements. She admired both of them, but right now, they were an obstacle to her studies.

How could she politely excuse herself from his presence after dinner and escape to her workshop? As much as she enjoyed their bed play—and admittedly, if she thought about it too long, she would forget work—she couldn't spend half her day in bed.

"Do you wish to linger with your brandy?" she asked as dinner ended, despising her timidity. She certainly couldn't ask if he wished to retire upstairs for ravishment. She flushed just thinking about it.

Dare stood and held out his hand to assist her from her chair. "No, but I probably ought to go to my office and finish up my work after spending the day away. Do you think we have enough staff for drawing a bath later? I am probably infested with fleas from that wagon ride."

The tension flowed out of her. She would have a few hours to set up a worktable, although the problem of the leaky ceiling needed to be addressed. "I'm sure Robert could carry the tub upstairs. We'll need to hire someone as large as him to take his place when he goes back to Ashford."

"Shall I order him to start filling it for you, my lady?" Dare asked with a leering lift of his eyebrow.

Oh dear, she must be strong and resist temptation, drat the man! "If you don't mind, I have a few things I must do as well. Perhaps. . ." A daring thought occurred to her, and she attempted a leer of her own. "We might share the water later?"

He chuckled and kissed her cheek. "I'll arrange that."

She held her cheek after he left for his office. What would it be like to exchange real kisses, the kind she'd despised when other men had tried?

Sadly, she would never know, unless someone proved consumption wasn't contagious.

Rather than pursue that dismal line of thought, Emilia went in search of oilcloth. She would have to ask Dare if replacing glass would fit into their budget.

DARE CARRIED his supply of Fowler's Solution out the back door to his workshop. The bottles had been sealed when he'd purchased them. He couldn't imagine anyone regularly adding poison every time he opened one. Cousin Peter might like to hasten his death, but his cousin had the spine of a jellyfish and the brains of a toad. It would never occur to him to use poison in such a premeditated manner—especially since it would have to include paying a servant to do the work for him.

Still, Dare needed at least to test whether the sealed bottles were dangerous, and it wasn't just the open one which might have been tampered with. And then he needed to determine what kind of poison killed vermin and if it was equally dangerous for people. Surely all the research Fowler had done hadn't killed anyone! The medicine had been available for decades, and the statistics on cures had warranted trying the solution on other diseases.

Dare almost dropped the lot as he passed the garden wall and saw a light flickering in the glass house. Did they have traveling Gypsies living here, poisoning bugs?

Remembering he'd found Emilia in there earlier, he cursed and set down the bottles. The crude conservatory had no doubt originally been a storage building, built with sturdy brick walls and small, high windows for light. The late Sir Harry had probably replaced a rotten thatch roof with glass to create a winter house for his plants. It looked like the light of a single lamp shining weakly through the front window.

He could hear faint hammering. The shed was too damn damp—and vermin infested—for his wife to use. And working outside at night. . . just invited trouble.

Just in case it wasn't Emilia, Dare checked the latch and found it open. Trying to see inside without being seen, he nudged the door with his foot until the opening revealed shadows and movement.

And humming, *feminine* humming. With a sigh, Dare kicked himself for imagining she had gone off to the parlor to embroider.

He eased the door open and watched as she stretched an oilcloth over a stick frame she must have created out of nothing. The woman couldn't cook a meal, but she could make a tent. It was a damned good thing they were living in rural anonymity. She would be a complete waste in a London ballroom.

"The frame needs crossbars or it will collapse under the weight of the cloth," he informed her, striding in and checking the posts she'd nailed to the table.

Instead of shrieking in surprise or yelling at him for intruding, his inimitable wife studied the weak frame and nodded agreement. "I don't have pieces long enough. And I fear the wood is rotten."

"I thought you were creating your laboratory at the abbey," he said with more irritation than he ought. "It's dangerous working out here at this hour."

She glanced up in surprise. "How? Will the mice eat me? I was wondering if I should sprinkle the leftover solution around the walls to kill bugs, but I was thinking it would be better to have a cat to catch the mice."

"Cats *kill* mice," he said dryly. "And strangers wander rural roads just as they do city ones. I was thinking of going back for my gun. You are not made of steel, my lady. These are perilous times."

"Times are always perilous," she said in irritation. "I have decided I need a place to work closer to home than the abbey. The abbey is good for practical application of my medicines, and should I ever have a microscope and the proper equipment, I can use the laboratory for studying how and why herbs work. But I also need a place to mix my herbs here. I cannot spend my evenings at the abbey."

"You cannot spend your evenings in a shed!" he protested. "You've led a truly sheltered life if you think women can wander anywhere a man can and be safe!"

"I can and I have," she said stubbornly. "Men keep everything to themselves, so I have to go out and fight for it. If that means walking the streets of London at night, then so be it. Although," she added with a grimace, "I usually took a footman with me. I just didn't think one was needed in my own home!"

Dare gritted his teeth and tried not to shout. "Someone may have tried to *poison* me. Your mysterious Mr. Crenshaw has robbed you after putting the entire staff out of work. We've not been here long enough to know if the villagers blame us or what other resentments might simmer beneath the surface. And vagrants and barn burners and madmen roam the countryside. You *cannot* be out here at night!"

"Poison you?" she asked, her eyes widening to mysterious midnight pools. "Your *medicine* may have poisoned you. I mean to experiment with that. But you cannot make me believe our servants put poison in that bottle!"

Of course she meant to experiment. Dare closed his eyes and leaned his hip against her makeshift table. It tilted. Cursing, he stood up again. "Come along then, tell me what boxes you need. We'll both work in the workshop. At least there, I can keep an eye on you."

"I don't want to be kept an eye on," she said resentfully. "And I don't wish to be blown up or stink of sulfur."

"I plan to experiment on the poison," he said in desperation, hoping to lure her to safety.

She wrinkled her nose and eyed him warily. "Just that? What hypothesis are you operating under?"

The one that says women are too vulnerable to be outside alone, but Dare bit his tongue. Looking around, he found an open crate and hefted it to his shoulder. "Come along. We can work one out together."

She hesitated, eyeing him as if he might attack her at any moment. Then with a look of dejection at her leaning tent frame, she began gathering up her few remaining boxes. "I believe your patent medicine consists of a dangerous substance mixed with less toxic ones."

"Do you have any notion of how to sort one substance from another?" he demanded, kicking open the door for her.

"First, I will test it on plants as well as vermin. It is obvious smaller subjects are more prone to die than larger ones. Humans are larger and apparently do not die outright. Is there some mitigating circumstance that might make the medicine useful for humans and fatal to vermin?" She filled her arms with smaller boxes and followed him into the night.

"You completely dismiss my theory that someone added poison to the bottle?"

"No, I cannot completely dismiss it, but that is easily tested. You need only pour some liquid from your unsealed bottles into a dish and leave it out overnight."

Damn, but the woman was clever—about experimentation, at least.

About financial affairs, Dare was fairly certain she had no understanding whatsoever. And if he did not find a way of completing the railroad land acquisition, they would be buried in debt by the time he stuck his spoon in the wall.

He'd finally looked over the survey maps. The tracks could cross abbey lands, or go further south and cross this property. He was fairly certain his wife would adamantly object to selling her family home—but the land part of her trust was in his control. He could do with it as he liked.

Thirteen

"COZY, BUT not as clean as I would like," Emilia said in exhaustion as she studied their evening's handiwork.

She'd swept out spiders and wasp nests from the walls, and worse from the floors. She was in desperate need of that bath Dare had promised. But he was equally disheveled and coughing hard after dragging together tables, hammering shelves into the walls, and unloading her equipment.

He pried open the seal on one of his medicine bottles and poured the solution into a shallow plate he set on the floor in a dark corner. "It will be enough tonight to test if the medicine is at fault. Tomorrow, when I have more light, I'll look at our victims under the microscope."

"I cannot say I am sorry to see bugs die," she said, wiping her hand across her dusty brow. "I am quite certain they are good for plants, but not in the environment I need to make medicine."

She checked on the field mouse they'd transferred to a small crate. It had burrowed into a nest of hay they'd given it for a bed. Using a dropper, she added more water to the tiny saucer, then added some cut up carrots from the neglected garden. The mouse stuck its tiny nose out and sniffed. Was it recovered already?

Dare wrapped an arm around her shoulders. "It's a mouse, not a pet. It will chew its way out soon enough." He steered her toward the door. "Medicine-making requires the controlled environment of a laboratory. This shack is little better than your garden shed."

"I know, but someday. . ." She sighed. "I am only fooling myself to believe my pharmacopeia will earn even enough to import ginger root to improve your cough medicine."

"Publish it under your initials. Men will believe it was written by a man. And yes, I know that's misogynistic. But not everyone can know you as I do, and you will admit that most women do not have your education." Dare locked the workshop, and she let him lead her across the stone drive to the back door.

Even if he didn't understand, it was a relief to know he didn't despise her for her unusual occupation. "First, I need the funds to have it printed," she admitted as they crept into a dark, silent house.

"*That* could be a problem. Color plates cannot be inexpensive. But we will worry about it another time. Tonight, we learn what can be done to produce a bath."

He started coughing again. Having learned that her desire for this man shielded her from his pain, Emilia wrapped her arm around his waist, enjoying the unfamiliar intimacy. Dare rested his arm over her shoulders as if she might truly be more to him than a means to an end. She'd always had family to keep her from feeling lonely, so she hadn't realized how much she'd missed by not being held.

Together, they staggered up the stairs in the illumination of their one lamp.

"We are very strange newlyweds," he said as they approached their chamber. "I am sorry that I have not provided a well set-up estate with a full staff for you, but even my own country house is as bad as this. We've not lived there in years."

"We didn't *plan* a real marriage," she reminded him. She didn't know what constituted a real marriage, but she was fairly certain theirs lacked the basic foundation of love. "Besides, I've never wanted more than what we have here. I love the lectures and libraries in the city, but I'll never be a social butterfly. Here, I can be eccentric as I like, and as long as we pay the merchants, no one complains. And if Bridey allows me to use the abbey. . . It's perfect. Or will be," she amended.

It would be a solitary life once he was gone, she admitted. Was it wrong to pretend that desolate future wouldn't happen? Or should she shield herself from caring for this man—whom she already cared about too much. She had never been good at emotional conundrums.

A single lamp glowed in their shared chamber. Towels and soaps and their robes had been laid out on the bed. A tin tub, scrubbed and shiny, waited in front of a low coal fire. On hooks over the embers hung buckets of water keeping warm. More pitchers of water waited on the washstand.

"This is almost like being at home," Emilia exclaimed, giving up her fears of the future for the delight of the moment. "Shall you go first before I use my scented soaps?"

Foolish question. Even exhausted as he had to be, her handsome husband offered a lascivious smirk and reached for her bodice fastenings. In the firelight his hair glittered like gold, and she was struck by a rush of desire.

"You will overexert yourself into an early grave," she tried to warn him, although the other half of her, the animal part that lusted, only half-meant it.

"Do I prefer quality to quantity of life?" he said in a rough-edged rasp, while releasing her bodice. Even his voice served to excite her. "That's an old question. At this moment, I choose quality,"

Quality, Emilia thought later, much later, after they'd soaped and splashed, and she now clung to her husband's neck and wet hair while he hugged her waist and bottom and pushed deep inside her. *Quality* should last forever, not be ripped away by the fragility of human flesh.

Even as the now-familiar quakes shook her, a tear rolled down her cheek.

It would be devastating to become too attached to this virile, exciting man, only to lose him.

THE NEXT morning, Dare watched his wife dress in old clothes for a day working with her herbs and his medicine—and a sadness wrapped around his heretofore nonexistent heart. Emilia was so dynamic, so brilliant, and so. . . Remembering last night's lovemaking, he considered simply putting a knife through his heart and dying while still in bliss. Consumption was a vile disease, and he did not want to diminish any of her brilliance with nursing his wasting useless self.

But he hadn't fixed the railroad problem or created an heir, so he couldn't die yet.

"Are you still feeling nauseated?" she asked, out of the blue, fastening her own bodice without need of her invisible lady's maid.

Dare thought about it a second. "I don't think so. The pain is still there, though. Perhaps I need to break my fast first."

She nodded understanding. "I am hoping it is the medicine that is causing the pain. I don't want to dose you with unnecessary medications until we know."

"You are not a trained physician," he pointed out rudely, needing to put a distance between them. "I'll travel to Edinburgh and find someone who has actual experience if I must."

"Take a written list of my medicinal ingredients for stomach pain and nausea if you go," she said with a shrug. "See what the experts say."

But he could tell he'd hurt her. He felt like an ogre, but it had to be said. It was bad enough that real physicians were poisoning him with proven formulas.

After they ate, Emilia was the first one out the door. Growling in exasperation, Dare followed her. He unlocked the workshop door, lit a lantern, and let her precede him. The windows hadn't been washed, and the gloomy day did little to illuminate the interior, but he held the lamp over the dark corner where he'd left the medicine-filled dish.

Dead bugs littered the dish and the ground around it. If mice had drunk from it, they'd crawled off to die elsewhere. Or recover. He'd have to deliberately poison one in a cage to know how much it took to kill a mouse—Emilia would probably kill *him* for the suggestion.

"What the devil is in that stuff?" he asked, lifting the saucer and grimacing at the contents.

"Bug killer," she answered pertly. "You have been drinking bug killer."

"I'm sure my physician will appreciate that report." Feeling murderous, Dare lifted a few cockroaches and carried them to his table. "We'll divide the bottles up. You can try killing weeds, and I'll see if I can discover what kills bugs."

She chortled just a little, although her brow was creased with worry. "Very useful ingredient if it kills everything noxious. I know quite a few plants that are deadly. So far, I've not killed any bugs with them."

"Give me a list of deadly plants, and if you have any specimens of them, give me those, too. I'll see if I can develop tests to match them against the medicine after I distill the water in it."

"Can you not just write Fowler, tell him his medicine kills bugs, and ask what he uses?"

"I believe he died some years ago, but the physician says the formula is in the latest edition of the pharmacopeia."

She sniffed and looked in on her mouse. "The formula is *that* old? The latest pharmacopeia was *reprinted* in 1809 and the recipes are positively medieval. I thought you were trying some new kind of solution. I'll look in grandfather's ancient library." She fed her pet vermin more carrots, then lifted her skirt and departed for the house.

Judging from her tone, Dare concluded he now ranked one rung lower than a cockroach, and he'd definitely better not poison her mouse. It would probably be easier on both of them if they remained at odds and fought attachment—as long as they still shared a bed. He wasn't about to give up that bit of heaven on earth. Emilia's quick, inventive mind worked in more places than a laboratory.

Picking up a dead insect, he calculated the best place to slice, then set up his lamps to examine the parts under a microscope. He'd need a live, unpoisoned bug to compare with.

Detecting poison was an entirely different field from detecting mineral elements, he feared. He needed more information. But if he'd learned how to identify opioids, surely he could boil medicine down to its essential ingredients.

Emilia returned with a heavy volume of yellowing pages, dropping it on the table and raising a cloud of dust. Dare coughed, held his nose, and looked up from his microscope. Having a female in his workshop was beyond distracting. The morning light illuminated her face so that it appeared to be translucent porcelain. Her old work gown clung deliciously to slender curves he had come to appreciate, and he had difficulty concentrating on what she was saying.

She flipped open to a page and pointed. "Fowler's Solution consists of arsenic oxide, potassium tartar, water, and lavender. It is recommended in paste for *psoriasis*." She said this last with distaste and disbelief. "Physicians are treating malaria and consumption with a potion for a *skin disease*?"

"Disease is disease," Dare said with a shrug, looking over her shoulder. "Maybe it's your lavender water that's poisoning me."

She elbowed him, hard. He kissed her ear in retaliation. At least she wasn't treating him like a crippled-up invalid. She'd just taken weeks off of his research by finding the formula, once he proved these were the actual ingredients in his bottles.

"What on earth is arsenic oxide?" she asked.

"Arsenic is a naturally occurring element in metals and minerals. *Oxide* means it's been chemically processed to add oxygen to it, but this does not say what form of oxide. There are several." Grudgingly, he added, "And they can be poisonous."

"So either Fowler's recipe has been poisoning patients for decades, or your apothecary used the wrong form of arsenic?" she asked.

"Or lavender water is deadly," he couldn't resist adding, circling her waist and pulling her back against him so he could plant kisses along her lovely throat and pretend he was healthy and not terrified of dying and leaving her alone. "Go play out in the garden where you belong. I'll stink up this shed oxidizing medicine."

"I've sent word to Bridey that I'll be over today. We need to develop a plan on how to move forward with the school. I'll check on the garden, then try out one of your new horses. Please don't poison yourself while I am gone." She kissed his cheek and wriggled out of his embrace.

Damn, but he enjoyed having her there to hug. "Take someone with you!" he demanded.

"I plan to."

She said it so brightly that Dare knew she didn't mean a coach driver or sturdy footman. He drove his hand through his hair as she departed, her nearly petticoat-less skirt swaying nicely over her well-rounded derriere. He wanted to lock her up where no one could ever hurt her, while knowing he needed to let her learn how to fly free.

He was under no illusion that stopping the Fowlers would cure his consumption. He'd simply lost one more hope of postponing death.

EMILIA STOPPED at the kitchen garden to see how it fared. The weeds had been hoed. Obviously, the spring planting had not been done, but there were volunteers of potatoes and onions from years past. The oregano and thyme had been unburied and trimmed.

Dare had said he'd talked to Mr. Arthur, but she didn't see the old man around. She vaguely remembered him as a friend of her grandfather's. He'd been ancient back then. He must be a hundred years old by now. She'd have to learn where he lived. Perhaps he was down at the hot spring garden today. If she had more time, she'd love to go down and look.

But she was no longer a child with no other task than wandering the fields. She'd have to trust servants to do their work while she did hers.

She stopped in the kitchen to talk to Tess. Mrs. Peacock sniffed her disapproval for Emilia's daring to venture below stairs, but Emilia wanted to be certain working conditions were satisfactory.

After verifying that Mrs. Peacock had made arrangements with farmers and the village market for the provisions she needed, Emilia pulled Tess aside. "I wish you to accompany me to the abbey. Can you be ready in half an hour? I'll speak to Mrs. Peacock and Mrs. Wiggs for you."

The girl could be no more than twenty. Emilia didn't know enough about Tess's delicate condition to guess how far along she was. The maid simply looked too thin and under-nourished.

Her features froze in fear, but she curtsied obediently.

"I've been told Tess writes a fair hand," Emilia told the suspicious cook. "I'm taking her with me to copy some medicinal recipes from Lady Pascoe's books. I may be gone until dinner. Please see that Lord Dare eats while I'm away. He's likely to forget."

Knowing better than to argue, Mrs. Peacock continued mixing her batter and merely nodded.

She was meddling, Emilia knew. But she was a Malcolm, and meddling was a family tradition. She hurried upstairs to decide whether she needed an extravagant calling gown, or if she might wear an old one and start right to work.

Deciding she only wore her fine gowns to force people to notice her, and she didn't have that problem with Dare and Bridey, she chose a comfortable muslin with modest sleeves and smaller skirts.

While Dare had been buying horses, Robert had found a gig for sale in the village. By the time she was dressed, the groom had one of the new horses harnessed to the cart, ready and waiting, much to Emilia's delight. Taking up the reins, she gave in to the thrill of independence. In London, she could go nowhere without an escort. Here, she could go anywhere, despite Dare's dire predictions. She'd driven her grandfather's gig all over when she'd stayed with him. She'd missed that freedom.

Tess climbed up beside her and folded her hands in her lap.

She'd tucked her thin, blondish hair into a cap, revealing a fine complexion and clear blue eyes. She might almost be pretty if she didn't always look so downcast.

"Mrs. Wiggs tells me you were an excellent student." Although she lacked any skill at small talk, Emilia attempted to break through the maid's silence as she drove down the lane.

"Yes, m'lady."

Hiding her grimace, she tried again. "Could you tell me about your schooling? How many years? Who was your teacher? That sort of thing?"

That roused the girl to cast her an anxious look, but she answered in a low voice. "The vicar has a school. I learned everything he had to teach, then helped with the youngers. I sometimes helped him write out his sermons in a clear hand, and I wrote letters for those that can't."

The tiny village that had grown up near the walls of Alder Abbey had no noble house besides the baronet's. Emilia was surprised to hear someone had provided a vicar's living. "There wasn't a vicar here when I was little. What's his name?"

"Oh, I'm not from Alder. I'm from Harrogate. I only came here because Aunt Mary asked."

Well, that prevented Emilia from learning more about the father of the infant she carried. Assuming Aunt Mary was Mrs. Wiggs, she thought she'd have to question that lady a little more. "It's good to have family looking after you," she said with what she hoped was reassurance. "I'm hoping you can help me and Lady Pascoe with our project. I'll wait until we are there to discuss it."

Emilia drew a little more out of the girl as she drove, but under the guidance of Dare's fine steed, the distance to the abbey wasn't great. He truly did have a knack for finding sturdy, if not flashy, horses.

Bridey greeted them with delight and led them straight back to the infirmary and school.

"I can hire workmen to fix roofs and partition schoolrooms and boarding rooms," Bridey said as they traversed the cloistered walkway. "But what I need to do is develop a system for accepting students and patients. Tess, I'd like you to help me with that."

Out of her element, the girl finally lifted her head. Emilia thought she saw a flash of the eager adolescent she must once have been, before humiliation and terror had beaten her down.

"How?" Tess asked timidly.

"I thought we should start with written applications. A good midwife should have the ability to write down her recipes and notes, and I want to start with the best students, so we need women who can read and write. Some will become teachers, so education is essential."

Given her height, and strong character, Bridey could be intimidating, but Tess seemed more interested than frightened. That was what Emilia had been hoping for.

She really wanted to start work on her laboratory, but with workmen running in and out of all the cubicles, she would only be in the way. So she settled for helping with the school.

A few hours later, Bridey helped herself to some of the bread and cheese a maid had delivered while she examined Tess's handiwork. "I think the student application looks sound. Now, let's start on the patient application."

Tess obediently lifted her pen to a new sheet of paper. She did, indeed, have excellent penmanship, and her spelling was accurate. She would be wasted as the housekeeper Mrs. Wiggs had hoped to make of her.

"Name, village, et cetera, at the top, of course, the same as the other," Bridey dictated. "Fill it in as if you were the patient, so we know how large the lines should be. Suggest anything you think should be there."

"Do we need to ask permission of the patient's parents, husband, or father of the infant?" Emilia asked, nibbling a bread crust.

"No," Tess said decisively, speaking out for the first time on her own. "Ask for the names of who is responsible for the patient in case of emergency, but don't force her to ask permission to be a patient."

"What if the patient is a child?" Emilia asked, offering the plate of cheese to Bridey and Tess before finishing it off. "Bridey really shouldn't take on that responsibility."

"If she's old enough to lie with a man, she'd old enough to take responsibility for herself and her child." Tess looked determined, then realizing she was speaking out of place, she ducked her head and began writing.

"Possibly," Bridey agreed. "Except I've seen twelve-year olds who have been raped. They have no idea of what's happening to them. At the very least, I need to know they have parents or somewhere to go once the babe is delivered."

Tess gasped, gulped, and reached for her water glass. "That's awful," she finally muttered. "You should have a line asking for the name of the father so you can cut off his cock."

Emilia exploded in laughter and Bridey sputtered. Tess began to look a little more fierce.

By mid-afternoon, it had been decided that Tess should stay at the abbey as Bridey's secretary, where she wouldn't have to carry heavy pots or scrub floors. Studying Tess's soft hands had convinced Emilia that the maid hadn't been born to service, but she still hadn't pried her background from her.

"I'd like to leave the original draft of my pharmacopeia here, if I may," Emilia said, nodding toward the metal box she'd brought with her. "This isn't all of it. Bessie still has more to copy, but the main part is done. Dare has reminded me that it isn't safe to keep both copies in one place."

Bridey took the box with delight. "There are stone cubbyholes here that are practically fireproof. We'll keep it as safe as possible. May I look at it?"

"Of course, that's the whole point! Having another expert look at it would be wonderful."

Before Emilia could say more, a dog's howl echoed off the stone cloister walls, startling all of them into glancing toward the doorway. Many of the older parts of the building had crumbled, so the central garden was no longer completely enclosed—which meant anyone could enter.

"That's Will's hound," Bridey said, setting the box on a shelf beneath a worn limestone counter built into the old wall. "He's been working with Pascoe's son on animal training, but I thought he'd gone out for the day."

"I'm assuming you mean *Will* is working with the boy, not the hound," Emilia said in amusement, relaxing. Dare's warnings were starting to work on her nerves.

"Well, actually, both. I'll explain later." Bridey stepped to the doorway, and in a few seconds, a huge deerhound raced up, tail wagging. She scratched behind the dog's ears and frowned. "Will, what have you been doing? Come over here and let me look. Where is Edward?"

A moment later a giant of a man loomed in the doorway. Emilia recognized him as an Ives immediately. She supposed she'd seen him at one time or another, but she didn't remember being introduced. One of Pascoe's bastard nephews, Will wasn't one of the city gentleman with whom she was more familiar. He was a dog trainer, if she remembered rightly, one who traveled about the country.

At the moment, he looked as if he'd been in a brawl. He nodded respectfully in her direction, then turned to Bridey, who was already clucking over a cut near his temple. "I brought Edward back earlier. I need to talk to Pascoe."

"You need that cut cleaned," Bridey retorted. "Sit down." She pointed at the stool she'd been using.

He hesitated. "It's probably too late now anyway." Under Bridey's glare, the big man sat as told.

"Tess, will you pull that bell rope over there?" Bridey indicated a long cord near the door. "Pascoe's been working on the bell system. It's far from perfect, but someone will come."

Tess fetched water from the pump while Emilia mixed balsam with alcohol and Bridey cleaned the wound. Pascoe arrived just as they were applying a bandage.

"Back to the good old days of terrorizing the neighborhood?" the baronet asked genially, not looking particularly concerned.

"Surveyors in the wheat field," Will said curtly. "Had a minor altercation. They're gone now."

"Surveyors?" Pascoe suddenly came alert. "From the railroad?"

Will nodded, then winced as Bridey cleaned his battered fingers with alcohol.

"Bl. . ." Pascoe caught himself and bowed to the ladies. "Forgive me, but I'm off to write Sommersville. The duke may know who is behind these trespassers. They do not have permission to lay their track through my tenant's field!"

Emilia watched him go with a frown of worry etched on her brow. "One of my staff mentioned they thought the railroad was going through my cottage. They can't do that, can they?"

Fingers taped, Will grunted and stood up. "These fellows thought they could."

Alarmed, Emilia gathered up her pelisse and bonnet. "I must talk to Dare. Perhaps we should all go to see the duke. I'm not losing my home just as I finally gained it!"

Fourteen

DARE GROUND his teeth as his stubborn wife drove into the stable yard—*alone*. He would admire the way Emilia handled the reins, except her bonnet had fallen down her back, and she looked disheveled and upset and was that blood on her sleeve? Frightened and furious, he crossed the stones and hauled her from the gig the instant the groom grabbed the horses.

"I *told* you not to go out alone!" He wanted to hold her close and ascertain she was all right, but he was unaccustomed to dealing with irrational panic roiling his innards. It was safer if he set her down.

"I didn't go out alone. I had Tess with me. But I left her with Bridey." She shook out her skirt as if he hadn't just manhandled her. She stalked toward the house, apparently expecting him to follow since she kept talking. "We must go to see the duke of Sommersville. There are *surveyors* in the fields saying they're laying a railroad track through the village!"

Frigging bloody damn hell. Had the investors believed he could twist arms so quickly? Time was of the essence in a matter like this. They may have assumed all was in order. Or else. . . His panic escalated.

A competitor was planning his own track.

Dare strode after his wife. "Fine. I'll ride over and talk with Pascoe. We'll make an appointment with the duke. One does not just ride up and say *hello, how are you*, to a duke! How do you know there are surveyors? Did you talk with them?"

"Mr. Ives-Madden did. He got into fisticuffs with them. That's how audacious they are! What are we to do if the duke isn't available?" She flung her bonnet and pelisse over a hook and looked at him with dismay.

"You have no reason to believe they will come through here. You've not seen any letters asking you to sell, have you?" Dare tried to think frantically if the consortium had sent any. Emilia's land hadn't been on the original path, so there was no reason to. But fisticuffs with surveyors didn't sound right at all. He wasn't in this to fight with landowners!

She halted at the bottom of the stairs, looking pale and frightened. "What if this Crenshaw person has done something despicable besides stealing money? Could the executors have sent *him* the letters to sort out?"

"I would think they would have told me if there was any possibility an offer had been made on the property. I questioned them thoroughly. I'll send a note to Pascoe," he said to calm her down. "He'll be able to reach the duke. Surveyors simply draw maps. They can't lay tracks."

She turned and flung her arms around him, resting her dark head against his shoulder. "Thank you. It would be awful to wait all these years to claim my home, only to lose it."

Emilia had *never* voluntarily thrown herself into his arms. Despite his roiling panic, Dare felt like a twelve-foot god having his independent wife turn to him. Feeling good about himself didn't happen much these days. He hugged her and rubbed her back. "They have to *buy* the land. They cannot simply steal it."

He'd write the head of the consortium while he was writing Pascoe. The investors he worked with were all honorable gentlemen. They wouldn't send ruffians to survey fields without permission.

He fought a cough and cursed. He needed this railroad done before he was too weak to gallop off to meetings. Without strong leadership, some of his investors might give up.

"Thank you. I'm sorry for panicking." She kissed his cheek, wiped her eye, and straightened bravely. "I've spent my life with books, and fisticuffs are out of my element. Thank heavens you don't indulge."

Since he'd indulged in more than his fair share of brawls in his reckless youth, Dare didn't have an answer for that. She only knew him as a weak invalid. Humiliating for him, to be sure, but reassuring for her, apparently.

"Let me know what Pascoe says. We really must hire a footman before Robert has to return to the marquess. We need someone to run messages to the abbey." She bustled off, leaving Dare in a cloud of lavender and frustration.

It was a hell of a lot easier dealing with women who had no interest in his business. It was bad enough he had to share his workshop with his distracting wife. Now he had to keep her out of his investments or she'd be telling him where to lay tracks so they didn't kill mice.

HER NEW LIFE as an independent married woman had advantages she'd never dreamed of, Emilia concluded as she happily dressed for a meeting with a duke two days later. She had considered marriage simply as a means of completing her research.

But now, aside from the interesting introduction of bed play, she was learning a whole new world outside of her books. Besides working with an accomplished herbalist and midwife like Bridey, she could meet *dukes*. And not just any duke, but one with the same professional interests and gifts as hers. She was nearly dancing with excitement at the opportunity.

Hearing the berlin pull up to the door, she dashed down the stairs to meet Dare. He'd buried himself in his office writing letters since the railroad incident. He hadn't even objected when she'd returned to the abbey alone to make more horehound drops for him. This morning, he'd dressed for his visit but had gone downstairs early to work on papers she assumed had to do with his business interests.

He'd been rather grumpy these last two days while planning for his meeting with a duke, but she'd happily worked around him. And in bed, she'd even dared send his poor stomach a little healing energy. He'd immediately been aroused, breaking the healing connection, but she thought the *wrongness* was receding from that area. Maybe, if she could just convince him of what she could do, he'd let her test his chest.

She wanted to make him proud of her today, so she'd worn her most fashionable afternoon gown and had Bessie help her with her hair. Sommersville was over an hour away, so she'd donned her best hat and matching pelisse to keep her gown clean. She didn't mind being a little warm.

Dare was just leaving his office, carrying his tall hat, when she reached the bottom of the steps. She halted to admire the dashing figure he cut when he bothered to dress like a gentleman. He wore his new gray wedding coat and his linen was a blinding white. She fancied he'd gained a little color in this past week in the country. He certainly didn't *look* weak, although she feared the journey would tire him.

"Where are you going dressed like that?" he asked in absent-minded puzzlement as he pulled on his gloves.

Emilia's spirits plummeted. "Is this not the day we meet with the duke?"

"Pascoe and I do," Dare said curtly. "But this is a business, not a social call."

"But it's *my* business as well. It's not just *male* business." Too upset to restrain herself, she hit him with her largest weapon. "Besides, the duke and I share a *gift*. I'm most eager to discuss it with him, even though I understand his healing talent has more to do with neurological problems than mine."

He frowned in confusion and continued toward the door. "We're not discussing health. You'll be bored to death. Even Lady Pascoe is staying home."

"That's because she is suffering morning sickness. Besides, she and the duke are old friends. They discuss medical matters all the time," Emilia protested, keeping up with his long strides. "I've never met him. I cannot communicate with a duke without an introduction."

Dare glared down at her. "Emilia, I'm sorry. I didn't know you had expectations of a social call. Some other time, perhaps. We don't have time for it today."

"Why is it all right for *you* to talk with a duke and not *me*?" Outrage, humiliation, and disappointment at being swept aside swamped her—especially after she'd just dared to reveal that she had a healing talent, and *he hadn't even reacted*! Was he not listening? She'd thought Dare, of all people, noticed her!

She stuttered helplessly, unable to express herself. She pounded her feeble fist on his broad chest until clearer words emerged. "You do not *understand*! The duke is a *Malcolm*. He's a *healer*. Do you have any idea how rare our gifts are? Perhaps he could give me advice so I needn't be afraid to use mine!"

She'd exposed her soul and was very much afraid she would burst into tears.

From Dare's horrified expression, he feared the same. "I have no idea what you're talking about. Sommersville is a physician, yes. But he does not practice medicine. We're to talk *railroads*. Now, I really must go."

She wouldn't cry. It was her own fault for not being brave enough to explain her gift or her fears. Her husband wasn't a Malcolm. He had no understanding. She'd known that when she'd married him.

But he ought to at least *listen.*

"Fine," she shouted after him. "Do not complain if I go visiting on my own!"

"Not until we hire footmen," he called back, before entering Ashford's great lumbering carriage and letting the marquess's footman slam the door.

Since he was taking their only male servants, he was telling her to stay home.

Not bloody likely. She was dressed to go calling, and by all the goddesses, she would go calling.

Perhaps she wouldn't attempt the duke today since he would be otherwise occupied, but there was one call they hadn't had time to make.

She located Mrs. Wiggs overseeing the parlor maid. "If you have a footman and groom in mind, could you send for them?"

"Jemmie and Luke," she said instantly, bobbing her capped head. "I told them to be ready, what with the new horses and all. I'll have them come around."

With that settled, Emilia returned upstairs to the office where Bessie worked. "I need you to accompany me. When the new groom arrives to hitch up the gig, we'll go visiting."

Bessie's eyes widened, but trained well, she didn't question direct orders. She bobbed a curtsy and hurried off to find hat and gloves.

Grimly studying her scarecrow reflection in a hall mirror, Emilia decided she looked suitably impressive to terrorize human vermin.

She knew the direction to Hadenton. It was just a matter of making a few inquiries before finding the corrupt Mr. Crenshaw.

"I'M DISAPPOINTED you didn't bring your delightful wives," the duke said as a maid laid out the tea table. "I am much more interested in how the infirmary fares than in railroads."

Dare tried not to drop his teeth in shock. Dukes weren't

supposed to dabble in female matters! Battling a cough after the long dusty drive, he let Pascoe respond.

"Bridey sends her best wishes and hopes you will invite her soon so she may discuss her next steps. But our railroad concern is more immediate." Pascoe poured the tea since there were no women to do so.

"Then you really need to speak with my son. Rainsford is far more familiar with that sort of thing than I am. He should be here shortly."

Tall, with a full head of silver hair, the duke was the picture of a distinguished aristocrat, but he didn't wield the overbearing authority of his station. What had Emilia said about his neurological interests? Dare had difficulty understanding why a duke would have any interest in such a menial profession as a physician. There was probably a story there that he was too impatient to learn.

The marquess of Rainsford arrived shortly after. Taller and thinner than his father, he carried himself with the languid grace of a privileged heir. After shaking hands, he poured his own tea and settled in a wing chair.

"I've had reason to look into railroad investments recently," the marquess said without prompting. "There is an association of bankers and merchants in Harrogate eager to establish their mineral springs as the new health spa, better than Bath. They believe railroads are their future."

Dare frowned. "Harrogate is no Liverpool. They have limited space inside the city for laying track. Goods can be unloaded in industrial areas outside the city. Materials are far more profitable to transport and less dangerous than passenger travel, which is what they're talking about. That can come later, after more investment has been made in safety. Buying property in town to establish passenger rail stations is an expensive venture as well. They're putting the cart before the horse."

Pascoe looked at him in surprise, but the marquess nodded sagely. "So I told them when I declined to join them. But the class of aggressive merchants involved are more concerned with building their businesses now than in waiting. Safety is not their issue."

"Neither are morals or ethics," Pascoe said dryly. "If this association is planning a railroad, they seem to believe all they have to do is lay track and worry about land ownership after."

"Developers usurp public roads and path easements," the duke said. "Had this same issue with the toll roads, and they're raising the question in Parliament again with the railroads. Communities have to step up and stop the wealthy merchants from grabbing what they can at the expense of the general public."

"That's easy for us to say," Dare said, having seen the other side. "We have power and access to wealth, but farmers do not. And they're not likely to think in terms of safety or long-term effects. An association of their friends and neighbors offers them cash for some part of their land, and they see a new roof for their house or barn."

"As *your* consortium knows," the marquess said dryly. "At least your group consists of respectable gentlemen who understand the value of agricultural land. You're to be commended for using honorable tactics and seeking wasteland. Have you and Pascoe found a way of overcoming Bridey's objections to selling abbey property for that final parcel you need?"

Damn. He had no idea how the marquess knew so much about his business. Dare started coughing and grabbed his handkerchief as Pascoe glared at him in surprise.

But Pascoe was a cautious diplomat. Instead of exploding, he let the marquess continue.

"Parliament is looking into an act that requires railroads to acquire government permits for building," Rainsford said, as if he hadn't just upset the applecart. "That could cost a fortune. You'd best hurry and complete the track before they have time to act."

By the time they left Sommersville, the gnawing in Dare's gut had worsened, and he was almost gasping for breath. He took a furtive swig of the herbal water Emilia had made for him, then sucked on a horehound. He didn't want to play the part of invalid while Pascoe rightfully rang a peal over him.

The baronet merely poked the opposite seat of the carriage and hummed thoughtfully.

"You heard Rainsford." Dare finally broke the silence. "It's a legitimate consortium of gentlemen. We attempted to buy the acreage we needed from the Crown before the king granted it to you."

"I have wanted to invest in railroads," Pascoe acknowledged. "I had just not thought of them at my back door."

"It will happen sooner or later." Dare leaned his head back and tried to control his breathing. "The race to the sea is too important. They've already planned a line from Harrogate to York. It's best to get in on the ground floor."

"Convince our wives of that, and I'll listen," Pascoe said dryly. "In the meantime, we're no closer to learning who is behind the contretemps in my fields."

"I've spent the last two days verifying that it's not my group," Dare said. "Next, we go to Harrogate, talk to bankers."

If his head did not fall off in the process.

Fifteen

EMILIA WAS a city girl who knew exceedingly little about horses and grooms. But now that Dare had learned Mr. Crenshaw's direction from the bankers in Harrogate, she was determined to confront the man. Besides, she needed to learn how to go about on her own.

In an excess of caution, besides taking Bessie with her in the gig, she had asked the new groom to accompany them on the second pony. She was glad to have them with her once they arrived at Crenshaw's "estate." It was little more than an overgrown field with a house not much larger than her own. The place had an air of shabbiness and despair that did not bode well for having her funds returned.

The groom knocked on the fading front door. Emilia could swear it took a full five minutes before anyone answered, but that could just be her fear talking. An elderly woman in a worn black gown and dirty apron finally answered and gestured for them to enter without even inquiring their names or business.

Leaving the groom to mind the horses since no one came around to help, Emilia led Bessie inside the dim interior.

"The master is not well," the servant intoned. "Come this way."

Without introductions, the housekeeper abandoned them in the doorway of a dark study. In a chair by the fire sat an extremely stout, balding man with a bandaged foot raised on a stool. He glanced up at their entrance with a frown. "I ain't got nothing to give to any funds for the poor."

"No, I gather you prefer to steal from them, Mr. Crenshaw." Rather than take a seat that had not been offered, Emilia remained standing. She didn't know what she'd expected, but this pathetic excuse for a gentleman had not been it. "I am Lady Dare, granddaughter of Sir Henry Malcolm. Are you the gentleman who was supposed to pay my staff?"

He looked a little shocked, then narrowed his eyes. "I don't talk business with females. They ain't got no understanding."

"I simply want explanations," she lied. She might not be good at small talk, but she knew how to maneuver around male obtuseness. "Why did you let my elderly staff go? They had every right to expect to live there as long as they wished. My executor provided for them."

"Shows what you know," he said, scoffing. "Railroad going right through that place. They were better off having time to look for a new place before the old one was torn down around their heads."

Emilia experienced a cold chill. Deciding knowledge was more important than the stolen wages she would never recover, she demanded, "I would like the names of the men who think my house is for sale."

That caused him to look shocked—and a little frightened. "It ain't already sold? Has to be. Mr. Weathersby wouldn't lie to me about an investment like that. He knows I need the blunt."

He thought her land had been *sold*? "Who is Mr. Weathersby?" she asked without inflection, hiding her panic.

"Banker in Harrogate," Crenshaw said with a splutter. "Bankers know everything that goes on. And there's Jeffries from the mercantile and a whole lot of physicians from the hospital. They've already started building the spa."

"I see. " Although she didn't. "Then perhaps you should take advantage of my visit today to ask for your investment back, because there will be no railroad through my property, *ever*. Instead of paying for my servants, did my funds go into investing in a spa?"

He squirmed. "I figured I'd pay back the estate once the investment pays off."

"No, you didn't," she said without rancor. "You planned to buy more wine and beefsteak and make yourself more ill. God has a way of punishing ill-doers. Get your investment back, Mr. Crenshaw. My husband will most likely sue you for our funds shortly."

She left the man spluttering incoherently. The visit had been a most unsatisfactory one, except for obtaining the name of the banker who thought he could steal her home.

"Bankers can do anything," Bessie said worriedly as they settled back in the gig.

"We're come this far south. We could go into Harrogate and question him." Emilia took up the reins but wasn't certain if that was a direction she wished to follow. She had no interest in finance or business and no notion of who the banker was who had handled her grandfather's affairs. This was why she had an executor. . . and *Dare*.

She was still furious with him, but not enough to drive to Harrogate, look for a bank, and confront a banker. She had never so much as been inside a bank before, much less talk to a *banker*. And there were physicians involved. She should ask Bridey if she knew any Harrogate physicians. Cautious research is what she did best.

"What I would really like to do," she decided, "is buy arsenic. I should find an apothecary."

"Strychnine works better on pests," Bessie said pragmatically. "They probably have that at the mercantile."

Emilia shivered. "One poison at a time, please."

Even with the side trip, they arrived home before Dare. Emilia changed into her work clothes and retreated to the laboratory. She couldn't test poison treatments on people or deliberately poison mice to see if she could cure them. But bugs. . . she might make concessions for pests.

She was fully involved in taking notes and trapping bugs when one of the new maids rapped at the door. "M'lady, his lordship is home, and he's took real sick. Do we call a physician?"

Emilia dropped her pen and pulled off her stained apron. "I'll be right there. Have someone heat water to boiling, please, and carry coals up to our chamber."

She hurried up the stairs, heart pounding. She could alleviate the symptoms of consumption to a small degree, but what if he had come down with an illness like pneumonia? She could easily kill herself attempting to fight both diseases. She'd have to send a note to Bridey, asking if any of the physicians in the area could be trusted.

She burst in on Dare just as his valet was helping him out of his waistcoat. His breathing was raspy, he was choking on his inhalations like an asthmatic, and he couldn't seem to stop coughing.

"Fetch brandy, James. I'll help with his undressing," she ordered.

"Do it myself," Dare argued through his coughs. "Don't need quacking."

One didn't smack the ill, although she was sorely tempted. "Lie down," she ordered. "Take pressure off your lungs. You've overdone it today."

He sat down and began tugging at his boots. Emilia straddled his leg and helped. By the time James returned with the brandy, Dare was sprawled on top of the covers in shirt and trousers, still gasping for breath. The new footman raced up shortly after, bearing a steaming pail of water and a cauldron that would hook over the grate.

The handkerchief Dare pulled away from his mouth was covered in blood.

Emilia tried very hard not to panic. She couldn't let him die like this!

She had no real ability to heal him, only prolong his life for a little while. She could die in his place if she tried.

He gulped the brandy. Terrified and hiding it, Emilia added herbs to the steaming water. She'd had them prepared for just this occasion. It took a few minutes for the aroma to fill the room.

"I could wish he was closer to the steam," she said worriedly to the valet and footman. The efficacy of herbs had been her foundation all these years, but sometimes—they were just not enough. She feared this was one of those times.

"Shall we call a physician, m'lady?" the valet asked anxiously.

"I'm right here," Dare grumbled. "And I don't want any more bloody quacks."

"I'll ask Lady Pascoe whom she recommends," Emilia murmured to the servant. "For now, let's see if the steam works."

"Just let me rest. I'll be fine," Dare said testily as the servants departed.

"No you won't," she retorted, hiding her worry. "Your lungs are weak. You've poisoned your gut. And even physicians can't tell you how to get better."

But he was in pain and his coughing was tearing his lungs apart. How could she do *nothing* when she knew she could help? His agony was ripping her in two.

The better, stupider half won. Swallowing her fear, she finally admitted, "I can ease the pain."

She waited for him to question. She had *tried* to tell him what she could do, but he hadn't listened. It was time to *show* him, although killing herself to prove a point seemed the very definition of insanity. And then there was the problem of what he would do if she proved she was what the world called a "witch." Best to find that out now.

"No opium," he said through another cough.

"Not yet, no," she agreed. Bracing herself for the pain, she sat on the edge of the bed. She slid her hands beneath his linen and placed them on Dare's still powerful chest. He burned with heat. His lungs barely pumped. She had no idea what tubercles felt like, so she could not sense them. When she actually concentrated on her healing gift and not lust, she felt his pain sting like electrical shocks radiating up through her fingers. The healing energy responded to the shock , almost melding her to him.

"What are you doing?" he asked crossly. "Leaning on me won't stop the coughing."

His voice distracted her from the pain, but also from the healing. "You'd be surprised," she said crossly. "Just be quiet for a change and let me experiment. It's dangerous, so I've not dared to do this much."

She didn't have the words to make him understand, so she spoke as she would to her sisters. "I almost died healing Lydia's asthmatic pneumonia, and that was only a partial healing. She still has asthma, but she recovered from the congestion. If you've contracted a pleurisy on top of the consumption, I might help that."

He tried to object, but he couldn't talk around the cough.

Closing her eyes, Emilia concentrated. She could not *see* inside him, but through her fingertips she received sensations similar to running her hand over a surface to determine its shape and texture. Some of the places she sensed seemed almost ragged. She reached through the muscular hardness of his chest, seeking the inner weaknesses that needed strengthening.

Conquering the cough enough to speak, Dare struggled for an upright position. "What the devil are you talking about?"

"Shut up or I will use opium on you," she said, irritated at being interrupted just as she thought she'd found a flaw. "If you won't listen, you can at least be quiet and let me work. But if I go catatonic, push me off."

"Catatonic!" He grabbed her wrists and pushed her away. Even in his weakened state, he was stronger than she was. "Have you lost your wits?"

"No, but I'm losing my patience." Now that she'd made up her mind to do this, she refused to give up. She placed her hands on her hips and glared down at the beautiful tousled visage that concealed so much damage. "Could you simply be quiet and trust me for a few minutes? I won't attempt more than that, if I can. Just lie there and pretend I'm trying to seduce you."

He glared at her through eyes almost gray with pain. Emilia waited. She had no more words that would convince him. Her stomach tightened, realizing she was asking him to trust a woman he'd only known a few weeks. But she'd thought. . . she'd hoped they'd reached an understanding.

He chose to mock himself by laying back against the pillows and saying, "I doubt a siren could seduce me right now. Do your worst."

DARE FIGURED he couldn't be any more humiliated than he already was. Why not let his lovely quack of a wife pretend she was performing magic by caressing his chest? He rather liked the soothing coolness of her hands against his over-heated skin. He wasn't as fond of the stink her herbal steam was sending up, but he wasn't in any position to argue with her knowledge.

If he lay here and conjured images of Emilia naked and on top of him, he could almost enjoy the massage. Had he planted his seed yet? He wanted to live to see her growing ripe and round with his heir. Or his daughter. He was used to having women around him and liked the idea of a daughter, but he *really* wanted to shove his cousin's nose in dirt by creating an heir.

Soothing heat seemed to wrap around his lungs where Emilia rested against him. The urge to cough lessened. Maybe she would move her marvelous hands further down as she had this morning, and he'd be aroused and ready for her. He could probably manage a good rutting if she stayed on top.

Lost in erotic daydreams, he didn't know how much time had passed. Only when her hands stopped moving did he recall her strange warning about *catatonic*. He forced his eyes open to watch Emilia swaying above him, looking strangely pale and unfocused.

"Blast it, woman! You'll lose my heir if you're making yourself sick!" He grabbed her wrists and yanked her down on top of him.

She collapsed without so much as a whimper. It wasn't like his intrepid wife to be so silent and unmoving. Terrified, Dare lay her back against the mattress. Her eyes were closed, but despite her almost bluish pallor, she breathed.

"Emilia?" He hastily unfastened her gown and corset so she could breathe easier. She didn't stir. "Emilia!" he almost shouted.

He could shout. Just a little while ago, he hadn't even been able to drag air into his lungs.

She didn't move.

"Emilia!" Panicking, he rolled out of the bed, opened the door, and shouted, "Bessie! James! Get in here now."

The servants came running.

The stinking concoction continued to boil and steam. Bessie used smelling salts to no avail. When neither of the stinking vapors woke Emilia, Dare panicked and sent Ashford's footman with a message to Bridey.

"Does she faint like this often?" he demanded, while fear added to the pain in his gut.

"Never, m'lord," Bessie whispered, looking as frightened as he felt. "I'll fetch cold compresses."

By the time Bridey arrived, Dare had positioned himself on the bed so Emilia could rest between his legs and lean against his shoulder. He was trying to pry water between her lips but she lifelessly resisted him.

"What did she mean, she goes catatonic!" he yelled the instant Bridey entered the room.

Still as regal as the countess she'd once been, Lady Pascoe raised her eyebrows. "Are you coughing?"

His wife was lying nearly dead in his arms, and she asked about *his* health? Dare couldn't bring himself to respond but merely glared.

Bridey rolled her eyes and reached for Emilia's wrist. "She's quite alive. This is the reason she does not use her gift as she ought. She puts far too much of herself into it."

She *what*? Remembering talk of gifts and healing, Dare glared at the imposing baronetess. How much of this folderol should he believe?

The part where his wife passed out was real enough. "Explain," he growled with impatience.

"Explain the circumstances in which this happened," Bridey countered, taking the glass from him and dipping a cloth into it. "And for now, I'd advise releasing her." She put the cloth to Emilia's lips and squeezed drops of water into her mouth.

Dare didn't *want* to release her. He had this irrational belief that if he held her, she wouldn't leave him. "She told me to let her work and not to let her go catatonic. What the devil is that supposed to mean? She wasn't *doing* anything!" Except pressing her hands against his chest, but that was a little personal to speak aloud.

"Pascoe said you were coughing so badly that he refused to go into Harrogate and took the carriage directly here. He was worried about you. From the smell of asafetida, I gather Emilia started the steaming kettle. Then what did she do?" Bridey poked him. "You're in my way. Move."

He gritted his teeth and gently lay Emilia back against the pillows so Bridey could reach her. "What does it matter? Will she stay like this? What can I do?"

In his man's world, he was competent and efficient and knew how to get things done. He should be able to cope with women and their foolish vulnerabilities. But he needed to know *how*. And why. That last part was causing him cold shivers as he released Emilia and moved to the edge of the bed. She looked so pale.

"Wait. Keep her lips moist. She'll come around eventually, I hope." Even Bridey looked a little worried. "She's not really used her gift in years, so it's difficult to say."

Dare kneaded his brow and tried to sort out this nonsense. "She told me she and the duke share a *gift*. Explain." He didn't know if he was ready to hear this, but he needed to know.

"They're Malcolm healers. We don't have many, for rather obvious reasons." Bridey nodded at Emilia's prone form. "So we have no one to teach us. Emilia has only told me a little, but I know she brought her little sister back from death's door and nearly died in the process. But if she was attempting to ease your cough, it's possible the energy she expended has simply left her exhausted. Let her sleep. Shall I stay to watch over her this evening?"

Remembering Emilia had told him the lady was in a delicate condition, Dare knew he should send her away. *But he couldn't bear to lose Emilia.* The realization stunned him. He didn't need more women in his life to worry about. She was supposed to take care of herself!

But if she'd made herself ill helping him. . . Dare rubbed his head in confusion. "I do not understand. What energy? All she did was help me undress and order servants about. I've seen her accomplish far more than that without falling asleep."

Bridey looked upon him with more patience than he felt. "*Healing* energy. It comes from inside, not from ordering servants about. You're not coughing any longer. How do you feel?"

Putting her hands on him had somehow made him better? That was not logical. "Be damned with how I feel! It's Emilia I'm concerned about! Have I done something to harm her? If she's with child, have I harmed the child? Tell me what to do!"

But he was feeling much better than he had when he'd arrived home. He'd barely been able to walk, and now he was breathing well enough to shout and rage. . . And he needed to *do* something.

Bridey raised her eyebrows and pursed her lips in thought. "Interesting question. Could her use of her healing power harm a child she carries?"

Instead of giving him an answer, she widened her eyes and looked into the distance as if she'd left her body. Dare could swear her eyes glowed. He feared he'd have to catch her before she fell. Pascoe would kill him of a certainty if his wife keeled over dead in his presence.

Just as he feared he'd have to make the effort, Bridey shook her head and returned to herself. "Her aura is quite healthy. She has an enormous potential for compassion which will get in the way of her scientific work, so we need to keep her out of the infirmary as much as possible. I cannot tell at this early a stage if she's with child. A child needs a soul before it becomes visible, and since she's not at Wystan with its plethora of spirits waiting for new life, that might take time. If you're eager for an heir, though, you might want to take her to Wystan."

He might as well be talking to a mad hatter. Dare stared at this intelligent woman with incredulity. "I do not understand a word you've said. Are you saying she's well, just asleep?"

"As far as my abilities are able to ascertain, yes. Let her sleep through the night. If she is not better in the morning, then perhaps we need to visit Wystan. Ashford and his wife are there, but they shouldn't mind the company. Wystan is healthier for Malcolm women who are carrying babes."

With a plan he might follow, Dare allowed himself to relax a fraction. "I just let her sleep, nothing more? And if she's not better, we go to Wystan on the morrow? And then she'll be well?" Which made no sense, if he thought about it, but neither did bottles of medicine composed of arsenic. At least a change of location wasn't poisonous.

"Life is full of uncertainties. We can never make promises, but yes, that nicely sums it up. I'll go home, tell Pascoe we may have to leave for Wystan sooner than expected, and we'll wait for word from you." Bridey tilted her head and looked at him askance. "Your ambition endangers your well-being, as well as that of others around you. Your aura says you're not a bad man, but you're consumed with a lust to succeed. Life is about more than success."

His *aura*. He would not ask what that meant. The lady let herself out, leaving Dare sitting beside his comatose bride and terrified out of his wits—provided he still had all his wits after that seriously strange conversation.

Fifteen

EMILIA WOKE slowly, trying to orient herself. She felt oddly empty. Her head rested on a muscled shoulder, so she knew she was with Dare. But she'd been angry with him. How had she ended up in bed? She couldn't remember.

The air still held the stench of asafetida, and she recalled his coughing spell. But he seemed to be breathing normally now. She must be getting used to him—immunizing herself in some way. She didn't notice his pain, although lust was always a factor. Curled up against his side, she brushed her fingers over his chest and tested his lungs.

Oh, yes, that's what had happened. She'd used her healing touch too long. Again.

But she'd survived! She hadn't died from her efforts. Had her bold insanity actually helped him?

With cautious eagerness, she confined herself to just testing to see if Dare's lungs worked better. Running her fingers over his sculpted chest, she could tell the injury was still there. She hadn't healed the damage. But he was breathing more as he ought, she realized with relief. Perhaps she'd stopped the pleurisy that had fevered him.

He had such a fascinatingly wide chest. . . She yanked her fingers back when he stirred.

Morning light was creeping across the bed. She'd slept all night? No wonder she was empty. She was hungry.

That Dare hadn't fled at her fit deserved a kiss. She pressed one against his bare shoulder. He stirred more, drawing her closer. She snuggled into him. His intake of breath said he was awake.

"You're alive?" he asked in a dubious whisper.

"Quite," she assured him, waiting with a lump in her throat for his reaction. She'd never used her gift outside family before, and they were prone to hysterics when she collapsed. Dare. . . She couldn't imagine what he'd thought. "I apologize if I worried you."

He squeezed her tight, and she could feel his heart pump.

"*Worry* is putting it very mildly," he complained. "You scared the devil out of me. Don't do that again, whatever it is you did. I'm not worth it."

She didn't know if she could make that promise. She was *proud* that she had overcome her fear of pain and death. She was even more gratified that her gift had helped.

Relieved that he didn't call her witch and shove her away in disgust, she kissed his handsome chest. "I truly try not to use my gift, but I don't seem able to resist when it comes to you. I've not been able to touch anyone else as I do you. With others, it's painful, so I just gave up trying. But even though I can feel your discomfort, you do not drown me in it. It's not refreshing, precisely, but I like touching you too much to stop."

"I'm afraid I'm losing my mind," he admitted. "I cannot understand half of what you and Bridey are trying to tell me. I used to have an exceptionally fine mind," he said in regret. "I hate thinking you'll be left taking care of a drooling imbecile."

For his peevish complaint, she laughed and pinched his taut skin. At least he wasn't calling *her* crazed. "You lack knowledge and experience, that is all. If you had studied Malcolm abilities as Bridey and I have. . . Wait, Bridey was here?"

"What else was I to do? You wouldn't wake up." He hugged her tighter, as if he really cared enough to worry about her, which thrilled her more than it should. She knew her family loved her, because they had to. She had not expected Dare to care what happened to her one way or another—especially after he'd so carelessly dismissed her yesterday.

"Sorry to cause you such inconvenience," she said dryly.

"You were passed out cold and looked like hell," he continued, sounding aggrieved.

"Thank you for the flattery." She knew she ought to be insulted, but she thought she preferred his frustration to her mother's tears. "I will attempt to look like a sleeping princess next time."

He glared at her for her facetiousness. "Whatever you did, don't do it again."

She thought about that—and rejected it. "I've been avoiding my gift all my life, substituting with studying healing herbs in hopes I can be more useful without risking my own well-being. I'm thinking that was a mistake. I should have been experimenting, looking for ways of touching that will not cause me to drain my energy."

He punched a pillow and sat up, looking stubborn. "I don't want you risking your life on anyone, even me. I prefer your studies."

Smiling, she stroked his masculine chest as she might rub a dog. "See, this does not hurt me. I'm not sure why yet, since I've not experimented. It may just be you or it may be my physical reaction to you. I have no way of knowing."

He growled deep in his throat. "I don't want you touching other men to find out."

She punched his arm. "Don't be selfish. What I need to do is find some way of grounding myself, so the healing current does not drain me. Once I'm connected, once I go really deep and feel the tissues healing, it's difficult for me to stop. My gift, my power, whatever this is that I possess, wants to keep healing until everything is perfect again. But doing so weakens me, especially in a case like yours, where the damage is too extensive. I'm not even certain what I can repair—tissues or just symptoms."

She'd been so foolish to waste all those years. . .

He hugged her and pressed a kiss to her head. "Then do not experiment unless one of your family is nearby to *ground* you. It does no one any good if you kill yourself, which reminds me. Bridey says she can't tell if you're with child, or if that caused you to faint. There was some folderol about Wystan if we want an heir and souls and more nonsense I cannot interpret. What did she mean?"

"That's not any easier to explain," she protested, snuggling against him. "Wystan was once a medieval Malcolm stronghold. It is filled with our journals, a place of retreat for Malcolm women when they're in the family way, and also a place to go if we wish to *be* in the family way. If you would like to understand us, you might go there someday and study what makes us who we are. But as we understand it, Wystan is full of the souls of Malcolms who have passed beyond the veil and who are eager to return their gifts to the world. Evidence over the centuries has proved that conception is guaranteed, whether wanted or not, if men are allowed loose in that tower."

He snorted. "That's a very convenient fairy tale. I like it. Bridey also told me that I'm too ambitious. Is she a fortune teller?"

Emilia chuckled at his offended sensibilities. She pushed away so she could meet his worried eyes. "Bridey is of Malcolm descent, like the duke and I. She reads auras—the color of the spirit inhabiting you. She says every color has a meaning, but that's all I know. But I don't need her to read your colors to know you're ambitious. I don't know why ambition would be wrong, unless it means you're the one allowing railroads to threaten our property. And in the meantime, I'm starved."

He still wore his trousers. She was still in her chemise. The servants would be in to check on them soon. There was no time for intimacies.

"I understand *medieval tower* and *journals* and *study*. But you seem to be saying we could go to this place and make babies?" Dare asked in interest. "Are we talking magic?" He cupped her breast through her chemise.

"No, we're not talking magic." She arched longingly into his caress, but she was too hollow to do more. "Unless you believe life is magical, which I suppose it is. Bridey had difficulty conceiving and never carried a babe past the first month or two, but after being with Pascoe in Wystan, she immediately conceived and seems to be carrying the child well. This is the kind of thing that happens there, with such regularity that we do not question why. It just is. We've spent a lifetime studying our family anomalies. You cannot expect to learn them overnight."

His brow puckered as he tried to comprehend. "I'm a man of science, but I accept that there are many things in this world that we have not studied sufficiently to comprehend. If I did not have this railroad business hanging over our heads, I'd fling you in the carriage and head for Wystan today." He hugged her close and kissed her hair.

Emilia graced him with her best smile, before the *railroad business* reminded her of yesterday's events. Reluctantly, she climbed out of bed to gather her clothes and explain what she'd learned from her visit to Hadenton.

She couldn't tell if her husband's fierce frown was for her or for Crenshaw, but she was fairly certain it wasn't because Dare was feeling bad. He seemed flushed with health this morning as he washed and dressed. She knew he usually called James about now to shave him, but he seemed more intent on what she was telling him. She thought. At least he wasn't telling her this wasn't a woman's affair.

"Weathersby is one of the bankers I spoke to about the estate funds," he told her. "He was the one who claimed Crenshaw was a gentleman your grandfather trusted. I'll have your executor sue Weathersby and Crenshaw for conspiracy and theft. But it is this belief that the house was condemned for the railroad that has me more concerned than the money."

"I am positive my father would not have authorized the sale," she said to reassure him. "I think Mr. Weathersby may be as much of a thief as Crenshaw and is just taking funds for an investment he can't afford otherwise."

"Very possible. Pascoe is the man to find out. But. . ."

He hesitated so long that she came out of the dressing room to study him with worry. "But?"

He sat down on the bed's edge. "Bridey is right. If we are being honest, I admit to ambition, sometimes to excess. I have invested a good part of my wealth in a railroad consortium building a line into Harrogate." He looked up with a guilty expression. "Our plans were laid out when the abbey lands were still in the Crown coffers. Now that they belong to Pascoe, we cannot finish the track. I stand to lose everything I invested."

"*You* are behind the railroad going through Alder?" Shocked, she couldn't absorb the immensity of what he implied.

"*A* railroad," he explained. "Railroads are essential. But we never planned a track through your land."

"But you planned one through Pascoe's lands and you didn't *tell* him?" Outraged, she wanted to fling him out the window. Had he been a stranger, she might have attempted to do so. But this was Dare. She had known his ambitions when she married him. "Were those *your* surveyors that Mr. Ives-Madden saw?"

"Not mine," he said forcefully. "I've ascertained that."

"So then it's all right?" she asked in relief. "No one will be destroying our homes and fields?"

To her dismay, he shook his head negatively.

"Even if I wanted to, which I don't, I can't throw away investor money by giving up now. And even if we did, there is another rail line to the north that wants to connect with Harrogate. Alder is in their direct path, so they will go through here one way or another."

Emilia fisted her hand over her middle. "So no matter what, we lose our homes?"

Dare shook his head. "The abbey fields make the best route, true. We've bought up land that is going to waste on either side of them. There is an alternative, if Pascoe won't sell." He held her gaze. "The tracks could conceivably go through some of *your* unused property. If Weathersby's association is considering that, then they are also talking to the northern rail line."

Emilia felt sick. If Pascoe refused to sell his property, Dare would go broke and his family would starve. If Dare's investors didn't lay track, then the men in Harrogate would—right through *her* land.

None of them had any understanding of what that meant. She gathered her courage and regarded him stonily. "I have no unused property," she informed him. "After we eat, I will show you."

"IT'S SWAMP," Dare declared, studying the wasteland land he'd considered an alternative to Pascoe's. He felt his boots sinking into soggy peat. "You could make a great deal of money selling off this worthless property. Why would you say no? Think what you could do to the cottage, the servants you could hire, the laboratory you could build. . ."

Here was a solution to their land problem! He could sell the consortium this swamp. Even if they had to build a trestle over it, they'd still make a fortune.

"I won't *need* a laboratory if I lose this land," his bewildering wife protested, lifting her old skirts above a pair of old boots and descending an embankment with the nimbleness of a mountain goat.

Dare was fairly certain Emilia was not insane. Odd, perhaps, misinformed, no doubt, but not insane. So she *believed* this swamp was more important than her studies. It would behoove him to figure out why or spend the rest of his limited life believing he'd married a crazy woman who would see his family starve over a swamp.

He slid down after her, catching her arm as they reached the bottom. She tugged him to a stop and pointed at their feet.

"We are walking on Sir Harry's garden. It's overgrown, but there should be stepping stones so we needn't crush the mosses." She crouched down and brushed aside ferns until she found a solid rock. With a gardener's expertise, she produced a pair of secateurs from her apron pocket and began clearing a path.

"It's a bog filled with bog plants," Dare argued, gazing at the lush greenery. He hadn't spent much time on his father's very small estate. He barely knew hay from alfalfa. But he knew a bog when he saw one.

She pointed to clumps of rounded leaves. "Liverwort, dozens of different species, some unknown anywhere else in the kingdom. Some species are excellent for improving blood circulation. Others are excellent for women who need it when they reach a certain age to balance out their ill humors. There's another species further on which makes an excellent tonic. I was waiting for this fall to harvest it to see if it might give consumptives more strength to fight the disease. My grandfather spent his life importing new varieties, learning their properties."

He saw *weeds.* "There is no profit in a crop of liverwort!"

"Sadly, no," she agreed, uncovering more stepping stones and proceeding toward the lowest part of the swamp. "When we start putting money above the needs of people, everyone loses. We'll kill off valuable herbs that could save human lives. What is the purpose of money if it can't buy health?"

Stunned, Dare studied the truth of this painful revelation. Weeds could cure him?

He'd spent his entire life learning how to turn everything around him into gold. Even now, he calculated the cost of building a trestle over this swamp. But what good would it do him or others if they died because the herbs they needed were lost?

He'd rather believe the herbs were quackery, but Emilia thought otherwise. And his wife had been right enough times that he couldn't simply discount her beliefs for his.

"We could move your plants closer to the house," he suggested, walking on the stones because she seemed to think it important. "We could dig holes and fill them with water. Weeds are hardy. I don't see the difficulty." He was practically pleading. There *had* to be a way.

She sent him a look of pure exasperation. "Put your hand in that stream you're standing beside."

Dare crouched down, pulled off his glove, and stuck his hand in the water. "Ah, thermal springs! But this whole area is dotted with springs. One isn't any more special than the other. I surmise you don't want to start a spa out here."

"You surmise correctly," she said curtly. "These particular mosses would not grow without the spring to keep them warm in winter." She pointed her cutters at a particularly succulent bunch of slime on the rocks lining the spring. "Those mosses have been known to prevent *infection*. Do you have any idea how miraculous that would be? Grandfather was unable to find a form in which it could be sold at an apothecary. It needs to be wet and green to work. But if we could hire a botanist, he might learn to grow it elsewhere. We could save millions of lives if we could fight infection. Just think of the soldiers who have lost limbs who might have been saved had this moss been available! But if you destroy the seed and the plant, the opportunity to save others will be lost forever."

Dare was feeling desperate. "Why should we sacrifice our futures for a few plants that probably grow elsewhere?"

"How many untouched hot springs do you know?" she asked with asperity.

None. And by the time they located one, it would be too late for the railroad.

Dare sighed and brushed ferns back from what appeared to be a carved stone overhanging the stream. He could make out a worn Celtic triple spiral covered in moss, giving evidence that this spring had been a source of water for thousands of years.

"My ancestors were reported to be Druids," Emilia said, coming to stand over him and admire the carving. "This land has been in our family long enough to make the legend believable."

"I am a man of science. I don't believe in water gods or Druids or even in ancient family history. But I respect your belief in the holiness of this place to you family." He bowed his head in despair, realizing he could never sell this land over Emilia's objections. She was his family now as much as his mother and sisters. *Damn.*

"Thank you," she whispered in what sounded like relief. "I hope someday to make you understand so that you'll know you did the right thing."

He'd be dead someday, but he didn't need to remind her of that regret. "I will talk to Pascoe and Bridey about their land," he said, placing the future of his family in the hands of others. "And then I shall go to Harrogate with a lawyer and have a good long talk with the banker."

"Lord Erran Ives is a lawyer. He might still be at Wystan with Ashford," she said. "I'll write Lady Ashford and ask if she'll send him down to talk with you and Pascoe. He's a lawyer with a powerful gift in his voice."

Dare scowled at her. "You're telling me that even men have these mysterious Malcolm abilities?"

She shrugged and smiled brightly. "One of Lord Erran's great-grandmothers was a Malcolm, one who would have adored this spring. He'll understand."

Dare offered his hand to help her up. She took it without hesitation, appeasing his ill humor. "I don't have the luxury of time for learning superstitions, but for you. . . I want to believe you are different, that you understand what I need. But in return, I know I must listen to what *you* need. I'm not a complete nod-cock. I understand quid pro quo."

Proving she was, indeed, a paragon of understanding, she acknowledged his declaration with a nod and said, "We can work together. I wish to understand arsenic. Why would a doctor put *poison* in a medicine and believe it cured people?"

And then she dropped his hand to crouch on another stone.

"Arsenic is a naturally-occurring element in soil and water," he told her as she removed a bottle from her apron and filled it at the stream. "It's quite possibly in that spring water, along with dozens of other minerals. Man has known about it for centuries. It's a byproduct of copper refining, for instance. It's been used in pesticides and medicines and may actually be as necessary to the body as fruits and vegetables, since many foods absorb it from the soil."

"A very complicated element," she said with a frown, tucking the bottle back in her apron. "You said there are different kinds?"

"Aye, and therein lies the problem. Arsenic combines with other elements to do different things. It's a preservative and a fixative in its most poisonous form. But as long as one doesn't go around eating wood and paint, it's harmless to humans."

"Paint?" she asked, looking up from gathering moss. "Wouldn't it hurt the people mixing the paint? I have a sister who decorates rooms. Are she and her workmen in danger?"

Dare shrugged. "Not that I know of, but I just read a Russian scientist's treatise on mad hatter syndrome that indicates the mercury used in making felt hats is poisoning the hatters. So it is possible that arsenic may be poisoning us in ways we don't understand."

"So, in the interest of progress and making money, we could all be killing ourselves?"

"Or we can be producing copper to sheathe ocean-going vessels so sailors needn't risk their lives scraping barnacles. And it shows exciting possibilities in the field of electrical conduction that could make all our lives easier in the future. We simply have to be careful of how we use our discoveries, not stop experimenting entirely. If your sister isn't drinking paint, then presumably, she is safe."

"I need more treatises on arsenic," she said worriedly, gathering her skirt and climbing up the hill. "I want to know what other symptoms it might cause. Could it have made your cough worse too?"

"I didn't start taking Fowlers for a very long time after I developed the cough," Dare warned her. "I doubt there's any connection. What do you plan to do with that water?" he asked, climbing up after her and wishing he'd thought to bring a bottle of his own.

"I'm not sure." His intrepid wife frowned and took his arm— something she was more willing to do these days he noted with pride. "Now that my pharmacopeia is complete, I'd intended to experiment and improve upon it. But this talk of minerals and arsenics and other naturally occurring substances. . . I want to know more."

"I can help you with those studies. I've been learning to separate elements in hopes of finding new ones. Once we learn the composition of our planet, we can better understand how the building blocks fit together."

Instead of yawning and changing the subject, she studied him with interest. Even men of his acquaintance hid behind newspapers when Dare expounded upon his theories. He waited to see how much she wished to know.

"How did you become interested in elements? Is there money in such discoveries?" She asked that last part skeptically.

He acknowledged her perceptivity with a nod. "There is seldom money to be made from scientific discoveries until some commercial inventor finds a way to put them to use and sell them. The steam engine took decades to develop and is just now becoming commercially viable. So, no, I do it because I like to know what makes things work. Until recently, I've not had time to invest much energy in a hobby that does not lead to a profit, so I've not made much progress."

"Consumption keeps you home now," she said sympathetically. "I understand the frustration of not being able to go about as one might like."

"Which is why you were angry with me yesterday? You didn't want to be left home?"

"Precisely," she said in a clipped tone that indicated she still wasn't happy with him.

Oddly, Dare realized he wanted her to be happy with him. He'd ignored the silly requests and complaints made by his family for years, but Emilia—didn't want to visit a duke because of his *title*. She wanted to visit a man who could *teach* her. Dare could relate to the quest for knowledge.

"Shall I show you how to separate out the minerals in your water?" he asked, with a degree of trepidation, but he was honestly eager to share his knowledge.

She halted in the middle of the grassy field, stood on her toes, and covered his cheek in kisses.

Dare thought that might be a *yes*.

"M'LORD, M'LADY, Lord and Lady Pascoe-Ives have come to call." One of the new maids stood nervously in the workshop doorway, apparently unwilling to enter the dim interior.

Emilia removed the protective spectacles Dare had ordered her to wear. "Oh dear, I had not thought they would arrive so precipitously. Take them tea in the parlor and tell them we'll be right there."

Dare growled irascibly and turned up the flame under his beaker. "It is almost boiling. Tell Pascoe to come out here."

Emilia glanced longingly at the workbench where he was showing her how to separate the elements of her spring water. "That is rude. We asked them to call, if you remember."

"Dying men don't have time to be polite. Pascoe won't mind." He didn't even look up from his work.

"You could be dying for years," she retorted unsympathetically. "That's just an excuse to have your way."

That caused him to look up and flash her the glaring white smile that almost made her swoon. "You are a woman of rare perception." Then he returned to work.

"I am beginning to think your doctor deliberately poisoned you," she declared, removing her apron.

"I love your concern and sympathy," he called after her as she left.

He shouldn't be able to make her laugh when she was angry with him, but he did. He was so brave in the face of death—it broke her heart but gave her courage as well.

She stopped to tuck her hair into its pins and dust the straw off her hem before she hurried to the parlor to greet their very first guests.

"You honor our humble home," she exclaimed as she entered.

Bridey was sitting on the ancient walnut sofa while Pascoe studied an old portrait. Emilia was relieved that Mrs. Wiggs and her crew had restored the parlor to cleanliness, if not fashion.

"Your letter expressed rather urgent concern," Bridey said, offering her a cup. "And we were worried about both of you."

Emilia settled on the sofa beside her and took the tea. "Thank you for helping Dare understand that I'm not a vaporish sort of female. He hasn't quite grasped all we're telling him, but he's willing to listen."

She turned to Pascoe. "He is in the workshop, distilling spring water, and asked if you would join him there."

Pascoe was a distinguished gentleman, garbed in the height of fashion for this call. His lips curled wryly at her request. "You make me feel right at home. That is exactly what one of my nephews would request."

"I'll have Aster trace Dare's family tree. Perhaps there's an Ives branch on it somewhere," Emilia acknowledged. "But I need for him to understand why it would be disastrous if a railroad was built across the property."

There, she'd said it. She didn't want Dare's family to starve, but the moss might help all mankind. She had no alternative.

"I'm sure Dare will explain that remark," Pascoe said with a laugh.

"But the railroad is one of the reasons we're here," Bridey added worriedly.

"I'll find Dare. You speak with Emilia. We'll see which of us has a glass thrown at our heads," Pascoe said dryly, bowing to Emilia before exiting.

"Glass?" Emilia asked, studying her teacup. "I rather like this tea set, and I'm not much inclined toward tantrums."

"That's why I thought I'd be safe here." Bridey removed her gloves and reached for a cucumber sandwich. "Pascoe has many correspondents and has made inquiries into the railroad situation."

"Oh dear." Emilia took a teacake. "Perhaps sugar will sweeten my disposition and prevent cup flinging."

"You'll need more than a teacake. The railroad association Mr. Weathersby is helping to finance has already started laying rail. They claim to have signed deeds from all the property owners along the route. Pascoe wants Dare to look at the survey maps, but the track appears to run through our tenants' field *and* your house."

Emilia felt as if she were wilting into the sofa's floral fabric. "They can't," she whispered. "My father would never have allowed it."

Gently, Bridey asked, "Are you sure Dare wouldn't? He has the right to sell your property that is not entailed, and since you're not male, there is no entail."

Sixteen

"*SIGN DEEDS?* I bloody well did not sell our land to a rival, no more than you did," Dare shouted, flinging his spectacles to the table.

"I had to ask." Pascoe leaned over the worktable to examine the beakers. "I don't suppose you've discovered gold in the water? It will take a fortune or two to fight a wealthy merchants association. We'll have to hire armed guards to keep their ruffians off our property."

"Give me a legal deed to your corner parcel, and I'll have my group start building before the Harrogate lot can even dream of claiming our ground." Angrily, Dare strode up and down the workshop. "I can't believe the audacity!"

Pascoe shrugged. "Both our properties lay vacant for years. They had every right to assume no one would notice, much less object. As Sommersville said, once a right of way is established, it's nearly impossible to recover."

"Well, it's *not* established. There is no road or path through this house or your field. They have no rights at all." Dare wanted to shout at the top of his lungs, but his lungs didn't have the capacity any longer. He considered punching a wall but he feared the building would fall on their heads.

"I've written Erran to look into it. But if it comes to an actual lawsuit, we have to be prepared to empty our purses." Pascoe shoved his hands in his coat pockets and pulled out the lining to show they were empty.

"And there's every possibility that Weathersby has a judge or two already in *his* pocket," Dare said bitterly. "Life's too damned short for this."

Pascoe nodded sympathetically. "True. So let's fire the first gun and see what happens. Write your consortium. Tell them I need a fair price to pay my tenant to buy his own field elsewhere. And I want shares in return for my cooperation. And a good wall to keep the cattle from crossing the tracks."

Dare wiped his hands on a rag and offered one to shake. "Thank you. You'll see we deal fairly with landowners. The abbey could have its own train station out there someday, once passenger travel is safe. It would be a boon to your wife's school and infirmary."

"I considered that. Plus, I decided it best not to upset the two of you by refusing my land and forcing you to use yours. Marital strife won't win us the support Bridey needs from Emilia's family. The physicians working with the hospital in Harrogate are likely to start protesting Bridey's unconventional school, and we need powerful people behind us."

"As I understand it, the Malcolms are already behind Bridey," Dare said in confusion. "You don't need me to have their support." Now the problem was resolved, Dare started toward the house and his wife.

Pascoe made an indelicate snort. "You really need to look into your wife's family history."

Dare shook his head. "History has nothing to do with anything. Even if I should be so desperate as to sell Emilia's swamp, I don't understand how it affects you and Bridey."

"Her family will blame *me* for not selling my plot. I'm an Ives. My family fought the Malcolms for centuries. Hostilities did not end until the women regained control of that drafty lump of stone in Wystan. Do not expect logic when it comes to family feuds."

Feuding with women? What could they possibly do except. . . Dare grimaced. In marriage, a shared bed could become a battleground. He understood that better than family feuds and history.

"Emilia's generosity will allow my family to have a home after I'm gone," he explained. "I cannot stand in the way of her dreams, if she believes that swamp is worth saving. Help me find a way to protect my investment, and I'll do whatever is necessary to help our wives," Dare heard himself saying. He hoped to hell he knew what he promised.

Picturing Peter gloating while Dare's mother and sisters starved, Dare locked his jaw in determination. Somehow, he'd find a way to take care of his wife as well as his family. Although admittedly, he'd nearly killed himself in succeeding this far.

Fighting from his deathbed did not seem very appealing.

"YOU CANNOT sell my land!" Emilia shouted at Pascoe and Dare the moment they returned to the house. "I will write my father and the executor and Ashford and the king himself, but you cannot sell my grandfather's hard work!"

Dare raised his eyebrows and exchanged glances with Sir Pascoe. Emilia almost took a painting off the wall to pound both men with it.

"Told you so," Pascoe murmured.

Bridey grabbed Emilia's hand before she could fling her favorite teacup. "That's his smirking cat-in-cream look. Let them speak before we declare war."

"Your father trusted me with your land for reasons," Dare declared indignantly. "I shouldn't have to justify my decisions."

If Bridey hadn't been holding her arm, Emilia would have flung the cup. "Why should I trust my father's decision any more than yours? I want you to promise to never sell my grandfather's land!"

"Even if we're starving? Or my family is in danger of starving?" The obstinate man crossed his arms and glared at her. "You would take that choice from me?"

"Yes, yes, I would. It's *my* land. Only I know its value. I want it deeded to me directly." Emilia crossed her arms and glared back.

"Wystan Tower," Pascoe said, seemingly senselessly. Then, when Dare didn't appear ready to commit to giving up any of his authority, he continued, "I am selling *my* land." He raised his eyebrows expectantly at his bride.

"We'll have smoking noisy engines running through the yard?" Bridey asked in dismay.

"Not so close as that," Pascoe said. "Give me the same chance you told Emilia to give Dare."

Bridey scowled, but the door knocker rapped. Emilia exchanged a glance with Dare, who shook his head. They all paused, waiting for the footman to enter with a card. He handed it to Dare, who scowled even worse than Bridey had.

"One cannot deny entry to pestilences if they are family, can one?" he asked. "The rest of you may want to sneak out the back way. If I kill him, you can pretend you never knew he was here."

Unsettled by the argument, Emilia shook her head at Bridey's and Pascoe's looks of concern. "Have a seat. You must meet Dare's charming heir so you understand his lack of hospitality."

Eyes alight with curiosity, their visitors returned to their seats and waited expectantly as the guest was fetched.

Peter Dare entered looking as dapper as Emilia remembered from the wedding. He wore a small blue jewel in his neckcloth and a rather garish gold watch on a chain at his waist. His attire was of the latest fashion and neatly tailored to suit his small frame. His smile didn't falter at seeing that Dare had guests.

After making the introductions, Dare asked rudely, "What do you want, Peter? It will be a long time until I'm at death's door. The country air agrees with me," he added acidly.

Emilia noted his cousin didn't look daunted but merely produced a packet of papers from his inner coat pocket.

"Your mother asked me to carry these to you. She was concerned that you have not written lately, and I had business in Harrogate anyway."

"What business did you have visiting my mother?" Dare took the package and began flipping through letters.

Peter shrugged. "I stopped to ask her if I could see the size of the townhouse. Annette is expecting our fourth child, and she's concerned the nursery won't be large enough. It's a shame the house can't be sold."

Emilia caught Dare's clenched hand and squeezed warningly, then spoke before he could. "How charming of you to think of Lady Dare at a time like this. I do hope you won't mind, but we were just on our way out. Thank you so much for carrying the messages." She rose so the gentlemen must also.

Pascoe, ever the diplomat, led the way. "What business takes you to Harrogate?" he innocuously asked the visitor as he steered him toward the foyer.

Following, Emilia kept a tight hold on Dare's fist. "Killing your heir won't help your mother," she whispered.

"My late father banked in Harrogate," Peter replied, "and my meager inheritance is still there, so I've continued the practice. They hold my mortgages. Every so often I travel up from London to reassure them that my prospects are still good." He put his hat back on and bowed to the group. "My pleasure, ladies, Sir Pascoe, Dare."

He rode off while Dare glared at his departing back.

"Obnoxious twit," Pascoe observed. "Does he have any income of his own?"

"His father left him a small property where he houses his wife.

Mostly, he borrows money, and he and his courtesan live on my expectations," Dare said with dryness.

"His poor wife," Bridey said generously. "Have you ever met her?"

Dare shrugged. "I wasn't invited to the wedding. I believe it was an arranged marriage when they were both quite young. Her father's property abuts his, and she brought him what must have seemed a decent marriage portion at the time."

"If he's dealing with Harrogate bankers, we need to be wary of him," Pascoe warned.

Emilia frowned at the possibility of Dare's heir conniving with the people trying to run railroads through her land, but she preferred to leave business in the hands of those who understood it.

"I will not let suspicion and distrust mar my days. Peter Dare is simply an annoying insect." She kissed Dare's cheek as their visitors prepared to leave. "We have better things to do. Bessie has almost finished copying my book, and I need to add the old pages to the ones Bridey already has. I'd also like to help with the infirmary as much as possible. The sooner the school is in operation, the sooner I can have my laboratory. Bridey has already said I might go with them."

"Let Ashford's expensive team eat them out of house and home," Dare said with callousness. "We have the gig now and don't need the berlin."

"Your generosity overwhelms," Pascoe said dryly. "But a crested carriage does add prestige when I harass the bankers. We've already sent word to Erran about the deeds, so let me work with him on that angle for now. You work with your consortium in securing my corner."

"You really ought to spend more time in the fresh air instead of writing letters, Dare," Emilia admonished. "But I do hope you'll arrange the deed to my *swamp* be entrusted to me." She tucked her portfolio of papers under her arm and waited to be assisted into the berlin.

As the carriage drove off, leaving Dare standing in the drive, glaring at the road, Emilia prayed he did not do anything foolish like ride after his cousin and beat him into a pulp for being a reprehensibly self-centered fop. Like mice, even fops deserved to live.

Surely, he would not sell her land. If he'd talked Pascoe into selling his instead, Dare had to understand how much it meant to her.

The carriage let them off at the rear of the abbey where Bridey had established an entrance exclusively for the school and infirmary. Pascoe went on with the horses to the main house.

"How is Tess doing?" Emilia asked as they followed the ancient stones to Bridey's office.

"She's marvelous! Quiet, but she handles the paperwork admirably. I have great hopes for her once she gains a little confidence."

She pushed open the door to where the topic of their conversation worked. Tess stood up, but Bridey gestured for her to return to her seat. "Put your pages with the others," she told Emilia. "I've been reading the pharmacopeia as I have time and making a few notes, but you've incorporated almost everything I know. It's a brilliant work."

"Thank you," Emilia said with relief, knowing Bridey's expertise equaled hers. "I need to ask Lord Erran if he knows the best way for me to publish it. I hate spending my own money to have it printed while our expenses are so uncertain. Dare is trying to make me understand budgeting." She added the papers from the portfolio to the metal box under the counter. "I am not very good at more than knowing what I can buy with the coins in my pocket."

Bridey laughed. "There speaks the rich girl who has been given everything she wants. Welcome to the real world. You're in luck this time. Pascoe sent a carrier pigeon to Ashford at Wystan yesterday asking Erran to come down and help us with this railroad affair. His wife's baby isn't due for weeks, so we expect him to jump at any offer to escape."

"When the tracks are laid, will we be able to take a train from here into town?" Tess asked with fascination, looking up from her work. "My father. . ." She ended that sentence abruptly.

They'd not been able to persuade more from Tess or her aunt about the girl's parentage. Emilia pretended to concentrate on removing her gloves. "Your father has interest in railroads?" she asked as if it didn't matter at all.

"They are supposed to be beneficial." Tess returned to her work.

The girl took *taciturn* to new levels. Emilia exchanged a look with Bridey and left Tess alone.

They were just finishing up their work at the end of the day when Pascoe and Lord Erran arrived. Pascoe was only older than his nephew by a few years, Emilia knew. They both had the strong cheekbones and dark Ives good looks. Pascoe was a little more lean and sophisticated. Erran was broader in face and stature and dressed more fancifully. His wife was an accomplished seamstress and did little to discourage his preference for embellished waistcoats and fancy linen.

"You made good time," Bridey exclaimed.

"You're only a day's ride away, and I was eager to escape the women and their nesting. Even Ashford is shouting for brighter paints and papers, demanding windows be installed where no windows should be. A summer day's ride is pure pleasure in comparison." Erran bowed to Emilia. "Lady Dare, my congratulations. Your husband has the respect and admiration of many."

Since the Ives men had barely acknowledged her existence until now, Emilia credited Dare with this new recognition. She curtseyed but let the men lead the conversation.

"Once Dare has approval from his consortium, we can draw up the property deeds," Erran said after Pascoe explained their agreement. "That's of no moment. But I'd like to talk with the men who believe they already own your properties, if indeed, that is the case."

Emilia listened intently. It wasn't Dare she had to fear but someone else?

"If there are forgeries, I need to see the signatures," Erran continued. "Everyone is trying to rush railroads into production before parliament can draw up restrictions, so they may just be bluffing and hoping they can obtain signatures. But a lawsuit needs to be constructed on evidence."

"We'll go into Harrogate tomorrow and work our way around town," Pascoe said. "Tell Emilia what you'll need from Dare, and he can have it prepared when we come by on the morrow."

Erran turned to the desk where Tess worked. "May I borrow pen and paper, please? I'll make a list."

Wide-eyed, the secretary pushed clean paper in his direction and sharpened a pen.

"Might I ask you about ways of publishing my pharmacopeia?" Emilia asked as he worked on his list.

He glanced up at her. "Don't strike the messenger, but you'd do best to have an accredited physician's name on the cover. But perhaps if you had letters from physicians who approve of the contents, you could use your initials, and I could talk to a few printers. I don't suppose you write articles for medical journals and your name might be recognized?"

"Sommersville," Bridey immediately said. "The duke would be the perfect reference. He writes articles all the time, and everyone knows him."

Emilia brightened. "Could you introduce me? I could show him the copy we keep here. Perhaps if we put his name on the cover—would he allow that?"

"If it would put a good pharmacopeia into the hands of apothecaries, I can't see why not. You could make your fortune!" Bridey said enthusiastically.

"Making a little money instead of spending it would be a pleasant change, but mostly, I want the information disseminated far and wide. We have so much to learn, that it's a shame physicians have only the old methods to fall back on. We need to keep adding to our knowledge!"

Bolstered by the sensation that she'd finally found friends who understood her, Emilia gathered up her belongings and prepared to leave.

She was excited and eager to go home, to see what Dare had accomplished, to see *Dare*. . . He'd *listened* to her and understood about her land and hadn't sold it!

For the first time in her life, she feared her heart was as engaged as her brain.

FEELING MORE energetic than he had in a long time, Dare contemplated the two horses in the paddock and wondered if he ought to ride into the village. It wasn't as if the nags were meant for galloping across field and stream, but he missed riding, and he hated being treated like an invalid. The village was less than a mile away. Once upon a time, he could have walked the distance.

He tried breathing deep. Was it really possible that Emilia could heal damaged tissues simply by touching him? He coughed and cursed when he drew too much air into his lungs. She was at least correct that she couldn't *cure* him.

Hearing the creak of the garden gate, willing to be distracted from his frustration, he turned and watched the old gnome totter out. The gardener was never around when Emilia was, but Dare had seen him puttering about occasionally. He still didn't know where the man lived.

To his surprise, Mr. Arthur toddled over to the paddock carrying a handful of greens.

"Dinbernt," he said between his missing teeth. "Give it to da miss."

Dinbernt? What the devil was dinbernt? "Shouldn't you give it to the cook?" Dare asked, studying the weeds he took in bewilderment.

The garden gnome doddered off, ignoring him.

Apparently being a viscount and lord of all he surveyed earned little respect from gardeners. In a vague way, he understood. The old gnome could produce food from dirt, whereas Dare could produce nothing particularly useful except money. In the gardener's eyes, he needed to earn respect.

Out of curiosity, Dare took the greens into the workshop and stuck them in water. He had a vague notion that greens, like flowers, might last longer in water. After a bit of study, he realized there were two types in this bunch, one straggly looking stalk that really did look like a weed, and a healthy bunch of thick leaves. He took one of each and carried them inside and upstairs to Emilia's secretary/maid. Bessie looked up from her work with surprise, then rose hesitantly.

Dare waved her back to her seat and presented her with the leaves. "Arthur handed these to me, said something that sounded liked *dinbernt,* and ordered me to give them to Emilia. What am I supposed to do with them?"

Bessie studied them, then paged through the drawings of the new pharmacopeia. "I am no expert but they look fairly common. I'm sure Lady Dare will know immediately. I know greens can be dried, but I really know nothing of the process. Perhaps you could simply lay them on her workbench?"

Dare studied the weeds with interest. "They can be dried? Of course, that is one way to mix them in elixirs. Interesting."

He studied the shelves of herbals in the office until he found one that sounded as if it might teach him the techniques of drying.

Whistling—he could whistle now at least—he carried the book out to his workshop.

Emilia found him bent over his bench when she came home. He knew the instant she entered. Her lavender scent gave her away, but so did her. . . Dare sought a word as he finished up what he was doing. His wife simply had a *presence* to which he was attuned.

Setting down his pen, he took her in his arms and pressed kisses down her cheek and throat until she giggled. Apparently, their earlier argument had been satisfactorily resolved.

"I have never known peppermint to cause arousal," she said breathlessly. "And what else is that you have there? Ginger leaves? How did you find ginger out here and why would you cut the leaves?" She broke from his hold to examine his workbench.

He chuckled, not insulted that her curiosity won over his lust. He knew he wouldn't be neglected once they were in their chambers.

He poked the weeds he'd spread out on a piece of tin over a lamp. "Your gardener handed these leaves to me and called them what sounded like *dinbernt*. I assumed there was more where these came from, so I've been trying drying techniques."

"Dinbernt? *Zingiber* is the genus name for ginger, although I don't know how he would know that. Perhaps Grandfather used the name and Mr. Arthur is combining the names of ginger and mint? The combination makes a soothing tea. He may be trying to help you.

"But if there is ginger here somewhere. . ." She looked up with excitement. "Would ginger grow in a hot spring? Or perhaps he has potted them and brings them in for the winter. But it is the *rhizomes* of ginger that I need, not the leaves."

"He came out of the garden carrying them is all I know. What is so valuable about ginger?"

"It is almost the perfect medicinal plant! It will be excellent for your damaged gut and for Bridey's morning sickness. It's shown some promise for inflammation from arthritis and other uses. It might even help prevent diseases like diabetes." She headed for the door. "But it's a *tropical* plant. I cannot imagine how he can be growing it."

Dare followed her. "How can you be certain it is ginger? It looks like any weed to me."

"Anything green looks like a weed to you. It is a good thing you have a cook or you would starve. I cannot be positive it is ginger until I have the root, but this looks like the specimens I have seen in drawings and the one plant I've seen in a botanical house. I cannot imagine it surviving in a kitchen garden."

The gate creaked as they entered the furrowed plot. Debris and weeds had been removed this past week, and neat rows promised vegetables in the future. Dare located the rounded leaves of the plant she'd called peppermint in a concrete box in a far corner. Even he was aware that peppermint was used for digestives. Arthur was trying to quack him too? Did that mean the old man accepted him? And why should he care?

Emilia surveyed the garden like a general preparing for war. "There." She marched toward a corner nearly concealed by what Dare thought might be a grapevine. Beneath the arbor, hidden among the leaves, was an old tin pail with a few tall stalks that appeared to be on their deathbeds.

Emilia cooed over them as if they were precious jewels, then dug into the dirt. "They won't be ready to harvest for a month or so, but I really need to see. . ." She produced a broken piece of misshapen root and glowed as if she'd been given riches. "Ginger! We have our own ginger! I really must speak with Mr. Arthur. Do we have any notion where he resides?"

"I have been wondering the same. He must have a burrow, like a rabbit. I don't suppose ginger is something we can sell for a profit?"

She granted him a look of disdain, which turned thoughtful. "I cannot imagine we can grow much of it. It will not survive the winter where it is now. It's usually imported, which makes it valuable. But if the hot springs could heat a small nursery. . ." Her voice trailed off as she considered it.

"There might be money in an herb crop?" he asked, knowing she had never considered how money was made.

"I truly cannot say," she replied in bewilderment. "All I have ever done is buy the more exotic herbs and roots from apothecaries, but they must obtain them somewhere. Do you think Mr. Arthur is suggesting we can save the hot springs garden by selling exotic plants?"

He did not have the years left necessary for learning a new trade. With a grimace, Dare offered his hand to help her up. "Let us wash and prepare ourselves for dinner. Perhaps I need to be teaching you how to survive in trade instead of how to distill arsenic."

"Ladies do not deal in trade," she asserted.

"Call it agriculture," he said. "Even dukes buy and sell cattle and grain."

"Their stewards and estate managers handle it," she informed him loftily, but he could tell by her tone that she was interested.

"Remember what Pascoe said, if it comes down to a lawsuit to save your land, we will need plump pockets. Your father is no longer responsible for you. I am. And when I'm gone, you must look after yourself. It's time you gain a little practical experience."

The look she sent him was so sad, it nearly broke his heart, and he was the damned one dying.

Seventeen

A FEW DAYS later, Emilia proudly stored the last of her draft pages in the box under the infirmary counter. "It is done," she told Bridey with satisfaction. "Have you heard from the duke?"

Bridey beamed. "He is most eager to see your book. But Pascoe says we cannot go alone, and he and Dare are all wrapped up in the railroad business. Has Dare given any indication how the negotiations are going?"

"Lord Erran has sent the documents to Dare's investors for approval. I think the next step is dealing with the northern railroad with which they wish to connect. Have you seen any more trespassing surveyors lately?" Behind the counter, where she could reach the wall of shelves that had been added just for her, Emilia pressed her pestle into her mortar to grind the peppermint Dare had dried so quickly. The sweet scent of mint filled the small office.

"Will is training the deerhounds to be guard dogs, so he's patrolling the back fields. He says he's seen no sign of trespassers. With any luck, our worries were for naught. And your lovely ginger has worked wonders with my morning sickness! Have you determined where your gardener is growing it?" At the desk by the door, Bridey signed her name to a document Tess presented her.

"I cannot find my gardener," Emilia said in frustration. "I've asked all the servants, and they claim not to know where he lives. I've studied the hot spring, and there are several places where ginger might be kept warm in winter. So I've decided that once the rhizomes are ready for dividing, I will experiment with planting them in pots and carrying them down there. It's the only thing close to tropical anywhere around, although a glass enclosure would be ideal."

"Once your book starts making money, perhaps you can build one!"

"I doubt my entrepreneurial ability," Emilia admitted. "I need Dare for that. I would rather look for cures for consumption." Thinking of the dynamic man who had so much to offer the world, she prayed his disease was in remission. Perhaps miracles happened and someone would find a cure soon.

Bridey gave her a sympathetic squeeze that only caused warning prickles. Of course, other than being enceinte, Bridey was quite healthy. "I think you are prolonging his life with your gift. He could have many, many more years."

Emilia fought a weepy smile and simply turned back to her grinding. She'd left Dare enthusiastically working on some new process for detecting arsenic. She had no notion what one did with such information but she was certain he would. She had ordered him to leave the door and windows open so he'd at least be breathing fresh air.

"Would you mind reading through my instruction manual while I talk to the workmen?" Bridey placed a stack of loose pages on the counter. "I know you've never assisted in childbirth, but the women who will be reading the manual will most likely not have much instruction either. You can tell me if I need to simplify more."

Emilia nodded. "Of course. Just leave them there. I'll finish this up and take the manual home with me to study."

After Bridey bustled off, Emilia tried to find the stillness she usually experienced when she was working with her herbs. She often used the steady beat of the mortar as a form of meditation, where she sought new ideas or perfected old ones. But somehow, she couldn't find that tranquility now.

Perhaps it was her uneasiness over Dare's health. She knew better than to weep over what couldn't be changed.

Even the scritch-scratch of Tess's pen irritated. Tess was silent, but she seemed permanently tense. She wrote each word as if it were her last.

Unable to make the kind of casual small talk that might draw out the girl, Emilia finished crushing the mint and poured it into the container she'd brought for it. She had the gig. She'd go home and read the manual and try to restore her strangely rattled nerves.

She turned off the counter lamp, leaving just Tess's desk lamp for illumination. Since the room was little more than a nun's cell, it had no windows, only the door to provide light, which was fine for storing herbs. She crouched down behind the counter to gather her gloves, umbrella, and the basket she used for transporting her plants. Deciding to add Bridey's manual pages to the basket, she reached to pick them up, but managed to drop them all over the floor. With the light off, she was literally in the dark as she scrambled about on her knees hunting for pages scattering in the breeze from the open door.

A shadow darkened the chamber even more, and Emilia froze.

"So, this is where you've been hiding," a male voice said in such detached tones that her blood curdled. "Your father sent me to fetch you and the book."

A chair scraped. Skirts rustled. Emilia was torn between listening and letting the intruder know she was present.

"Crenshaw," Tess whispered in what sounded like fear.

Crenshaw? Emilia chose to stay hidden. This was not the gouty old Crenshaw she'd met. This man sounded young, and from the shadow blocking the door, he wasn't small or crippled.

"Come along with you, then. I don't have time to waste. Where's the book you told your father about?" The shadow entered the small interior, allowing daylight to filter in again.

Emilia tried to make herself smaller behind the counter. What book? Had Tess told her father about the *pharmacopeia*?

"It's gone," Tess said in a wavering voice. "They took it to the duke."

Definitely the pharmacopeia. Why on earth. . . ?

"You're lying. You always look at your feet when you lie. Where is it?"

The smack of a hard hand against soft flesh and Tess's cry had Emilia scrambling about, looking for a weapon. If only she could reach the bell pull. . .

Tess wept while Crenshaw slammed the cabinet doors under the counter. The book box was the only thing under there. He couldn't miss it. With nothing else to use, Emilia grabbed her basket, stood up, and swung it hard at the head of the man just standing up, her precious book box in his arms.

"Pull the bell, Tess, pull the bell!" she shouted as she beat the man soundly with braided straw.

Understandably, he was more startled than harmed. He grabbed the basket and flung it against her wall of shelves, sending jars crashing to the stone floor.

Tess yanked on the cord so hard they could hear the bell ringing in the kitchen.

Crenshaw grabbed Tess's arm and tugged her toward the door. "Your pa said to bring you home with the book. I've got the book. Now come along before you stir up them dogs."

Outraged at the audacity, Emilia leaped at his broad back. The man was built like a stone monolith. She couldn't find purchase but wrapped one arm around his neck and yanked at his hair. He dropped Tess long enough to swing his elbow backward, knocking Emilia off like an annoying pest. Free from his hold, Tess stomped his boots and kicked at his shins while wrestling for the box, but he was just too big. He shoved her aside.

"Hell, if you don't want to go, I don't want you anyway. I've had juicier pieces than you. But this book will keep these nobles in their places, not interfering with us that earn our way."

Terrified that he would escape, Emilia screamed and grabbed his arm, trying to force him to release her box. "That's valuable only to me, you oaf!"

He snorted and flung her against the wall. "If you want it back, you tell that man of yours to call off his fancy lawyers." He strode out.

Tess collapsed on the floor in a puddle of petticoats and noisy sobs.

Seeing servants and even Pascoe running from the main house, Emilia peeled herself off the wall and pointed at the man running down the rear drive. "He hurt Tess and stole my book!"

Pascoe slowed down. "Are you all right?"

"I'm fine. I'll take care of Tess, just catch the wretch!"

Given an excuse for action, Pascoe raced for the stable while the servants ran down the drive. Thinking that should do it, Emilia crouched beside Tess. She feared hugging her, but touching only her chin, she gently tilted the girl's poor bruised face toward the light. Pain leeched off her in such agonizing waves that Emilia could barely maintain her grip.

"I have some arnica and witch hazel that might help. Did he hurt the babe?" She couldn't differentiate the pain of the bruise from Tess's terror and grief, but she released her chin and reluctantly touched the girl's growing belly. She couldn't discern anything that indicated danger, although she was fascinated by the stir of life beneath her fingers.

Realizing she was in danger of being sucked in, she tore her hand away.

"I'm sorry. I'm so sorry." Tess stayed where she was, rocking back and forth with misery.

"Why would your father want my book?" she asked, because logic calmed her, even if it didn't help Tess.

Tess shook her head. "I wanted him to know I was doing good." She wept harder.

Emilia tried to puzzle that out but couldn't. "Is your father an apothecary who can use the recipes?"

"A physician! He can *sell* your book." Tess wrapped her arms around herself and struggled to stop weeping. "I think he has something to do with the railroad," she whispered in shame.

A physician? Emilia started to worry, but Tess came first. Surely Pascoe would ride down the young criminal. "Is Mr. Crenshaw the father of your baby?" she asked, knowing she didn't know how to ask as judiciously as someone like Aster or Bridey might.

Tess froze, then nodded as color filled her pale cheeks. "He said we'd marry as soon as the railroad made him rich."

"And then Sir Pascoe and Lord Dare moved in, and railroad progress halted," Emilia said, as much to herself as to Tess.

Tess nodded, gaining a little more confidence. "I told him it didn't matter. He didn't need to be wealthy. That he'd find other investments. But he. . . he called me names and walked out, even after I told him about the babe."

This time, Emilia did hug the girl. When the hug only brought sharp prickles, she helped Tess to her feet. "You are better off without Mr. Crenshaw, I promise. I'm sorry to say that any man who would strike a woman is a coward and little better than an animal. You could not know that before, but think on it now."

"My father hit me when he learned of the babe," Tess whispered, staggering to her feet, only to collapse in her chair and bury her face in her hands. "It's all my fault. I knew better. I was raised proper. But Charles was so handsome, and no one hardly ever looks at me and. . ."

Emilia patted her shoulder. "You're not the first and certainly won't be the last to fall for a handsome face. We're all animals in some ways. It's our nature. You'll know better next time and look past his face to see a man who is good to you."

Thinking it was a very good thing that they'd married *before* Dare turned his seductive charms on her, Emilia couldn't condemn this young girl for falling for kisses and promises.

She fixed a poultice, using some of the foreign arnica her grandfather had grown after receiving seeds from an herbalist in the Americas. Unlike ginger root, it thrived in his garden now. By the time Tess had a compress held to her bruise, the servants were trickling back—empty-handed.

Bridey arrived. Emilia looked up hopefully but her friend's dire expression did not bode well.

Bridey shook her head in answer to Emilia's silent question. "I think Tess should go to her room and lie down. We probably ought to fix her some lavender-chamomile tea to help her calm down."

Looking shame-faced, Tess was easily persuaded to return to her room while a maid ran to fix the tea. Bridey paced the cell until the girl was out of hearing.

"What happened?" the baronetess demanded.

"I could ask the same," Emilia replied, leaning against her counter. "Did Pascoe not catch up with the brute?"

"The wretch had a horse waiting outside. By the time Pascoe had his saddled, the thief was long gone. We don't know the fields and woods here as well as the thief does, apparently. Pascoe sent a groom back to say he's asking questions along the road toward Harrogate, but capture is not imminent."

"We know who he is. We just need to find out where he lives," Emilia said, not believing it would be that easy but trying to relieve her pregnant friend. "I should return to Dare, tell him that his plans are being threatened." Emilia explained all she knew from Tess's halting information.

Bridey's fierce expression enhanced her appearance as a red-haired warrior. "But you still have the fair copy, don't you? We'll need to take it directly to the duke. He'll stop anyone else from publishing it."

"I think it may be more complicated than that, but I don't understand how," Emilia said, crouching down to pick up spilled papers. "Crenshaw used the book as a threat against lawsuits. I need to ask Dare what that means."

"Countersuits, probably, or pressing charges against us for practicing medicine without a license, or witchcraft, for all we know. They seem desperate." Bridey sounded furious as she stooped down to help with the papers.

"Witchcraft? That's ridiculous."

"I've had my own village turn against me on such charges," Bridey warned. "Once people are afraid, they'll steer away for no good reason at all. People are not brave. They find safety in numbers and the familiar, and what we are doing is not usual. Once rumors begin, the school may never open."

Emilia knew Bridey's past gave her reason to fear the worst, but she simply couldn't accept that all their hard work would come to naught because of one brute. She might curl up and die along with Dare if she believed her book was truly lost.

"I will not believe people are so stupid and cowardly as to hide behind bullies. If so, then we can fight them by being brave." With the papers gathered, Emilia stood. Her basket had been crushed, so she shuffled the manual into an orderly pile. "And there is nothing of witchcraft in a pharmacopeia. I think they are just desperate. My concern is for poor Tess—to be so used by her father *and* her lover!"

"There is your compassion and optimism speaking again. If you'll use your head, you'll realize that she is the one responsible for telling people about your book," Bridey warned. "I do not know if we can trust her again."

"I have spent my *life* writing that book. I will spend the rest of my life defending it, if necessary. We will take her with us to confront her father," Emilia said, trying to prevent panic but fearing she sounded like an hysteric. "If Crenshaw was telling the truth, that's where he'll take the book."

"Sommersville first," Bridey suggested. "Then we will tackle Tess's father."

The yip of hounds ended any planning. William Ives-Madden appeared in the doorway, holding the leashes of straining dogs. "Do you have anything the thief handled?"

"Besides me and Tess?" Emilia asked, shuddering. "And the book he stole?"

Mr. Madden was nearly as large as Crenshaw, but his wide chest tapered to a narrow waist and hips, and even though he was dressed in a farmer's jerkin and leather, he carried himself with the same air of nobility as his relations. He bent her a wry look that hid his concern. "He hit you?"

"Shoved me." She pointed at her smashed basket. "I don't know if straw helps, but he crushed that."

She thought he might have growled, or perhaps that was his dogs. He let them sniff the basket, sniff her, and sniff the ground. They took off howling at some silent command, with William fast on their heels.

"How do they know which smell is which?" Emilia asked, preparing to leave. She needed the comfort and safety of her own four walls. And Dare. How would she tell Dare?

"I think Will talks to animals much as Pascoe's son does," Bridey said. "Who knows what he tells them?"

"I'm not sure I'll ever become used to the idea of men having our gifts." Emilia kneaded her brow. "I don't suppose we can teach them to write down what they learn in journals?"

"Doubtful," Bridey said with a little more cheer. "I think Pascoe smells emotion. Do you think men will even admit that they have moods?"

Feeling abysmally lonely and wishing Dare might whisper reassuring words of a love he would never feel, Emilia shook her head. "I doubt they even know what emotion is."

With that, she packed up to return to her husband, who enjoyed her bed but gave all appearance of forgetting her existence just as every other man she'd ever met did. Was it worth the effort to fight for his attention?

IN THE STABLE yard, seeing Emilia climb from the gig mussed, wide-eyed, and terrified, Dare felt his gut spasm worse than it had full of arsenic. He dropped his paperwork and rushed outside in his shirtsleeves. She threw herself into his arms and clung to him, trembling.

Fear wrapped his heart. What the deuce could make a woman as head-strong as his wife tremble? He drove his hand into her hair and held her against him. "Who do I have to kill?" he growled. And he meant it. He would throttle whoever had frightened her.

"They have my book!" she cried.

He couldn't tell if she was terrified or furious. Either way, rage bolted through him. Her book? He understood enough to know that from her perspective, they might as well have killed her.

"They're threatening us! *He hit Tess!* I hate this, I hate this, I hate this," she cried, burying her face in his linen.

Dare rocked her back and forth, trying to soothe her without having any notion of what she meant or what he was doing. His rational wife did not descend into hysterics for nothing and someone had to pay.

While the new groom rushed in to tend the pony, Dare led Emilia inside and ordered tea. Mrs. Wiggs took one look at Emilia's tear-stained face and began snapping orders.

While Emilia spilled her dreadful story, the housekeeper ran in and out with the tea tray and handkerchiefs, wearing a grim expression. Dare wanted to jump up and beat the threatening coward, but Emilia clung to him, and he couldn't let her go while she was in this state. Even the tea didn't settle her as she kept repeating and adding to her story.

When she finally calmed, Mrs. Wiggs marched in. "Tess is a good girl," she said stoutly.

Emilia nodded and wiped at her eyes with a soggy handkerchief. "She was trying to make her father happy for her. It's not her fault."

It damned well sounded like the girl's fault to him. She'd told her father about Emilia's book. She'd had no right. But Dare kept his mouth shut, knowing he could do nothing that wasn't already being done. His inability to gallop about the countryside as he pleased, limiting his options, grated.

The housekeeper nodded, satisfied. "Her da is my cousin's son. I'll give you his name and direction. I never liked the man, and I don't want that girl anywhere near him, but if Tess can get your book back, I'll tell her she must do so."

"Thank you, Mrs. Wiggs," Dare said, dismissing her. Now that they had some notion of where to find the book, it wasn't his biggest concern. That anyone would hold his wife's work as ransom for his behavior irked him, but he didn't consider it a serious threat. *Shoving* Emilia, however, required retribution—and it would have to wait. That riled him even more, but his business was more urgent. Beating a coward into mash had to wait.

He kissed Emilia's tear-stained cheek, wishing he dared kiss her as she deserved, but he wouldn't risk her catching his disease. "I must go to Leeds to finalize the railroad documents so we can begin laying track. I'm hoping you will go with me. When we return, we'll take care of this problem for once and for all. No one is treating you like that and getting away with it. Crenshaw and

Tess's father and anyone else involved will pay."

Her eyes were purple pools as she gazed up at him. "I just want my book back," she whispered. "I don't want him selling what I've spent my life working on!"

Dare patted her shoulder. "He only has the draft. There isn't much he can do. Erran can take the original over to Sommersville. Your book is fine. But violence is not. Pascoe and I will handle this."

She narrowed her eyes and pulled away. "Did you not just say you were going to Leeds?"

Dare had a suspicion he'd said something wrong, so he phrased his reply with care. "The investors are meeting there instead of London in deference to my health. I think I can safely take the gig that far without consequences. You can come along to quack me all you like."

"When?" she asked, setting her cup down.

"Tomorrow," he said warily. "The investors from the northern line are there to finalize the deal. We have everything in place. We need rail to be laid as soon as possible to prevent any more threats to our property or Pascoe's. We can't let this ridiculous ransom attempt halt our plans."

"I see." She rose stiffly. "My business, like your health, is of less importance than your investments. I entered this marriage understanding that money must be your priority. I have no right to ask you to change. I don't think I can accompany you tomorrow. If you'll excuse me, I have a headache. I think I'll have my meal sent to my room."

Her room? Her *room* was with him. What the devil did she have to be angry at him for? He hadn't hit her or stolen her book. He'd told her he'd take care of the bullies when he got back. What more could she possibly want from him? And she was bloody well right that she had no right to ask him to change. He damned well wasn't dead yet. He'd secure his family's future, and then he'd think about dying in peace.

Eighteen

DRY-EYED BUT with a lump in her throat, Emilia watched Dare ride off in the gig the next morning. Theirs wasn't a real marriage, after all. He had his business and she had hers. Believing they had any sort of partnership just because they enjoyed bedplay was frighteningly weak of her. She had always stood on her own when it came to her work.

Even though she thought her healing was helping Dare, she also had to accept that she wasn't a miracle worker. She might keep him alive longer, but some day he would die and leave her alone. She had known that from the start, but these past days of seeing him so healthy had blurred reality.

The idea of his inevitable death was appallingly shocking now that she knew him so well. Her heart was in danger of breaking if she didn't find some way of shutting out her feelings. She must maintain her independence and her goals, just as he did his. If it meant the loneliness of sleeping in separate beds as they had last night, so be it.

Wiping at tears threatening to blind her, she lifted her chin in defiance.

She would defend what was hers—except he'd taken the gig. She needed a carriage if she was to drive into Harrogate and find Tess's detestable father. She wanted her book back, even if it was just a draft. Her pages had controversial notions that a man steeped in old-fashioned methods might not accept. That he could change her writing was her worst fear. He could change it, sell the book as his own, and no one would believe that a *woman* had written it.

She sent their new footman to the abbey and requested the loan of the berlin. She dressed plainly but formally for her call on Tess's father. A physician was not a nobleman. He was not even necessarily a wealthy man. She didn't wish to intimidate with outer trappings, but with conviction and guilt. Once faced with the real owner of the book, he had to see his threat was an empty one.

The berlin arrived bearing Bridey and Tess. Lord Erran rode

along beside it. He swung off the horse and asked for the remaining copy of the finished manuscript. Knowing she could trust Erran to deliver it to the duke, acknowledging that it was no longer safe here, she sent him in to Bessie.

Emilia was more concerned with the occupants of the carriage. "Bridey, you cannot go with me!" she exclaimed in genuine distress as the footman opened the door. "Neither of you should be out riding in your conditions!"

"Don't be silly," Bridey said dismissively, inching over on the seat to make room for her. "We're not made of glass. This carriage rides so smoothly, it's no different from walking. I'm the midwife here, and a better judge than you."

But Bridey had miscarried before. Emilia would have nibbled her nail if she hadn't been wearing gloves. Dealing with people was so much more difficult than plants.

"If you don't climb in, we'll go on without you," Bridey warned. "I'm having a strong word with Dr. Thomas, and Tess needs to confront him as the woman she has become. He cannot keep treating her as an object to be dragged around at his whim. The man needs correcting."

"Where are Pascoe and Mr. Madden?" Emilia asked in resignation, climbing in.

"They have gone in search of young Crenshaw. But Dr. Thomas must be taught that threatening us is *not* acceptable."

As the former Countess of Carstairs, Bridey had almost single-handedly run a village and large estate. She knew more of these matters than Emilia ever would. If she was to learn to stand on her own, she should take lessons from her friend.

Taking a deep breath, folding her hands in her lap, Emilia admitted her other concern. "Dare took the gig to Leeds to finalize the railroad negotiations. I fear he will make himself ill, and I won't be there to help."

Guilt ate at her for the decision to allow him to go alone. If he had one of his coughing spells. . . She tried to tell herself he did not have asthma. He would come out of it. She prayed.

Bridey nodded in understanding. "Men make their own choices and we must suffer for them. It's not easy finding a common ground where we are both comfortable with decisions that affect us equally."

Finding out that it was her *nature* to care didn't make her decision easier. That she'd made her choice in anger didn't help. She simply had to hope she was right to send him alone so she could pursue her own concerns—as he had his.

The ride into Harrogate was tense. Gray clouds reduced the August heat, but the rain didn't break before they reached town. Tess gave directions to her father's house. The street was narrow and the wide berlin filled the pavement once it halted at a modest three-story town house.

With a footman and driver accompanying them, Emilia felt safe enough climbing out. Tess had come from a solid home and an educated family. It was just confrontation that she was bad at.

But with Bridey and Tess at her side, she couldn't turn back. She nodded at the footman to rap on the door. A maid in a long white apron answered. Her eyes widened at sight of Tess.

"We will see Dr. Thomas," Emilia said stiffly, handing over her card. Technically, a viscountess ranked over a baronetess, so her card bore more weight. Bridey's experience and composure meant more than a title, but that was hard to prove with a bit of paper.

The maid scurried back moments later to lead them down the hallway—not into the parlor but into a study. The doctor preferred familiar male territory for this battle, Emilia realized in amusement. She was probably hysterical. She clasped her gloved hands to keep from flying apart.

Tess's father wasn't a tall man. Gray hair rimming his bald pate and wire-rimmed spectacles on his nose, he wasn't even an intimidating one. But he was full-chested and twice Tess's size. Tess cringed when he rose from his chair.

For that alone, Emilia wanted to slay him like a dragon. "Dr. Thomas," she said coldly. She didn't know how to do pleasantries, but she knew how to make demands. "I have come for the draft of my pharmacopeia that young Crenshaw claims he was taking to you. That was badly done of you, using Tess's eagerness to please against her. I suggest that you apologize to her or you will most likely lose your daughter's faith."

"I don't know who you are and have no idea what you're talking about. No daughter of mine would have behaved as she has done. I have no daughter anymore. You will leave and take that wicked creature with you."

Tess whimpered. Bridey caught her shoulders and hugged her.

"Your daughter was seduced by a piece of rubbish *you* allowed into your home," Bridey said haughtily in her most cultured upper-class tones. "*You* are the one at fault for contaminating an innocent. Tess is an intelligent asset to my home, and I welcome her heartily. If you turn your back on your own flesh and blood, it is your loss. We are offering this opportunity to make amends. It may be your last chance to do so."

"And who the deuce are you?" Thomas demanded, glowering.

"Brighid Pascoe, Baronetess of Alder Abbey, and the woman who will claim this gem you are throwing away," Bridey declared grandly.

The physician's expression turned red and ugly. "The witch who thinks to teach women how to be physicians! You may go to the devil with my daughter. We will have you up at assizes the first time you touch a patient!" Thomas shook his fist and rudely took his seat, as if they were mere servants.

Emilia wanted to bash him over the head with his own books. While Bridey lashed out with words, Emilia searched the room for any sign of her manuscript on the messy shelves and found none.

Deciding he wasn't worth courtesy, she waited for Bridey to set him properly in his place. Then it was her turn. She leaned forward with her palms on his desk. "The Duke of Sommersville is in possession of the final manuscript. Keeping the draft is foolish and will only serve to raise the ire of the duke and my husband. You do not want them as enemies. Do not dig your grave any deeper, sir. Return my manuscript."

"I haven't seen Crenshaw in days," Dr. Thomas declared angrily. "Your accusations are an insult. I will have the authorities in here if you do not leave at once and take that baggage with you. She is ruined and of no use to me now. You are welcome to her."

Tess made a strangled sound, then caught Emilia's arm and pulled her aside so she could face her father directly. "Charles *forced* himself on me that last time we met," she said, the words barely loud enough to hear. "I told him I was carrying his child, and he tried to rid me of it by beating and raping me. You are the company you keep. I can no longer keep company with men who treat me as if I'm no better than a dog."

She spun around and walked out proudly, although Emilia saw tears streaming down her cheeks.

That had taken strength. Emilia admired the child for her courage and wished she knew how to be the same.

All she had was her husband to throw at him. That was unsatisfying. With no other weapon but her wits, Emilia straightened and offered an unpleasant smile. "The draft pages are missing antidotes for the poisonous herbs in some of the formulas. I trust you are knowledgeable enough to know which ones so you don't poison your patients. Should we receive any more threats, Lord Dare and the duke are prepared to take you to court. Good day, sir."

Behind her, Bridey made a rude snort. They both hurried after Tess.

Once in the carriage, Bridey broke into gales of inappropriate laughter. "The look on his face when you told him he would poison his patients was priceless and well worth our journey."

Catching her breath beneath the laughter that kept erupting, Bridey shifted to the backward-facing seat next to Tess and hugged the crying girl. "You were *magnificent*, my dear. He truly does not deserve you. It's a pity we cannot choose our relations, but I would be proud to call you little sister."

Tess turned into her shoulder and wept. Not certain that her feeble attempt at wit was worth laughing over, Emilia leaned out to order the carriage back to the abbey.

She wasn't satisfied, but Bridey and Tess shouldn't be taxed any more this day. They had accomplished what they'd set out to do, but Emilia still didn't have her book. She wanted to grab Dr. Thomas's ears and rip off his head for causing everyone such grief. It would have been nice if Dare had been there to accompany her, but she was no longer relying on him. Let him make money and feed his family and go his own way.

She wanted her *own* reputation for fighting back so no one dared cheat and steal from her again.

By the time they returned to the abbey, she'd made up her mind. After Bridey and Tess descended, Emilia stayed inside the carriage.

"Won't you come in with us?" Bridey asked worriedly. "If Dare is gone, you shouldn't be alone."

"I will spend most of my life alone," Emilia said. "I'll learn to cope. I have some errands to run, if you don't mind my borrowing the carriage."

Hardly in a position to argue, Bridey waved her off, although she frowned as she did so.

HEAVY CLOUDS rolled across the sky as Dare drove the open gig down the road, sipping from the doctored water Emilia had mixed for him. That he had strength enough to handle the horse said the fresh country air had been good for his lungs, but a drenching downpour would probably ruin all the gains he'd made.

He winced at realizing he was actually considering the effect of rain on his health. Once upon a time, he had ridden through blizzards to complete a deal without giving the risk a second thought. Only old men worried about a little rain. Old men and *Emilia*.

Thinking about his anxious wife, the one who *hadn't* shared his bed last night, he cursed at his own lack of understanding. He'd foolishly wanted her to share his triumph today as he finalized his dreams. They could have had a celebratory dinner, then enjoyed the luxury of a fine inn with big tubs and hot water and a comfortable bed. He wanted to shower his wife with the wealth he'd worked so hard to earn.

Emilia had no interest whatsoever in wealth.

Worse yet, she had spent the better part of her life creating an important book that could change medicine, a book for which she well deserved recognition—and someone had *stolen* it from her. She'd wanted his understanding and aid, not his wealth.

He stewed over the notion. Admittedly, he didn't need his wife's support as she did his. A railroad might not be an earth-shaking event, but it would do more than enrich his pockets. It would change lives for the better. He had a right to feel disgruntled that she didn't respect the importance of his endeavor. But he was feeling disgruntled because Emilia wouldn't be with him to share his triumph.

How had he fallen so low that he needed a woman to help him celebrate? Once a deal was done, he'd always been happy to go out with a few fellows to a tavern. Some good beef and fine wine had always been enough before.

It wasn't enough now, Dare realized in dismay as he urged the horse on. He craved Emilia's rare laugh, her astonished look of approval when he did something fine. She made him feel as if he was special and not just the man who provided food for the table.

Of course, she also made him feel lower than a worm for not helping her retrieve her book. He'd simply assumed finalizing his investment was more important than a draft copy of a book. But she'd been uncommonly distressed. Protected as she'd been all her life, she'd never been mistreated, so he had simply brushed off her tears as hysterical and temporary. Except—Emilia was not the hysterical sort.

Worse yet, it was just now occurring to him that the fool woman might get it into her head to retrieve the book on her own. Alarmed, he pulled on the reins as the pony reared at a flash of lightning ahead.

The book wasn't important as long as the copy was on its way to the duke, but *Emilia. . .*

Damn, but this marriage of convenience was becoming seriously inconvenient. Somehow, he'd let Emilia become well beyond important to him—and with his short life span, he had to consider that more closely. For these past weeks, she had been the sun that brightened his day and the fire that heated his nights.

She was damned well the reason he wanted to live forever.

Popping a horehound in his mouth to prevent his chest from seizing in panic, Dare turned the gig around. Hadenton wasn't too far off this path. He needed to have a talk with old Crenshaw anyway. He might be late for his meeting in Leeds, but if he timed it right, he'd miss the rainstorm. And if he were really lucky, he'd be there if Emilia took it in her head to confront the old goat and his son.

Praying the fool woman had stayed home, reluctantly admitting that she probably hadn't, Dare lashed the reins and sent the pony trotting down the lane to Hadenton. He wished he had a real horse, but a single coughing spell could spill him on the ground. He didn't think his pride could handle the fall—or his head, should he hit a stone. Perhaps he really was growing old to think like that, or maybe just more mature. He didn't want Emilia nursing an invalid with a broken head as well as lungs.

There was the crux of the problem. . . he'd not cared what happened to him before. He'd never had reason to consider how his family would feel if he broke his neck.

Marriage was smothering the devil in Dare.

It was a good thing he only needed this one last deal to reach his goals or he'd be giving away concessions because the other fellow needed the money more. Women softened the head—but the nights, the nights were worth it. Remembering Emilia rising over him wearing nothing at all—was akin to all the world's natural wonders rolled into one.

If she had just been good in bed, he might beat back this weakness, but Emilia had a rare mind, one that delighted and helped him. And there it was. . . her eagerness to help. How could he not love a woman, a partner, who wanted only to help for the sake of helping? Not out of pity, not because she wanted something, but because she had the same interests as he did.

He had no choice but to return her favor. With a few inquiries, he found the drive to Crenshaw's estate. Leaving the gig out of sight, Dare tucked his pistol in his coat, wrapped in a cloak against the wind, and trudged up the drive. He'd learned early to spy out the lay of the land before entering strange territory. He didn't like surprises.

Keeping to the shrubbery, he walked around to the rear where the stables were. More carriages than he would expect Crenshaw to own were lined up along the stones, and the paddock had several horses milling about. He didn't see an excess of grooms, but if his surmise was correct, the men inside weren't wealthy nobility but merchants and bankers who drove their own rigs.

To his dismay, but not to his surprise, Ashford's crested berlin rolled up the drive as Dare considered his next move. He could hope it was Pascoe, but he knew it was not.

So much for any element of surprise. He couldn't imagine what his wife intended, but he was insanely eager to find out.

With a spring in his step, Dare emerged from the shrubbery just as a footman helped Emilia from the carriage. He admired her attire with pride at her grasp of the situation. Instead of wearing one of her grandiose gowns with the flying sleeves and bouncing petticoats to flaunt her grandeur, she was dressed in a modest calling gown that any merchant's wife might wear. Dare thought she'd have been better off with a suit of armor if he gauged the meaning of this meeting rightly, but modesty had its own protection.

The rain started just as he reached the drive and the footmen rapped at the door.

"We'll both be drenched by the time they answer that door," he complained as he joined her.

"Dare! What are you doing here? You shouldn't be out in this." Emilia drew her cloak tighter, but rain watered the roses in her hat.

"Neither should you. Nor should you be here." He stated the obvious. "Crenshaw has all his cronies inside. This is not the time to confront him."

He saw the uncertainty, recognized her desire to retreat, then watched as she lifted her jaw and marched up to the entrance without him.

Grimacing, he joined her. "So, it's to be like this, is it?"

"I did not ask you to come," she pointed out as the door finally swung open. "I am perfectly capable of taking care of my own problems."

"Just as I'm perfectly capable of taking care of my own health, right?" He didn't know where that had come from. He handed his card to the maid waiting in the entrance.

Emilia sent him a sidelong look of puzzlement, but didn't have time to question. Dare placed his hand on her back as they strolled after the maid back to a room where male voices rose in anger. This would not be a pleasant visit. He wished he could carry the damned woman to the carriage and heave her in, except Emilia would most likely stove in his head if he tried. He had to admire his wife's courage in coming here.

While the maid attempted to catch the attention of her shouting employer, Dare took the time to study the room's occupants. He recognized Frederick, the elder Crenshaw, from Emilia's description of her earlier visit. He knew Weathersby, the banker he'd talked to in Harrogate. He assumed the hulking young bull snarling in the corner nearest to them was Charles Crenshaw, the man who had threatened women and shoved Emilia. Dare set his sights on that one. The others appeared to be physicians and merchants of small interest to him.

Finding a gnarled hiking stick leaning against a table, Dare picked it up and slammed it against the wall, causing paintings to tilt. The noise startled the argument into silence. Everyone in the room turned to glare at them. Dare took off his wet top hat and bowed grandly. "Good day to you, gentlemen. Pardon my intrusion, but I have come to retrieve my wife's property, if you would be so good as to return it."

Emilia glared at him as well, but there wasn't a chance in hell that this group would listen to a woman's plea. Dare practically bounced on his toes in anticipation of the confrontation to come. He wasn't completely soft yet.

"Who the devil are you and what are you talking about?" the gouty old man Dare had identified as Frederick Crenshaw demanded from his place by the fire.

Looking properly horrified, Weathersby leaned over to whisper to him.

"Ah, I do apologize, gentlemen. Not all of us have been introduced. I am Lord Dare, and this is my lovely wife. We have lately moved into Sir Harry Malcolm's home in Alder, the one Mr. Weathersby and Mr. Crenshaw were supposed to be looking after and apparently sought to sell to their investors for a railroad instead. You'll be seeing the lawsuit papers about that shortly."

Dare could sense the younger Crenshaw easing in his direction. He placed his bulk more directly between the bully and Emilia before speaking over the astonished murmurs. "Young Crenshaw here apparently took it into his head to stop the lawsuit by beating up on the mother of his child, shoving my wife, and stealing a draft of her pharmacopeia. I will leave it to his respected elders to deal with his behavior, but *I want my wife's book back.*" His drew his smile into a threatening frown as he made his point as clearly as possible.

"We have no notion of what you're talking about," an older man with mutton chops said querulously. "We are a legitimate group of merchants banded to aid our town in obtaining the transportation it needs to grow. What right do you have to make these accusations?"

"Witnesses and evidence, sir, which will hold up in court. The Duke of Sommersville possesses the final draft of the book in question, so there is absolutely no worth to the one Charles stole except for sentimental reasons to my wife."

"Well, there is some danger to anyone *using* it," Emilia added in her best professorial voice. "The pages on antidotes for the poisons in some of the formulas weren't quite complete and are not in the stolen copy, which renders the book rather dangerous."

Dare had to fight back a grin but gave her a look of appreciation he didn't think she noticed. She was too busy glaring at the men glaring back at her. His lady might not be charming but she didn't mince words.

Several of the unknown men continued to declare they knew nothing, but Dare noted Crenshaw and Weathersby remained silent. He considered taking the stick to someone's head, but with Emilia present, he'd have to make violence the last resort.

Before Dare could do so, Emilia turned to the young culprit looming over them. Dare was madly relieved that he'd decided to deviate from his plans to come here first. Brutes like young Charles weren't restrained by gentlemanly impulses toward ladies.

"I was there when you slapped Tess and stole my book," Emilia informed him in no uncertain terms, lifting her delicate chin. "You *saw* me. Just hand over my property, and I will not press charges. Tess will have to make her own decision."

"I dare the whore to press charges!" the younger Crenshaw said in an angry rumble. "I don't have your damned box of papers." With a ferocious grin of triumph he declared, "I burned your Satan's bible!"

"I don't believe you, sir," she retorted. "The box would not burn. Show it to me."

"You're calling me a liar?" The bully tried to shove past Dare.

Very Big Mistake, Dare decided. He was more than ready for a good brawl. Without a second thought, he braced his legs and plowed his fist straight at the larger man's genitals.

Even when he'd been stronger, he'd known better than to break his knuckles on a muscular breadbasket. Aiming low was dirty, but effective. His blow was not light and it was deadly accurate. Soft tissues crunched.

Crenshaw curled over with a howl of pain. A few members of their audience jumped to their feet, but mostly, they were either already standing or refused to relinquish their comfortable chairs. The elder Crenshaw shouted uselessly and waved his cane.

"That's for pushing my wife around," Dare said, stepping back. "The next blow will be for stealing her property if you don't return it."

"Fisticuffs is no way of carrying on civil discourse," one of the merchants said nervously.

"Stealing books and forging papers is not a civilized manner of doing business," Dare retorted, gripping the heavy staff and backing Emilia out of the study so he had room to fight back.

Behind them, the maid scurried to answer another knock on the door. Dare hoped this wasn't a younger contingent. For now, he thought the odds were pretty equal. The old men wouldn't lift a hand.

"My son is no thief," Crenshaw protested loudly. "He is only protecting his home and family from criminals like your wife who would practice medicine without a license. And from yourself, sir, who would steal land from the hands of honest merchants with your sharp city lawyers."

Young Crenshaw uncurled and came up roaring, aiming his massive fist at Dare's jaw. The brute had the advantage of several stone over him, and a healthy constitution. Prepared for the bully's reaction, Dare stepped aside. Using the young man's momentum against him, Dare bashed the sturdy staff against the back of his attacker's head, driving him to the floor.

Being quick on one's feet was useful when outweighed and outmatched. Had Crenshaw's fist connected, he most likely would have broken bones. Instead, the bully sprawled on the floor, knocked stupid but not senseless.

"Emilia, return to the carriage, please," Dare commanded, standing over the brute while he shook his head and regained his senses. "We cannot reason with animals. We'll find the magistrate and press charges."

She sensibly stepped into the corridor, leaving him an exit. The men he faced were either muttering to each other in dismay or staring helplessly. Not one offered to come to Crenshaw's aid, or his own. In disgust, Dare refrained from kicking the rogue at his feet. "Gentlemen, you are a disgrace to King and country. You'll be hearing from my lawyers."

As he turned to leave, Emilia screamed. Dare only had a moment to follow her gaze before the flash of silver from the floor slashed his thigh to the bone. Young Crenshaw's massive fist yanked the blade out, prepared to strike again. Thinking only that he couldn't die and leave Emilia unprotected, Dare gripped the pistol in his pocket.

As he crumpled, he pulled the trigger without even taking aim. His attacker was close enough that the bullet couldn't miss as Dare fell across him with a groan. This wasn't how he'd planned on dying.

Nineteen

EMILIA COULDN'T stop screaming. Dropping to her knees, she tried to tug her husband off the murdering thief, but he was too large and heavy. Blood was everywhere, and her eyes blurred with tears. "Dare, *Dare*, damn you, you cannot die on me now! Someone give me bandages. You're doctors, curse you, help, please!"

She wasn't a physician, but she was pretty certain the blood gushing from Dare's leg was a death sentence.

Big hands reached from behind her, hauling Dare off Crenshaw and dragging him into the hallway. Dare groaned and tried to grab his leg.

Weeping at this sign that he lived, Emilia deliberately shut out the young brute on the floor with a raw gunshot wound in his gut. The sight made the contents of her stomach rise in her throat, but his thieving companions could deal with him. It was Dare who concerned her now. . . *Dare wasn't even supposed to be here.*

"Give me his neckcloth," a familiar male voice commanded.

Pascoe. While the room behind them erupted in shouts, Emilia did as told, nearly ripping the cloth from Dare's throat. He feebly attempted to aid by lifting his neck so she could unwrap the linen. She wept more as her fingers brushed the strong column of his throat.

"Sorry, love," he whispered. "I wanted to be a hero for you."

"I don't need heroes," she told him angrily, fighting her tears. Her anger wasn't for him. He wasn't the one who had started this. Her anger was at men in general and civilization as a whole and at herself for being so useless. "I need *you*. Don't you dare die on me."

Pascoe ripped off his own neckcloth to pad the wound and tied the second one around Dare's thigh.

Dare gave a half laugh "Dying is inevitable, my dearest. I'd rather go this way than languish on a sickbed, spitting blood."

"I ought to let you croak for that heartless remark," she retorted. "Think of your mother and sisters and stay alive!"

"Will, help me carry Dare to the carriage," Pascoe ordered.

"That's all the doctoring I know. We'll have to take him to Bridey."

"What about. . ." Emilia glanced down at the hulk sprawled across the study entrance. One of the strangers she assumed to be a physician was leaning over him, but young Crenshaw did not appear to be breathing.

Pascoe grabbed her elbow and turned her away. "Evil brutes come to bad ends. If you have any gift at all, use it on Dare. He will bleed to death before we reach the abbey otherwise."

Not a single man turned to help them or protest their departure. The silence was almost deafening as Mr. Madden and Pascoe carried Dare down the hall to the berlin. Outside, the deerhounds waited. They must have been tracking the thief.

Emilia didn't listen to the discussion of who would do what. She merely climbed in with Dare, set his big leg over her lap, and pressed her hands to the wound. The warning prickles immediately became shocks of agonizing pain traveling up her arms. His thigh was far too large for her to circle, even with both hands.

In another time and place she would have been embarrassed at publicly embracing a man's thigh. Even a week ago, she would have been terrified to pour her energy into a man as vital as this, with the power to suck everything she was and could be into him.

"Don't go catatonic on me," Dare warned weakly, shifting and breaking the dangerous connection. His face looked pale but handsome as ever, causing her tears to fall again. "I'm not worth it."

The bandage beneath her hand had already turned soggy with blood. Ignoring his warning, Emilia pressed her palms harder over the gaping tear. She focused her attention on the beat of his pulse in the long column of his throat. A small curl of brown hair teased over his shirt. It stirred familiar lust as she watched it move with the draft. Pascoe climbed in across from her, and she barely noticed.

"You are worth saving," she murmured, concentrating on Dare's pulse and not the energy pouring from her. Did his heartbeat weaken even as she watched?

She couldn't tell him that she feared her gift couldn't save him. She'd never attempted to stop blood or replace it. She didn't really think it possible. But if she could keep him alive until they reached Bridey. . .

Dare groaned as the coach jolted to a start, and his eyes closed.

"His coat," Emilia said. "I need more padding."

Pascoe took off his own and handed it over. "I'm sorry we were so late arriving. We let the dogs practice tracing Crenshaw's scent. We know where he hid the book, but we had no way of digging it up or carrying it."

The book seemed so meaningless in light of Dare's wound.

Again, she'd been hopelessly selfish. He hadn't had time to ride to Leeds and back. His meeting was going on without him. With his pain consuming her, it was hard to concentrate on his pulse and her energy. Thinking was out of the question. She relied on instinct.

"The railroad," she said, closing her eyes and letting pure energy pour through her fingers. "Papers in his pocket? Send someone."

"Don't let her pass out," Dare muttered through another groan. "She'll kill herself."

"You believe me." Distracted by that notion, Emilia took a breath and released him long enough to see if she was in danger of fainting.

She was light-headed and exhausted already. She didn't think she could keep this up until they reached the abbey, even though the team appeared to be galloping at full speed. She nearly fell off the bench as it took a turn at a reckless pace.

"If I live, we'll go to Wystan," Dare suggested.

She understood the lascivious thought behind his amused whisper, and her insides melted. "It's questionable whether your humor or your lust will be the first to kill you," she warned.

Ignoring their whispers, Pascoe rummaged through Dare's coat pockets, producing the oil-cloth protected packet of papers. "We'll run Erran ragged at this rate, but we'll arrange the meeting, although I think Dare has taken the fight out of that group of slugs back there."

Emilia wanted to cry out her horror of the death she'd seen right before her eyes, but Dare's life was more important than her fears. She returned to pouring herself into stopping the bleeding.

"THE ARTERY is nicked. You should have bled to death almost instantly. I don't know how you're alive," Bridey said in what sounded like awe.

Groggy and in excruciating pain, Dare heard her from a distance. Ascertaining from his crude surroundings that he was in the abbey's infirmary, he struggled against his weakness but couldn't lift his head. "Emilia?"

"Lying down. I had Tess feed her beef broth and bread, but she really needed to sleep. You must be made of super-flesh to survive this wound, even with Emilia's gift."

He could feel her needle stick into him, but he was too far gone to care about pain. "Will Wystan be a safer place for her?"

The needle stopped piercing him for a moment. "That's a good thought. It's a day's hard drive, though. I'm not sure you'll be better for the journey."

"She shouldn't be alone," he insisted as much as he was able through the haze. "She's special."

"I'm glad you finally realize that." The needle returned to jabbing him.

When he died, he wanted Emilia safe with family, not a target for vengeance. Not all men were good losers.

"I'LL MAKE HIM live," Emilia said fiercely, brushing Dare's over-long golden hair back from his forehead as the berlin drove the final stretch of the journey to Wystan in the dark. Lantern lights bobbed like fireflies in the gloom, barely lighting the road.

"He's dying," Bridey warned her. "His lungs are weak, and he's lost too much blood. His heart doesn't have the strength to work much longer."

They'd employed the makeshift mattress-bed to carry him again, with Emilia sitting at Dare's head and Bridey in the small space at his feet. Pascoe had remained behind with Lord Erran to handle the railroad business, but Mr. Madden rode along side of the carriage with his dogs. Emilia didn't fear the travel. She feared losing her husband.

"He should have years more to live," Emilia said in determination. "I will do everything in my power to see he gets them."

"You will kill yourself in the process," Bridey warned. "A body cannot expend that much energy and not weaken. You will do to yourself what disease and injury is doing to him. And if you should be with child. . . We have no notion what damage you can be causing a fetus."

"I'm not dead yet," Dare muttered, showing signs of consciousness for the first time in hours. "I'm about to starve though."

Emilia grasped at this straw of hope, wanting to believe he was stronger. She rummaged in her basket and produced the meat and cheese Bridey had recommended if he was able to chew. She wrapped them in a thin slice of bread and held it so he could nibble without moving.

Looking determined, Dare grabbed it from her hand and tore into it. She didn't know if it was possible for a man his size to look weak, but he was decidedly pale and unshaven. The ache around her heart deepened.

She wanted to have faith in her abilities, but she didn't, because she knew Bridey was right. He was weak, and this insane journey wasn't helping.

He wouldn't let her take the half-sandwich away after he finished chewing. "If eating will make me well, I will eat. I have unfinished business to take care of."

Emilia wanted to smack him and cry at the same time. She wasn't normally so irrational, but he drove her to madness. "Hire a man of business," she said callously.

"I will, for that sort of business." He lifted the sandwich and tore off another bite.

Her cheeks heated as she worked her way around that and realized what other sort of *business* he meant. Bridey chuckled, so she'd understood too.

"You need blood in your body for that sort of business," Bridey informed him. "You'd better hope Emilia already carries your heir."

He transferred his sandwich to his other hand and clasped Emilia's gloved one, lifting it to his mouth to kiss it. "I need to show you. . ." He hesitated, apparently searching for words. "I can change. I did not understand how special you are before. I do now. I only wish I could kiss you to prove it."

Emilia's heart ripped in two and tears slid down her cheeks as Dare closed his eyes and passed out again.

They arrived at Wystan Castle near midnight, but servants had the door open and lights lit before the carriage halted. Mr. Madden and a footman carried Dare on his makeshift bed into the towering hall and up the stairs. Emilia tried to absorb some of her surroundings so she at least knew where to go in the morning, but stone and tapestry all blended together in lamplight, especially when she couldn't tear her gaze from Dare.

He was weaker. He was barely breathing.

A footman helped strip Dare's big body down to his shirt. Bridey cleansed and wrapped his wound again once he was settled. "I don't see any sign of infection, but he's warm. Call me if he worsens."

Unused to hugging, Emilia awkwardly wrapped her arms around her friend. Bridey actually felt *good*, as if sending her healing vibrations. She had so much to learn—and Dare was the one who had taught her to reach beyond her fear. "Thank you a thousand times. Go rest and take care of that babe. There's nothing else you can do."

"I'm sorry." Bridey touched her cheek, then followed a servant into the corridor, leaving Emilia alone with her fears.

So, this was what it would be like to be alone—empty of laughter, lacking dancing eyes and masculine irritation, without argument or intellectual fascination, with no kisses or impromptu hugs. It did not seem possible that such a force of nature as Dare could depart without leaving an earthshattering gap in the world.

Trying very hard to be as strong as she knew she could be, Emilia stripped down to her shift and crawled in beside Dare's lifeless body. The last part of the journey had been too much for him. Even now, the fresh bandage showed traces of blood. She tested his brow for fever and brushed her fingers over his broad chest to test his lungs. Then knowing she was already drained and weak, she applied her hand to his wound again, endured the agony, and applied what energy she had left.

"Don't leave me," she whispered, and a single fat tear fell on his chest.

DARE HEARD people whispering. He recognized gentle hands rubbing him with scented soap and water. He tried to thank his own personal angel of mercy but only managed a croak. He thought she kissed his rough cheek but darkness closed over him again.

The next time he felt her near, he struggled to wake. He was certain he needed to tell her something important. But the words didn't come, and he only managed to squeeze her hand. She spoke in a low murmur that sounded both angry and sad and hopeful all at the same time. That was one of those things he loved about her. Oh right, that's what. . .

Fighting free of the darkness another time, Dare realized the *room* was dark, not him. How long had he been here? A gentle pressure wrapped a warm glow around his heart, and he knew Emilia slept beside him with her hand on his chest. Amazed that he believed in the impossible miracle of her gift, he prayed she hadn't descended into that dark place she'd gone to before. He kissed her hand and put it on the bed. He needed her alive and awake.

The next time he woke, the sun cut a diamond pattern across his covers, dogs howled below, and the walls echoed of children screeching with laughter. He was starving.

"Emilia?" he asked tentatively, working at the covers in vague hope of removing them to search for her.

"We made her go play with the twins. She was turning into a wraith in here."

Dare didn't recognize the voice but it was almost celestial in its mellifluous beauty. He pried his eyes open to study a slim, dark-haired woman of tawny complexion holding a sleeping infant over her shoulder.

"Good morning, my lord. I'm Celeste, Erran's wife. We were unable to attend your wedding because of this one." She patted the infant. "Her name is Serena Malcolm Ives, although Erran insists on calling her Siren."

Dare was too muddled to know how to respond. His head ached. His leg hurt worse. "Erran is here?" he finally worked his tongue into asking, although all he wanted was Emilia.

"The whole family is gathered," Celeste said cheerfully. "The marchioness could have her babe any day now. It takes an entire village to keep Ashford from tearing walls down with his bare hands."

"Is that supposed to make sense?" Dare asked warily. "Or am I too ill to comprehend?"

"Ah, you don't know the marquess very well," she said, rising. "I'll send for Emilia. Pascoe's twins are leading her and Will's animals a merry chase, but it is probably time for them to settle down."

She signaled a servant, and Dare reserved his strength for Emilia's arrival. He lay there feeling the warmth of the sun through the room's mullioned window, the pull of air in his lungs, the beating of his pulse. He was alive. He gave thanks to whatever superior being took credit, closed his eyes, and clung to consciousness.

Even with his eyes closed, he knew the moment Emilia entered. The room filled with the scent of lavender, and the air practically vibrated with life. He held out his hand, and she placed her slender one in it. He breathed fully for the first time in recent memory.

"I'm alive," he told her, because that seemed most important.

She laughed softly, leaned over, and kissed his bristly cheek.

"For now," she said solemnly. "We'll see how well you fare once you are up and surrounded by Malcolms and Ives. Your mother is rather overwhelmed, but your sisters are holding up amazingly well."

"My mother?" Dare asked in incredulity, forgetting the next important thing he meant to say.

"Of course, she feared for your life as we all did. Your daunting family took a mail coach before we could send a carriage. Are you up to a little broth? Or are you tired of it? We've been spooning it down you for a week."

He summoned the strength to open his eyes again. His beautiful wife perched on the bed near his hip. The sun caused her black hair to gleam almost blue to match her glorious thick-lashed eyes. Pink colored her cheeks and lips. "You don't look like a wraith," he told her.

She laughed. "Thank you, I think. You do though. We'll set you to chasing the twins as soon as you're well."

"Will I be well?" he asked, testing his leg by shifting it toward her curvaceous bum.

"Your leg is healing," she said with obvious relief. "And you're awake again. Bridey says those are very good signs, if we keep you from any more brawls."

In other words, the consumption hadn't magically dissipated, but he might have years ahead, if he took care of himself. Dare brought her hand to his mouth, kissed it, then tugged her toward him. "I'm not ready to leave you just yet. Tell me what to do so I may recover to annoy you for a while longer."

She folded up beside him, kissing his cheek, hiccupping on a sob. "I've been so frightened. I'm not ready to lose you yet either. I don't think we've taken enough time to learn each other."

"That's it. We'll get to know each other so well that we'll hate each other before I die," he crowed. "I can do that. Now, I want more than broth, please." He hugged her tight and covered her hair with kisses.

Twenty

"I HAVE BROUGHT samples of the wallpaper and fabric we'd like to use to repair the study." The dowager Lady Dare presented the box of colorful paints, papers, and fabrics as if they were jewels.

Emilia smothered a laugh at Dare's stunned confusion. He was up and around now, looking so much better, but it was hard to keep him from pacing the hall with the marquess. Restlessness was his nature, and he needed an outlet. His mother obviously knew that about him but didn't quite comprehend his interests. Emilia didn't think decorating would hold his attention long.

"The colors are interesting," she said for him. "Such brilliant greens! Will you re-do the settee and pillows as well?"

While her mother-in-law chattered of her plans, Dare limped around the private parlor of their suite, his physical presence and energy nearly vibrating the small chamber. His leather trousers were loose enough to conceal his bandage. His valet had arrived with a trunk full of clothes, but Dare was still wearing unstarched linen and a loose tweed coat, all that this rural outpost required. He was shaved and his hair had been properly cut so he looked as healthy as any of the Ives men wandering in and out. Her heart swelled with joy just watching him—even knowing the pain he concealed.

He finally stopped behind Emilia to toy with her hair. Once, she might have been annoyed that he loomed over her, but no longer. Having him almost healthy and strong was worth all his masculine intimidating tactics.

"I thought you were looking for a new house," Dare said in irritation. "Why should I decorate for Peter? Give the sample box to him."

To everyone's surprise, Dare's cousin had accompanied his mother and sisters to Wystan. Had he known at the time, her husband would probably have recovered just to taunt his heir.

Once he'd proved he wasn't on his death bed, Dare had sent Peter into Harrogate with Lord Erran. Concerned there might be forged deeds floating about, Erran was still tracking down

Weathersby's investors. Since Peter knew businessmen in Harrogate, Dare had thought he might be useful, but Emilia knew that mostly he wanted to drive his annoying insect of a cousin out of the house.

"We don't intend to move until we must," Lady Dare said, essentially refusing to admit he would die. "It's our home."

"Fine then, re-do the whole house, if it makes you happy," he told her. "I'll talk to the bankers about increasing your household allowance."

His mother beamed as if he'd bestowed the moon and stars upon her. "You are such a dear boy! I thought we should update the salon for Isolde's come-out next year. I'll leave these with you so you can tell me which you prefer."

She hurried off to pass the good word to her daughters—just as Dare had planned, Emilia knew. Her husband was a conniving sort. She tilted her head to look up at him as he stalked the room. "She is so beautifully easy to please. How on earth did she have a son like you?"

"Bad luck, I'd say." He placed his hands on her shoulders and kissed the top of her head and brow. "How long must we stay here? Now that the negotiations on the railroad are completed, I would like to return to my workshop."

"The duke has promised to visit here soon to tell me what he thinks of the pharmacopeia. We're hoping he'll arrive in time for the birth of Ashford's heir. Might we stay a little longer?"

"So Wystan magic can create an heir for me?" he asked jestingly.

"You need to rest more and you know it," she said in disapproval. "You are only just now out of bed and aren't able to stand long on that leg, much less engage in vigorous activity."

Their lovemaking had been limited to hands and mouths while Dare recovered. She still held hope of Wystan magic though—when the time was right, and he was strong.

"I think we can do just as successfully at home, but I know you wish to meet the duke," he acknowledged, sliding his hand down to her breast. "Shall we practice magic tonight?

She grew warm just thinking of it. "Perhaps, if you rest yourself today instead of pacing like a caged tiger. Why don't you use one of the spare rooms here for your experiments? They may not have custom-made glassware, but surely they have plenty of everything that might substitute."

"I was testing arsenic compounds, looking for a means of showing visible evidence of its presence. I need a source of heat, various minerals to combine it with, and of course, products containing arsenic."

"I thought the problem was that almost everything contains arsenic? The castle is full of lamps of all sizes to provide a flame. Borrow glasses from the kitchen. What minerals do you require? Could you ask Ashford? He controls mines all over this area. He might know where you can obtain what you need. Besides, it would give him something to do besides shouting at the servants."

Which he was doing now, apparently. They could hear the marquess's bellows from the far end of the corridor, followed by his wife's laughing reply.

"You are a brilliant woman with strange relations," Dare said, coming around the chair and holding out his hand to help her up.

"Ashford is merely a cousin-in-law. You're the one whose mother hauls wallpaper to your deathbed. You should hold *that* over your fire and test for elements. It's a most noxious green and I don't know how you can tell her to cover your walls in it."

Dare gave the box an evil look. "I hated that paper in the study."

"So you kept scorching it." She laughed and kissed his glower away. "Without you around, it will remain on the walls for a hundred years. Perhaps you can convince your mother it's the wallpaper's fault for scorching too easily, and she should paint the walls a nice bright cream. Now I must pay my respects to Christie. She grows bored confined to her chambers."

"She doesn't sound bored," Dare said, listening to the laughter filling the corridor. "She sounds as if she's driving Ashford crazy. So I will heroically rescue him while you entertain his lady. If vile odors fill the air, don't say you weren't warned." He hefted the box of decorating material, placed a hand at her back, and steered her into the mayhem of Wystan Castle.

"ARE YOU TRYING to make yourself ill?" Ashford demanded, peering over Dare's shoulder as he set a makeshift beaker over a flame.

Taller, broader, and more muscular than most men, Duncan,

Lord Ashford, overwhelmed the small chamber with just his physical presence. His authoritative presence was even larger. Dare still ignored the mighty marquess.

The gas and smoke from his last experiment permeated the air of the windowless closet Dare had appropriated for his work. He assumed the chamber had once been a priest's private chapel, deconsecrated in Cromwell's time. The stone altar was perfect for his workbench.

As the contents of the beaker began to burn and smolder, Dare coughed and waved the stench from his face. "I'm already sick. I don't think smoke can make me sicker. Am I bothering the ladies?"

"Down here, you're only bothering the rats. But this rot smells damned poisonous. What do you hope to accomplish?"

"A better way to poison rats? Mostly, I'm trying to determine how to detect different arsenic compounds so physicians won't keep poisoning people with their quackery. Arsenic trioxide, for instance, creates arsine gas when treated with nitric acid and zinc." Dare captured the smoke from the heating wallpaper in an awkward contraption created out of a glass decanter and the hollow stem of a broken wine glass. "But gas isn't visible and doesn't prove anything except to me. I need discernible evidence."

"That smoke is damned visible and stinks worse than garlic. I'm regretting sending for the chemicals. Why the devil are you testing wallpaper?"

"I'm also testing paint, water, herbs, and anything else the women hand me, but the wallpaper is particularly fascinating. Look at how the paint changes color. How the devil are they making these dyes? Hand me some of that charcoal over there."

Only after Ashford handed him the lump in wry silence did Dare realize he'd just ordered around one of the most important men in the kingdom. But the talk of poisonous *smoke* had ignited a new theory.

"Are you not stretching your distaste for this wallpaper a little far?" Ashford asked, apparently unperturbed by being reduced to the task of coal carrier.

"Cover your nose," Dare ordered, using his own handkerchief to do the same. "Fragments may escape this contraption." He added the charcoal to the beaker.

They both watched as a shiny black powder formed inside the tube from the smoke of the heated wallpaper.

"Damn, I didn't expect that," Dare whispered, watching the particulate floating into his makeshift beaker. *"I've been poisoning myself."*

Holding linen over his nose, Ashford peered at the black powder. "Or your mother has," he added helpfully. "She chose your wallpaper, did she not? Are you saying that powder is poison?"

"Arsenic, if I do not mistake. I'll have to test further. I just did not think. . ."

"Arsenic? Are you sure? We sell copper to paint and dye manufacturers, but not arsenic," Ashford offered. "Can you be poisoned with copper?"

"Arsenic is a naturally occurring element often found in combination with copper. The process by which they're creating this pigment. . ." Dare began scribbling notes. "There is a very good possibility that the *copper* contains arsenic. I need to find out more about their process."

"And you have been regularly burning your wallpaper?" Ashford asked in astonishment. "And breathing these particles?"

"Just heating the wallpaper would release the gas. My study is decorated completely in this noxious green. The dye could be in the wallpaper, the paint, the fabric on my chairs! I've spilled chemicals on them, smoked them, heated them, thrown water at fires and soaked them since my youth. And all this time, they've been giving off arsenic in gas and dust and fabric lint! I have been inhaling poison all my life."

Ashford leaned over, turned off the lamp, and shoved Dare toward the door. "Remove yourself now, go breathe some fresh air before you keel over."

As they hit the corridor, a clear celestial song echoed down the stone staircase. Ashford paled.

"It's time!" With only that warning, he loped off.

"I WILL NEED you here when my time comes," Bridey had explained as she ordered Emilia to accompany her in the birthing of Ashford's first child. "I've done my best to train the Wystan midwives about cleanliness, but your knowledge of herbs is superior to mine, and your gift is beyond valuable. The marchioness is strong and healthy and this should be an easy birth for you to learn from. I have not been so fortunate, so I want the best talent available when my time comes."

Emilia understood Bridey's desperate desire for a child of her own. Pascoe's twins were adorable. He had his heir. But that wasn't the same as having a piece of one's self to love and nurture and provide hope for a brighter future. For her own reasons, she was more than a little interested in learning about this next step in being a wife and woman.

So Emilia joined the other females in the castle in lighting candles, chanting, and welcoming the new infant into the world. Celeste's gifted voice soothed and celebrated at the same time. A modest woman of large and generous nature, Christie, Lady Ashford, seemed delighted with the entire ceremony and joyfully joined in the chant when she was not gasping with her contractions.

As lavender incense perfumed the air and music vibrated the walls, Emilia sensed the stirring of the castle's ancient spirits. It was almost a physical sensation of a veil lifting between worlds, combined with sensual anticipation. Maids and ladies alike held hands and repeated the old songs, occupying a timeless universe with all the centuries of women who had come before.

The ceremony kept the men at bay until the cry of the newborn pierced their songs and the air shivered in jubilant triumph.

"A boy," Bridey cried in delight, lifting the red, kicking infant into the air for inspection. "Ashford has his heir!"

"And I will call him Malcolm," the marchioness announced, holding out her arms for the babe.

"Over my dead body!" Ashford roared, forcing his way past the barrier of women as they released each other's hands and allowed him in.

Emilia chuckled, and at a nod of approval from Bridey, she slipped away.

Appearing amazingly healthy in an unfastened coat and waistcoat that revealed his wide chest, Dare waited impatiently in the corridor. "Now," he demanded, his hungry gaze practically ripping her clothes away before he lay a hand on her.

"Now, yes," she agreed, feeling the excitement shivering the old walls. Tonight, the spirits walked.

Twenty-one

EMILIA INHALED deeply of the musky scent of Dare's shaving soap. She loved that he didn't use the sweet soaps other men used, or perhaps his natural scent neutralized the perfume. Whichever, the fragrance was seductive in itself. When combined with the knowledge that he'd bathed and shaved while waiting for her... He made her feel *special*, as if he truly noticed her preferences and cared enough to indulge her. Nothing could arouse her more than to know that this brilliant, dashing man considered an uninteresting creature like herself worth his time and trouble.

When he led her back to their shared chamber, and she saw what else he had done, she nearly wept in disbelief at his attention to seductive detail—for *her*. He'd lit the room with flickering lavender-scented candles, filled glassware with every flower blooming in the village, and had a hot bath steaming before the fire.

"I think I'll keep you," she murmured senselessly, wiping at a tear threatening to roll down her cheek. She swung around, stood on her toes, and hugged his neck while spilling kisses over his jaw.

When Dare's mouth deliberately covered hers, she nearly expired of shock and pleasure.

They'd been married for over a month, and they'd not once properly kissed. His mouth was hot and demanding, and she nearly swooned from the sensual power of his hunger. Beneath his insistence, she parted her lips, and the sweet invasion of his tongue shot desire straight through to her womb. Who had time for a bath at a time like this? She tore eagerly at his neckcloth.

His hands worked the fastenings of her bodice while she tugged his linen loose. She groaned beneath the intense torture of his mouth as Dare backed her toward the bed. Emilia took advantage of his unfastened coat and waistcoat to run her hands over the linen covering his chest, until he undid his placket buttons so she could tug the shirt free of his tight trousers.

He rewarded her by bending her back against the mattress and plundering her breasts through her chemise. The ribbons came loose, and soon he had her nipple in his mouth, suckling, until she cried surrender.

They were supposed to be going slowly, but the night air filled with song and vibrated with seduction and it had been so long... The flickering light gleamed in his honey-gold hair and revealed his broad, bare chest beneath the half-open shirt, and she wanted to lick him all over.

He had other plans. Emilia cried out as Dare tugged her skirt and petticoat up, and cool air caressed her thighs. She felt as if she would die of emptiness if he did not join her now. Wrapping her legs around his hips, she urged him toward her. He hastily finished unbuttoning his trousers. She whimpered with need as his male organ brushed her female petals.

"I wanted to do this properly, my love," he murmured, coming up for air and letting a draft blow across her aroused nipples. "I have a speech prepared telling you how much I adore everything about you, how you've changed me for the better, and how much I will love you until the end of time. I don't think I can remain coherent to speak it properly. Thank you for being mine."

He *loved* her? Emilia was beyond thought. Grabbing the front of his shirt, she tugged him down so she could kiss him again.

As his tongue invaded, she opened for him, and wept in joy as he pushed past her petals to fill her. She didn't have words, but this, she could do. She rose up against him, milking him with her inner muscles as he pounded her with need—until they both shattered and cried each other's names.

THE BATH WATER was only lukewarm by the time Dare undressed his beautiful wife and dipped her into it. Emilia leaned against his shoulder and submitted to his ablutions while her silky hair caressed his skin. He loved sliding the soap over her, exploring every inch of this magical woman who had given herself to him.

"I am not hurting you, am I? I love touching you." Now was a fine time to think of that, he knew, but she had allowed him so much already... He needed to adjust to knowing that being special came with consequences.

"I'm learning the differences in healing connections and personal ones," she murmured. "This is just blissful."

Just because he could, Dare leaned over and kissed her plush lips again. He had missed what felt like a lifetime of soul-melting kisses, and he couldn't have enough.

"I didn't think it could be like this," she continued, stroking his jaw. "No books explain how it feels to love and be loved. My heart feels as if it might explode with joy. And my head wants to know why you decided kisses are now allowed. I love you and your kisses." She brushed her mouth against his.

It was a few minutes later and the bath was even cooler before they gasped for air.

She'd just told him she *loved* him, even though he had done nothing but give her grief since she'd known him. "Women are beyond contrary," he protested, pulling her from the water so he could dry her off. "How can you love a man who marries you for your money, plans to die on you, runs off to play with trains when your life's work is in danger, and then foolishly almost dies in a brawl?"

He was afraid if he told her how stupid he actually was, that she'd flee as fast and far as she could.

She laughed. She actually laughed at his idiocies. Then she went on to explain. "Because he is the same man who doesn't mind if I spend my time beating up herbs, working with a school that will most likely have me vilified, and who turns around and misses an important meeting to help save my life's work. And because you *see* me and care enough to give me this bliss." She gestured at the flickering candles and bouquets. "You do not need me to simper and flatter to know I exist."

"It may be the smashed herbs and vilifying that causes lesser men to look the other way," Dare said in amusement. "It takes a brave man to stand up to a woman who proposes to him on sight. The world is full of cowards."

She beamed dreamily as he carried her to the bed. "And you are no coward. You face death with such manly courage that I cannot help but love you."

"About that. . ." He tucked her beneath the covers before padding around the room, snuffing candles. When he joined her in the bed, he took her in his arms and whispered in her ear, "It's possible that I'm not dying."

She shot upright, suddenly wide awake. "*What?*"

Dare prayed he'd done everything right, even though he'd bungled the speech making. Heart pounding a little too hard, he propped himself up on his elbows and admired her pearlescent breasts in the moonlight. "Will you kill the messenger, even if he loves you?"

She chuckled and leaned over to push him back against the pillows. Her long black hair stroked his chest. "Do you think I've exhausted myself keeping you alive just to kill you for any reason?"

He gathered her against him and inhaled deeply of her lavender scent. "I love you. I would never have met you had I not thought I was dying. I cannot regret what we've done. But I do regret worrying you and my family when it's possible I've simply poisoned myself."

She dug her sharp elbows into his chest. "Explain yourself."

So he told her of his experiments and the possibility that he'd breathed in arsenic for years.

"So you may not have consumption, are not contagious, and you may live forever?" she asked in excitement. "I just need to keep you from breathing when you work?"

He laughed and cradled her against him, luxuriating in the press of her breasts into his chest. "I'll create some sort of mask to filter out fumes. I need to experiment more, write a paper to warn others."

She snuggled down at his side. "It is all too much to think of just now. I am about to explode like an over-filled balloon from all the wonder of what the future might have in store. A *lifetime*. . . It is so very hard to imagine. But these last days, I have discovered how much I would miss living with an impossible man."

Satisfied just to hold her and know she wouldn't flee at the possibility of a lifetime of explosions and brawls, Dare closed his eyes and drank in the wonder of the night.

The celestial notes of a lullaby drifted through the walls. The walls hummed with excitement, Dare thought sleepily. Were they spirits? Was the place haunted?

Beside him, Emilia uttered an excited *Oh*. She grew momentarily still, which jarred him from foolish dreams. Fearing he'd hurt her, he sought her hand. He found both of them covering her abdomen. "Are you all right?"

She kissed his jaw. "Your child just quickened. As it says in the journals, I *felt* it. It's like being handed a miracle."

Dare froze, fearing to disturb her or the spirits or the child she couldn't possibly know about this early. But the magic of the night and the woman whispered of truth and miracles, and he wanted to believe it with all his soul. "I will trust anything you tell me this night."

She laughed softly. "And question in the morning. But you will see I'm right. My courses are often late, but I've had none since we married, you realize. It's possible. And I *felt* the spirit enter me."

"If it's possible," he said with a contented sigh at this explanation, "I love you more just for your mystery. Sleep. You have to save your energy to bake my child." He said that with a pride and satisfaction he'd never experienced in all his years of success.

EMILIA CRADLED Ashford's lusty, bellowing heir. In the bedchamber, Bridey examined the new mother. Emilia was grateful for Bridey's confirmation that a new white aura resided under her heart, but Malcolm instincts had already told her of the life she carried. Now, she needed to grasp the challenges she faced—a forever husband and a child.

She needed her cousin Aster to explain how she managed all her new duties of wife and mother but still kept up with her astrology studies. But Aster had gone home with Theo to oversee the estate harvest and Theo's growing glass manufactory.

"When Serena cries without reason," Celeste said in sympathy as Emilia awkwardly try to quiet the squalling infant, "I try to imagine what gifts might be upsetting her. Do you think Ashford's son might be gifted?"

"I think he's large enough to be three-months old and won't need anything except his fists and title to move mountains," Emilia said dryly, watching the boy wrinkle up his face for another tempest. "Have they settled on a name yet?"

"At the moment, the list is an eternity long. He may need a brain larger than even his broad shoulders can carry to remember them. The weight of all those ancestors is heavy." Celeste placed her sleepy daughter over her shoulder to rub her back.

"It's a little terrifying to know we hold the future in our hands." Emilia offered her finger for the infant to suck, thus distracting him.

A servant tapped at the door to announce, "Lord Erran has

returned and wishes to visit. And Lord Dare wishes to accompany him."

"We're dressed. Allow them in," Celeste called.

The men filled the feminine salon with their masculine energy and the aroma of fresh air and horses. Both exuded subdued excitement. Dare looked healthier than Emilia had ever seen him. Color had returned to his skin, although he was not as naturally swarthy as the Ives men. His gaze fell instantly on her and the babe, and his eyes lit with a lovely azure.

"Practicing?" he asked suggestively, but pride beamed from his expression.

"If your son is as demanding as this one, then you will have to tend him," Emilia said sternly. "It's a good thing Christie is big and healthy or this child would exhaust her within days. Do you have news you wish to impart? The two of you are practically spilling over with excitement."

Dare settled on the settee beside her and gestured at Erran. "You did the work. You may have the honors."

Erran shrugged and leaned over his wife's shoulder to examine his sleeping daughter. "It is odd how honors no longer matter so much when one is blessed."

Celeste kissed his jaw, then smacked his hand. "Tell us, O Smug One."

The usually stern lawyer flashed a brilliant grin. "Your wish is my command, your highness." He straightened and rested a hand against his wife's chair back. "The duke is thrilled with the pharmacopeia. He has endorsed it fully, which made my task simple. I have negotiated a deal with a publisher who will be pleased to release it under the author name of E.M. Dare, *botanist*, and under the auspices of the Duke of Sommersville. The first printing will be enormous. If he sells even half of it, you will have a nice nest egg for feathering your laboratory."

"Mixed metaphors, old man," Dare said, hugging Emilia.

Without his hold, she might have floated straight to the ceiling. She sat stunned, unable to speak the volumes of gratitude that needed to be expressed.

Dare laughed and spoke for her. "Emilia is preparing a speech in her head that essentially says thank you a thousand times over. We are deeply in your debt."

Emilia poked him with her elbow, reddened, and nodded agreement at the same time. Her tongue was lost. *Published*, at last!

Erran took a seat on the arm of his wife's chair and lifted his sleeping daughter. "We'll make Dare earn it back when the next election comes around. In the meantime, Will and his dogs have dug up your box with the draft copy and left it with your secretary. And Dare's cousin Peter has been all that's helpful in opening doors in Harrogate. Given the scene of carnage you left behind, it wasn't an easy task."

"How is Mr. Crenshaw faring?" Emilia asked, finally able to express her sorrow.

Dare hugged her tighter. "You are not to concern yourself with him. He carved his own path, and it is a greedy, crooked one. In related news, I've had my consortium working with Erran on our Harrogate problem. I hadn't realized Peter's wife is related to several merchants in the area. There's a story for another day, but apparently, I have underestimated him to some extent."

"Not to the extent that your cousin is a callous termite," Emilia interjected.

"Selfish, entirely," Dare agreed. "But not stupid and more honest than Crenshaw. We may set him up as our man of business in Harrogate, give him something better to do than complain that I'm not dying soon enough to suit him."

"What did your cousin do?" Celeste asked impatiently.

"Mostly, Peter is a fountain of information. For instance, he told me that our gardener, Mr. Arthur, is actually Arthur Crenshaw, father to the wretch who took your funds and threw out your servants. Our gardener *owns* the house Frederick Crenshaw and his ruffian son occupied. Mr. Arthur is an old friend of Emilia's grandfather. They worked on the bog garden together, and he's kept it up all these years. The executor didn't know that Frederick Crenshaw wasn't the man specified by your grandfather as his trusted agent. The banker knew and didn't care."

Emilia could only stare at him in disbelief. "I remember grandda's friend. Is that why he's been hiding from me?"

"We should let Peter tell the story over dinner," Erran suggested.

"He's back?" Emilia blinked in astonishment.

"He's to escort my family to London," Dare acknowledged.

"He's eager to return to his family, so my mother is packing as we speak."

"His family?" Emilia asked faintly. "The one measuring your home to see if it suits?"

Dare chuckled and kissed her forehead. "As I said, he might be more useful than I thought possible. I've been rather goal-directed for a long time and hadn't really paid him much attention."

"Goal directed being a polite way of saying obsessed with money and success?" Emilia asked with amusement, willing to be distracted.

"Ashford loves a good story," Celeste added. "We have much to celebrate, so let us do it properly. I'll see if Christie will be up to joining us." Leaving Erran holding their daughter, Celeste removed the squirming protesting infant from Emilia's arms. "Go, say farewell to your family."

"I love you, my published author and celebrated botanist," Dare whispered, holding out his hand to help her up, then kissing her until her toes curled.

Titles meant nothing to her, but his kisses. . . Emilia sighed her pleasure. A lifetime of kisses was the only payment she needed.

Twenty-two

EMILIA WAS in the Wystan library searching for a volume to keep Lady Ashford entertained until dinner when William Ives-Madden entered the medieval hall carrying the odor of dog, horse, and sodden wool. Since this illegitimate Ives relation seldom graced Malcolm homes, Emilia followed her curiosity to the door to greet him.

"His Grace is on his way." Mr. Madden took off his hat and shook it much as a wet dog does. His hair was lighter than most Ives, with a touch of gold.

Like Emilia, this Ives was not much of a talker. "Shall I ask the kitchen to hold dinner until he arrives?"

He nodded curtly. "I've a message from Pascoe to Ashford."

Pascoe had stayed at the abbey to finish business. Emilia knew Bridey and her husband had been exchanging pigeon messages, so he knew about Ashford's heir. She didn't know why he couldn't have sent another bird messenger instead of his nephew. Still, it wasn't her duty to worry over the mystery of Ives ways. "Ashford and Dare are busy poisoning each other, I believe. Why don't I have the housekeeper show you to a room where you can wash up. You can join us for dinner too."

He looked as if he might balk, but his Ives curiosity won out. "Poisoning?"

"You can ask them. Dare is apparently very proficient at poisoning himself. I hope to ask the duke if he might verify his lungs are merely damaged and not consumptive." Emilia signaled a servant, who led Mr. Madden away.

In excitement that she might finally meet the duke, she had the requested journals delivered to Christie while she ran up to her own room to change. A noted and Malcolm-gifted physician, the duke had actually given her dreams his blessing. Now she needed him to say that Dare was right, and he wasn't consumptive. She wanted their child to have a father to help him grow to adulthood.

A little later, Dare caught her nervously trying to decide

between a black lace ribbon above the bodice of her violet gown or the silver chain she'd worn since her come-out.

"I need to buy you jewels," he said, kissing her temple and teasing a curl of the coiffeur a maid had created for her. "Amethysts?"

"I have no notion what they are," she admitted. "I never dine with dukes and have little reason for jewels most times."

"You could become a celebrated author and dine with kings. You must have jewels. Why don't you wear both those pieces of flummery? They draw the eye to your lovely throat and make me want to ravish you all over again."

Gratefully, she kissed his cheek. "A man of decision, thank you."

At the duke's insistence, they held their informal dinner in the upstairs parlor so the new mothers didn't need to be far from their infants. When Emilia entered on Dare's arm, she nervously scanned the company. The duke was quite visible. Tall, slender, with distinguished silver-gray hair, he probed Mr. Ives-Madden's thick hair with practiced fingers. Emilia almost erupted in laughter at the taciturn William's dour expression.

"It doesn't take a physician to determine that my brother has a skull as hard as rocks," Ashford said, handing them wine glasses.

"All Ives have skulls hard as rocks," the duke retorted, jotting notes on some papers he removed from his pocket. "But some, like William here, have pockets of intelligence."

Dare and the women laughed. William looked relieved to have the duke's hands off his head. His brothers, Lord Ashford and Lord Erran, merely saluted the riposte with their wine. As host, the marquess introduced Emilia to his distinguished guest.

Emilia curtseyed in awe. "Sir, I cannot express the extent of my gratitude for what you have done for my pharmacopeia." She'd practiced that line the whole time she'd been dressing so as not to be left completely tongue-tied.

He took her hand and patted it. "Your book is brilliant. I am delighted that you thought to let me see it first. Working with Bridey, you can annotate and edit and update it regularly, and it will be a boon to mankind."

He turned to Dare. "I understand you are undertaking the chemical end of medical science. Will you also be publishing your discoveries?"

Emilia could see her husband was taken in astonishment at the notion that his hobby might be thought beneficial. She squeezed his elbow until he nodded acknowledgment.

"If I have anything worthy of publication, of course. I have not my wife's experience, but I am hoping to have more time in the future for experimentation." At the duke's questioning look, he continued. "If my theory is correct, I may have longer to live than expected. I have just come to suspect that my consumption may be the result of arsenic inhalation."

"Is there some way to know for certain?" Emilia asked what Dare would not.

The distinguished physician listened with interest. "After dinner, I will listen to your lungs. Arsenic, you say? Now there's an interesting theory."

Lady Ashford called them to the table, and the conversation became more general. Lord Erran had been successful in winning the election of one of Ashford's pocket boroughs, so there was discussion of labor laws and banning slavery from British soil. The duke had examined Ashford's eyes and found them recovering from the blow that had caused temporary blindness.

Ashford announced that his son and heir was to be named Alan Dunstan Russell Ives in honor of his ancestors and Christie's father.

Christie counter-announced that he was to be named Alan Duncan Malcolm Ives in honor of her husband and mother.

The duke wisely withdrew from the debate. While he and Dare left to determine a possible diagnosis, William and Erran cornered Bridey and Emilia.

"The animosity and suspicion toward your plans for the abbey are high in Harrogate," Erran stated without preamble. "Having their plans for a railroad rejected has not improved your relationship with the community. I understand that's not your fault. I'm just warning you."

Bridey. . . bridled. Emilia couldn't think of a better word.

"I am not giving up my school," she said emphatically. "Pascoe says he will support me no matter what I choose to do, and I choose to go forward."

"I stand with Bridey," Emilia said. "I don't understand how men can feel so threatened by a few powerless females. It's silly."

"Crenshaw," William said.

Erran nodded at this reminder. "Pascoe sent us to warn that Frederick Crenshaw is crying murder. I have gathered depositions from the witnesses. He has no grounds for charges. But rumor, insults, and innuendo are more interesting than facts, and the town is more inclined to believe one of its own."

"Arthur Crenshaw," William said tersely, prodding the tale along. "And Peter Dare."

"Locals," Emilia cried. "They can speak for us."

William nodded approval at her understanding.

"Neither is considered a man of substance," Erran warned. "Arthur, your gardener, is seen as eccentric at best, mad at worst. Peter Dare has no title or position, only a large mortgage on his small estate. While his father-in-law is a respected landowner, Peter's relationship with him is. . . not close. There is animosity over his estrangement from his wife, although I've met the wife, and she and Peter seem to be on good terms."

Emilia puzzled over this revelation. If she'd been Peter's wife, she would have run him through the heart with a meat cleaver for haring off to London and raising a family with his mistress.

Dare and the duke returned before she could respond. The duke continued on to talk business with Ashford, but Dare hugged Emilia's shoulders. "The duke claims he can find no trace of consumption, that I might live a hundred years if I don't overexert my damaged lungs."

Emilia covered his face in kisses. "I will learn how to heal lungs," she declared boldly. "His grace says I must not fear my gift, and that he can teach me techniques to make it less daunting. You will be my experimental lesson until I can trust myself."

Dare laughed and hugged her hard. "Thank you, I think. I am glad I can be useful. Now, what trouble can I cause to remove all your long faces?"

Erran and William congratulated him with enthusiasm. And Bridey cried. When Emilia turned to her in concern, her friend waved her handkerchief in dismissal. "I become weepy over everything these days. Pay no heed to my tears. I am thrilled for you both, and Dare, I welcome any aid you can offer. We are apparently about to be destroyed by small-minded merchants and uninformed physicians."

"And your cousin Peter is not wealthy or established enough to be influential," Emilia added.

"I had a long talk with Peter before he left. His case is unusual and not one he wishes bandied about," Dare said with a warning in his voice. "If I can swear you to secrecy?" At nods from all his listeners, he continued, "Peter and his wife married when they were very young, to save Susan from her father's abuse. Men terrify her. She lives comfortably with a female companion in the small house Peter's family left to him. She has no interest in marital relations. She and Peter are friends, and she has encouraged him to make his family elsewhere."

"Your poor cousin," Emilia said in horror.

"Poor Susan," Bridey added. "We must beg introductions. She will need friends."

Dare looked on them with pride and relief. "Good, because my next task is to make the railroad profitable, and I will need to do so through connections in Harrogate."

Bridey narrowed her eyes. "We will not stop the school so you can make peace with bigots."

Dare shook his head, and Emilia regarded him with love, trusting that his inventive mind had already sought solutions that would not leave her behind.

"While the school and railroad are being built, we will begin building relationships with the town. I will make Peter my man of business and establish him as a man of consequence."

"And his. . . his children and their mother?" Emilia asked.

"They will have to continue to live in anonymity, unfortunately. But he assures me they will be delighted to move near Harrogate if I'm so evil as to continue living," Dare said with a smile. "He's really not a complete termite, and he has the kind of character that deals well with small minds. As a matter of fact, Arthur Crenshaw has agreed that I might rent his estate for Peter's use. It seems he and his son have had a falling out, and if I'm willing to find some other use for Frederick—somewhere in the Antipodes was his suggestion— he will be delighted. Your gardener is quite an entertaining man."

"Now I am fascinated," Erran said. "You are almost Machiavellian in your manipulation. What do you intend to do with that bitter, gout-ridden old goat who wants to charge you with murder?"

Dare shrugged. "I've had him brought up on charges of theft. He is currently sitting in gaol, awaiting arraignment, so Mr. Arthur is free to return to his own home if he so chooses. I've ordered the locks changed so his son can't usurp it again. I have left it up to Arthur to decide how he wants his son punished. He is considering sending him to a sister in Scotland if I drop the charges and can't find a place for him on the other side of the planet."

The men laughed and pounded him on the back. Dare didn't cough once.

"You are employing your formidable mind for the good of all and not for profit," Emilia crowed in delight.

Dare hugged her. "As you will soon employ your gift for others. We will be a national treasure."

The laughter and cheering aroused the marquess's curiosity. While the others hastened to tell Ashford the story, Dare took Emilia's hand and led her from the room.

"Tonight, we will explore the chemistry of magic," he murmured, leading her down the corridor.

"That should take a lifetime and more," Emilia agreed happily.

The ancient walls of Wystan hummed agreement.

GET A FREE PATRICIA RICE BOOK

Thank you for reading *Chemistry of Magic*
Would you like to know when my next book is available? I occasionally send newsletters with details on new releases, special offers and other bits of news. If you sign up for the mailing list I'll send you a free Patricia Rice novel. Just sign up at **http://patriciarice.com/**

If you enjoyed this story, try these PATRICIA RICE books!

The World of Magic:
The Unexpected Magic Series
MAGIC IN THE STARS
WHISPER OF MAGIC
THEORY OF MAGIC
AURA OF MAGIC
The Magical Malcolms Series
MERELY MAGIC
MUST BE MAGIC
THE TROUBLE WITH MAGIC
THIS MAGIC MOMENT
MUCH ADO ABOUT MAGIC
MAGIC MAN
The California Malcolms Series
THE LURE OF SONG AND MAGIC
TROUBLE WITH AIR AND MAGIC
THE RISK OF LOVE AND MAGIC

Historical Romance:
The Rebellious Sons
WICKED WYCKERLY
DEVILISH MONTAGUE

Praise for Patricia Rice's novels

MAGIC IN THE STARS

"Rice packs her tale with whimsy humor and mayhem … and takes her readers on an amorous adventure in this magical tale."— Joan Hammond, RT Book Reviews 4 1/2 top pick

FORMIDABLE LORD QUENTIN

"another gem …with touches of whimsy, astute dialogue, a bit of poignancy, passion and sensuality —fast-paced tale of love and laughter." –Joan Hammond, RT Reviews

"Rice has crafted her novel with plenty of witty, engaging characters and a healthy dose of romance. Clever Bell is a splendid protagonist, and readers will cheer her efforts to get men to take her seriously and treat her as an equal." –*Publishers Weekly*

MERELY MAGIC

"Like Julie Garwood, Patricia Rice employs wicked wit and sizzling sensuality to turn the battle of the sexes into a magical romp." -Mary Jo Putney, NYT Bestselling author

MUST BE MAGIC

"Rice has created a mystical masterpiece full of enchanting characters, a spellbinding plot, and the sweetest of romances." *Booklist* (starred review)

THE TROUBLE WITH MAGIC

"Rice is a marvelously talented author who skillfully combines pathos with humor in a stirring, sensual romance that shows the power of love is the most wondrous gift of all. Think of this memorable story as a gift you can open again and again." *Romantic Times*

THIS MAGIC MOMENT

"This charming and immensely entertaining tale…takes a smart, determined heroine who will accept nothing less than true love and an honorable hero who eventually realizes what love is and sets them on course to solve a mystery, save an entire estate, and find the magic of love." *–Library Journal*

MUCH ADO ABOUT MAGIC

"The magical Rice takes Trev and Lucinda, along with her readers, on a passionate, sensual, and romantic adventure in this fast-paced, witty, poignant, and magical tale of love." *Romantic Times* (Top Pick, 4 ½ stars)

MAGIC MAN

"In this delightful conclusion to the Magic series, Rice gives readers a thoughtful giant of a man who can bring down mountains, but with gentle touches can make the earth tremble for the woman he loves. This is a sensual, poignant, humorous and magical read." *Romantic Times*

About the Author

WITH SEVERAL million books in print and *New York Times* and *USA Today's* bestseller lists under her belt, former CPA Patricia Rice is one of romance's hottest authors. Her emotionally-charged contemporary and historical romances have won numerous awards, including the *RT Book Reviews* Reviewers Choice and Career Achievement Awards. Her books have been honored as Romance Writers of America RITA® finalists in the historical, regency and contemporary categories.

A firm believer in happily-ever-after, Patricia Rice is married to her high school sweetheart and has two children. A native of Kentucky and New York, a past resident of North Carolina and Missouri, she currently resides in Southern California, and now does accounting only for herself. She is a member of Romance Writers of America, the Authors Guild, and Novelists, Inc.

For further information, visit Patricia's network:
http://www.patriciarice.com
http://www.facebook.com/OfficialPatriciaRice
https://twitter.com/Patricia_Rice
http://wordwenches.typepad.com/word_wenches/
http://patricia-rice.tumblr.com/

About Book View Café

BOOK VIEW CAFÉ Publishing Cooperative (BVC) is an author-owned cooperative of over fifty professional writers, publishing in a variety of genres including fantasy, romance, mystery, and science fiction. Since its debut in 2008, BVC has gained a reputation for producing high-quality ebooks. BVC's ebooks are DRM-free and are distributed around the world. The cooperative is now bringing that same quality to its print editions.

BVC authors include New York Times and USA Today bestsellers as well as winners and nominees of many prestigious awards, including:

Agatha Award

Campbell Award

Hugo Award

Lambda Award

Locus Award

Nebula Award

Nicholl Fellowship

PEN/Malamud Award

Philip K. Dick Award

RITA Award

World Fantasy Award

Writers of the Future Award

Made in the USA
Middletown, DE
17 April 2017